Items should be returned to the library from which they
were borrowed by closing time on or before the date
stamped above, unless a renewal has been granted.

**Swindon** BOROUGH COUNCIL

SBC.LIB 02

# Fresh Blood

**edited by Mike Ripley**

**& Maxim Jakubowski**

**BLOODLINES**

First Published in Great Britain in 1996 by
The Do-Not Press
PO Box 4215
London SE23 2QD

Collection © 1996 by Mike Ripley & Maxim Jakubowski
Foreword © 1996 by Mike Ripley

All stories and introductions © 1996 by respective authors
with the exception of:
'A Piece Of Cake' © 1991 by Russell James
'Calling Cards' © 1991 by Mike Ripley
'Nightmare In The Street' © 1996 by Estate of Robin Cook
All rights reserved

ISBN 1 899344 039

British Library Cataloguing in Publication Data. A catalogue record for
this book is available from the British Library.

Printed and bound in Great Britain by The Guernsey Press Co Ltd,
Guernsey, Channel Islands

# *Fresh Blood:* Contents

# Mike Ripley

## *Foreword*

Nineteen-eighty-nine was a good year for British crime fiction for those who were watching and waiting. The watchers were able to spot first novels from exciting new authors. There was Mike Phillips putting a black investigative journalist on to mean streets previously untramped in Britain; while Philip Kerr put his private eye hero on to some of the meanest streets ever — those of 1936 Berlin. Denise Danks tackled computer crime and warned of new technology to come. John Harvey created a credible ensemble cast of policemen and established Nottingham as the new crime capital of the country. Russell James gave us an uncompromising (in both style and content) view of a Britain where the police seemed to be on permanent leave.

For those who had been waiting for something new to happen in British crime writing, here, surely, was confirmation of earlier signs. Mark Timlin had already launched private eye Nick Sharman on an unsuspecting south London and Ian Rankin had produced the first of his Inspector Rebus thrillers set in an Edinburgh not seen by visitors to the Fringe. In 1988, Michael Dibdin won the Crime Writers' Gold Dagger for *Ratking*, the first of his Italian Zen novels; the same year in which a dedicated crime and mystery bookshop, Murder One, opened in London.

Something was happening.

Avid crime readers had already noticed a new direction in American crime writing. Elmore Leonard was the name to drop; James Ellroy the one to watch; Charles Willeford, Carl Hiaasen and James Crumley had already achieved cult status. The private eye novel seemed to be sewn up by Robert B Parker and Sara Paretsky, but readers (and film makers) were rediscovering their heritage with a growing interest in Jim Thompson, Charles Williams, David Goodis and other sadly neglected exponents of *noir*.

The British new wave also had a *noir* icon in the shape of Derek Raymond (Robin Cook), a hard-hitting social novelist of the 1960s who had re-emerged in the '80s as a crime writer with his bleak and uncompromising 'Factory' series of novels.

And by 1990 it all seemed to be coming together. Critics had long been in agreement that while the British remained supreme at the *detective story* (and Ruth Rendell was doing amazing things with the psychological chiller), the most interesting developments in more 'realistic' crime writing were coming out of America. This was something confirmed by the appearance of Walter Mosley, but perhaps now there was a domestic product which could hold its own.

Jim Huang, writing in *The Drood Review* in the USA, identified a trend emerging among British crime writers to portray 'today's Britain with an edge'. John Williams, interviewed in *The Guardian*, described the new wave with basic pragmatism: 'If Elmore Leonard can write about the mean streets of Detroit, there's no reason why Mike Phillips or Russell James or Sarah Dunant or whoever can't write about the mean streets of Tottenham or Holloway. After all, guns and crack aren't getting any less popular in Britain, are they?'

George Thaw, then of the *Daily Mirror*, remarked: 'There is a new face to British crime writing. You might not like it, but this is the future.' And in the *Daily Telegraph*, Hugo Davenport identified the new wave as: 'bent on dynamiting the decorous tradition of the English country house detective novel.'

A handful of writers involved in this trend/reaction/new wave whatever - attempted to join together to promote the new face of British crime and, of course, themselves.

They acquired a brand name — 'Fresh Blood' — which was always a reflection of a fresh attitude (or bad attitude as some said) on the part of the writers rather than on their age.

As a group, 'Fresh Blood' was informal, based loosely on London. There was no constitution, no membership fee, no manifesto, no permanent meeting place. 'Members' did not have to like one another; in fact in publicity terms, it helped if a member actively disliked at least one other. There was one meeting in a pub in the West End and one dinner in the badlands of Beak Street on the fringe of Soho. Neither actually ended in violence, but legend has it they did, so print the legend.

Michael Dibdin came up with the name 'Fresh Blood' but this shouldn't be held against him. A 'Books In Print' catalogue for 1991 was produced and distributed through bookshops where we had contacts and, through friends in *Sisters In Crime*, to librarians in America. Five of the new wave — Phil Kerr, Mike Phillips, Mark Timlin, Michael Dibdin and myself — even made it as male models in a photo-shoot for *GQ* magazine on what the hardboiled crime writer was wearing that year.

And that was about it, really.

Television claimed several of us, radio too, for both adaptations and original scripts. At least one made it to Hollywood, two on to the bestseller lists and one was mentioned in the same breath as the Booker Prize. Two — Ian Rankin and then Denise Danks — won the Raymond Chandler/Fulbright Scholarship to tour America. Maxim Jakubowski reverted to his fiction roots and made the giant leap from editor to author (and then the much more lowly jump from author to critic). Thankfully for the rest of us, he didn't give up the day job and continues to sell crime fiction from Murder One, when not gallivanting off to film festivals or drowning in the seas of erotica.

There was an attempt to compile an anthology of short stories, each one starting 'There was fresh blood on…' as a joint exercise in self-promotion. But this didn't appeal to everyone, and certainly not to publishers, who all said there were too many anthologies of short crime already and no market. Gradually, enthusiasm for the anthology faded, although almost all the stories written for it eventually found a home, and, ironically, there have probably been more collections of short crime fiction published since than in the previous decade.

And now, five years on, there's another one.

*

Why now? Can *Fresh Blood* still be fresh?

Oh yes. Just as there was a distinctive new wave of writers appearing around 1988/89, there is an equally distinctive second wave (second spurt?) of new writers emerging now. Since late 1994, Stella Duffy, Jeremy Cameron, Graeme Gordon, John Tilsley, Nicholas Blincoe, Colin Bateman and Lauren Henderson — and no doubt others — have published first novels, all with a clear, individual voice and all, harking back to 1990, showing Britain 'with an edge'.

Some of them are represented here, some with their first-ever short stories. All will become better known.

So what distinguishes these new waves of crime writing? It is not simply a more realistic approach to violence — many a traditional detective story writer gives you the full gruesome details these days.

Perhaps it is simply that these are not traditional detective stories. Few have conventional policemen or even conventional private eyes as heroes or heroines, and they often deal with far from conventional crimes. Rarely is murder at the heart of the story, and definitely not in the traditional 'whodunit' sense.

The crime novel today is no longer a simple puzzle of detection. The authors in this collection (and others) try to show the consequences of crime in today's real world. Their central characters tend to be urban and mobile rather than rural and in a closed social circle, and 'outsiders' (outsiders make the best observers) even if they are professional policemen. Many are young or youngish, few have responsibilities in the conventional sense, some have less morals than the villains they take on. The crimes they investigate or become involved in are often resolved outside the law. Some are not resolved at all. The characters in these stories don't realise they are committing crimes and wouldn't care if they did. They have no concept of being caught and no fear of being punished. Many crimes take place continuously and are simply accepted.

Just like life, really.

*

This particular sample of Fresh Blood attempts to show some of the varied voices at work in the new wave of British crime fiction, with each author providing a short introduction to his or her contribution.

There are no bodies in libraries here; no amateur detectives; no neat moral solutions.

There is, however: sex and violence (Stella Duffy, Maxim Jakubowski), professional criminals at work and play (John B Spencer, Ian Rankin), violence as black farce (Graeme Gordon), a robbery which goes badly wrong (Mark Timlin) and one which seems to go horribly right (Nicholas Blincoe), a disturbing and downbeat Inspector Resnick story (John Harvey) and an object lesson in who not to trust for young London blacks (Joe Canzius).

From Denise Danks, a sample of work-in-progress with the first chapter of a forthcoming novel and from Chaz Brenchley, a novella showing that however young, the past can always catch up with you. To represent the work of the late Derek Raymond, the critic and journalist, John Williams, has selected an extract from a novel previously unpublished in English.

For old time's sake, Russell James and I both offer the stories we wrote for the original *Fresh Blood* anthology which never saw the light of day five years ago.

The wait — and the chance to welcome new blood — has been worth it.

*Mike Ripley, March 1996.*

# Nicholas Blincoe

## Notes

Nothing very stupid has ever come out of America, except for their serious obsession with psycho-analysis. I don't know how they got hooked. In the fifties and early sixties, they still knew that shallow and casual was the best way to treat Freud's macabre little case studies. Crime writers and film-makers, especially, yanked Sigmund Freud's chain and produced a raft of black comedies that turned the psycho-meister's theories inside out.

I have a terrible memory for names and, until recently, tended to lose every paperback I read so I can't provide a reading list. It's probably enough to mention Hitchcock and films like Psycho or Vertigo. That mix of sex and psychosis, black-comedy and everyday-horror seems to me to be the essence of Noir.

I wrote My Mother Was A Bank Robber in an attempt to up-date the noir of the 1950's. Once I finished it, I wondered how I was going to justify its place in an anthology of realist fiction. I came up with two answers, one too serious and one too casual.

Firstly, the realist genre was long ago colonised and glamourised by film-makers, feature journalists and TV producers. If my writing reads as though it's realist, it's because I enjoy using the kind of effects achieved in films, journalism or on TV. And because I can't see any other way to write truly contemporary fiction.

Secondly, a realist story that didn't have sex, psychosis, comedy and everyday horror would have so little life; who would read it?

# My Mother Was A Bank Robber

## by Nicholas Blincoe

### I

She knelt on the pavement outside the Spar Superstore on Finchley Road, struggling with the hood-catch of my old pushchair. Mum was twenty-two then; a young mother with her hands full, trying to unpack a child and a box of groceries into the back of her Cortina estate. The engine was running, the car was nose-out towards the oncoming traffic. When two armed men came running out of the bank, she jumped for the car and ditched everything else: the box, the baby, the pram. The men dived in the open back, scrabbling to hold the door closed as she swerved across the traffic. The car's rear-end swiped my pushchair as she hauled to the left. The eye-witness said she was heading north towards the A1. They were no more help: too concerned looking for the remains of the baby she'd hit as she zoomed away. The pram was empty. I was at home with my Grandma.

They dumped the Cortina in a side-street off Child's Hill. Mum had another car waiting for them there, a Morris Minor. They looped back to town at a crawl, through Hampstead and down into Chalk Farm. That weekend, one of the men started mouthing-off in a pub but it was another five weeks before the police caught Mum. A photograph taken outside the Old Bailey shows a blond woman in a thigh-high dress, smiling towards the camera. The same photo appeared in most of the papers, especially the Sundays. It was only two years since the film *Bonnie and Clyde* so everyone was hyped for her story. When I was older, I read the clippings and found out the rest. I've played the scene-of-the-crime reconstructions through in my head. I didn't need to be there.

My memory kicks in around 1970, soon after Mum was sent to Holloway. She got three years, I was eighteen months-old. Back then, Holloway was red-brick and solid Victorian. When I visited I'd come on the overland from Willesden, badly slowed by my Gran. Mum would be waiting in the big hall. The room was unbelievably noisy. The whole of the prison stank of shit and cabbage. Most people grow to hate that smell but I never have. From the stone floors to the high ceiling, the place rang with laughter. It's the only way I can remember it, each week in seamless continuity so I don't know if I'm remembering her first day or another day. She always looked the same: her hair scraped back, no make-up, skinny, big-eyed, smiling, hands in front of her on the table.

She lifted a hand and waved with her fingers as I came charging down the steps. I was on a pure high, bouncing through the hall like a space-hopper in my one-piece padded baby suit.

Mum stayed in her chair throughout, keeping watch as I ran around. I was out of control, tripping over chairs and running like crazy. A friend of Mum's caught me and started tickling through the quilted material. I was screaming with laughter and kicking my legs around. From the far side of the room, I heard my Mum shout, 'Have you got him, Jo?'

'Yeah.'

'Then spank his arse and send him back.'

I was laughing, screaming *No No No* as Aunty Jo turned me upside down. She started chanting 'Who's a naughty boy, then?', scoring alternate syllables with a fat slap on my padded bottom. Three spanks and I was turned upright, totally hysterical with the giggles. Aunty Jo ruffled through my hair and wet-kissed my forehead. She shouted, 'He's a good kid really. Can I keep him?'

My Mum said, 'Sure. You keep him, Jo.'

But no one would let her. There was always someone else ready to grab for me. The second my feet touched the stone, I was off again, straight into another pair of arms. That's how it was. Aunty Jo, Aunty Maureen, Aunty Frankie and the rest, they couldn't get enough of me. They were my friends, families, neighbours. I grew up knowing their names and their stories, just like I knew the stories of the lezzas who guarded the doors.

I spent my childhood wondering what a boy had to do to get sent to a woman's prison. It was years before I realised I wasn't seeing the whole picture; like maybe the girls didn't spend every second of the day laughing their heads off.

Something my Mother said brought it home. She told me, watching me grow up was like playing with a flicker book. She flipped the corners of the pages and my picture changed. Except she did it so slowly, one page a week, she always lost track. The way her voice cracked, it tore me up. I even remember when she said it: Cookham Wood, June 1987, when she was eight years into her twenty for armed robbery and grievous assault.

But she had it wrong. She imagined I had another life in the pauses between my visits. I didn't. I was eighteen and the whole of my life could be boiled down to one long, fixed shot of an endless visiting hour. The shot established my Mum was in prison but told me nothing else because nothing ever happened when I was in the frame. For the bigger picture, I relied on Women's Prison films.

The titles are the giveaway: *Woman Hunt, Women in Chains, Women Without Names, Women Without Men, House of Women, Love in A Women's Prison, Prison Without Bars, Bare Behind Bars, Girl Behind Bars*. I bought anything with 'Girl' in the title: *Jailhouse Girls* and *Delinquent Schoolgirls* were obvious selections, *Girl On Approval* and *A Nice Girl Like Me* were lucky finds. But films like *So Evil So Young* or *Sunday Daughters* came down to pure intuition. I swear I could smell the prison, the shit, the cabbage and the hot cat-fights.

## II

Mum began hitting banks again the day her first stretch ended. Her new partners were called Charlie Warren and Derek Pease but she tagged them the Karamazovs. Charlie was the driver, Mum had graduated to shotgun. She would walk into the bank ahead of Derek, dressed in kitchen sink drag and a waterproof headscarf. She needed to cover up if she was going to play the part of a hopeless old cow, waiting in line with two heavy bags. When Derek came charging through the doors, waving his shotgun and shouting like a loony, everyone would freeze. They never noticed Mum haul out her sawnoff. She would hammer on the nearest cash window, one time only, hard enough to shake the glass. It rarely broke but sounded so loud everyone was sure a shot had been fired. By the time the counter-girls caught their breath, they were looking down the barrel of her gun.

In seventy-seven jobs, Mum only ever had to shoot two people. In total, she shot a few more before she was caught but her tactics were psychologically sound. When adrenaline kicks in, the only buttons are fight and flight. There is no middle route, it's not a multiple choice scenario. Once the bystanders copped Mad Derek, it was down to the law of averages: half would swing one way, the rest would swing the other. But the shock of seeing Mum brandishing a double-ought sent them all into paralysis. They'd know, whichever way they'd swung, they were cooked. Mum bagged the swag and sailed out of their lives. Derek held the rear, following her to the pavement where Charlie was waiting in the Karamazov sledge. Then off they'd go, sleigh-bells jingling in the snow. It was her life, until it all went wrong at a road block, three hundred yards the wrong side of a job in Hornsey.

They were dragged out of the car by armed cops and driven in chains and gaffa-tape to police central. Charlie cracked after three seconds' hard questioning. The trial was a wash-out. The only drama happened outside court when Derek Pease slipped custody. He was free for six months. The papers said he was caught climbing aboard a Russian boat in Ipswich. When Mum read it, she said her Karamazov gag must have stoked his taste for romance. Maybe it had, but her jokes went down less well with the judge.

She went back to Holloway in 1979, sentenced to twenty years modelling prison pinnies and share-wear lingerie. The black eye and broken nose she got in her first month completed the full ensemble.

The sight of her there, her face half-beaten and swollen, sent my Grandma into a freak. Her twitching hand grazed my shoulder, as though she hoped she could brush me away and ask the serious questions mother-to-daughter. She wished I'd start running like I used to when Mum was last inside. I didn't move. I fixed on the bruising and I stared. I was ten-years-old and nothing like the same skittering satellite of energy and emotion I was as a toddler. There was a buzz about the place and I was tuned to it. I knew that no one, least of all Mum, cared about the black eye.

Over the months even Gran gave up waiting for an explanation. By the time the bruises disappeared, Gran had accumulated a whole stack of new questions and an hour a week is not enough time for an openly Oprah exchange. Mum was fine. She was still joking and still shouting to her friends. I had a new set of Aunties, just as good as the first. My Aunty Jackie would always go on about how pale I was, didn't I ever go out? Aunty Ruth would ask what I'd been doing, hitting puberty a bit too hard? Jackie and Ruth were both toms, but Aunty Ben was more innocent. She was a Nigerian lady who got twelve years after she was caught at Heathrow with a wodge of smack up her privates.

I remember Aunty Ben asking me what I did all week. I told her I'd been watching the telly.

She said, 'What do you like, love?'

My favourite programme was *Within These Walls*. She'd never heard of it but it got a big laugh off everyone else. We were still laughing when the cripple came hobbling down the steps into the visiting hall.

The room went quiet for a second, then erupted into a sneer. There is no other way of putting it. The cripple kept her eyes on the floor and carried on limping to her chair.

The moment I saw her, everything clicked. She used to sit at the far end of the hall, outside the circle of my Mum and her friends, among her own people. She'd been a kind of off-screen presence, a heavy-duty shadow that I knew to avoid. And despite only having a dark image of her, I knew she had never limped. Now, her left leg was three inches shorter than the other and she needed two sticks to get around on her own.

I said, 'What's up with her?'

Mum said, 'She's been up the infirmary.'

'What happened? She done her leg?'

'Just the one, but she shattered every bone. The only way that slag's ever going to get back on top is to sleep her way there.'

That's how my Mum came to be a boss. From then on, she ran every wing she was ever put in. It made things easier, especially for Gran. She continued to ship-in chunks of dope and bags of pills but the amounts became larger and she no longer had to worry about being discreet. At the end of the visiting hour, a rough lezza called Winifred would hand my Gran a wad of money, minus twenty per cent. My Mother always gave the screws their cut directly, it made for good working relations.

## III

The Seventies began and ended in prison, that's the frame for my decade, my Mother's Holloway Sandwich Trick. In the middle years, the Karamazov boys saw more of her than I did. She was too busy chasing money with a smoking sawn-off to topple into domesticity. I lived with Gran and shaped my weeks round the Sunday episodes of *Within These Walls*. When Mum went down for the second time, I took it well. I pictured her as the star of her own long-running show, another weekly serial for me to look forward to. My appetite for prison drama was getting more intense. Now, it's out of control.

This is my Top Ten:

1. *Yield To The Night* (Diana Dors playing Ruth Ellis).
2. *The Weak And The Wicked* (Dors again, re-teamed with the same director, J Lee-Thompson).
3. *Caged Heat* (*Charlie's Angels* on amphetamines).
4. *Jackson County Jail* (Redneck rape classic).
=5. *Bare Behind Bars* (Hi-speed Spic flick with all the ingredients: cat-fight, fire-hoses, naked-in-solitary).
=5. *Second Chance* (Catherine Deneuve as crazed jail nymph slut).
7. *And God Created Woman* (Not that good actually, but Rebecca de Mornay strips).
8. *High Heels* (Would have been a Top Three if the prison sequence wasn't so short).
9. *Dyke Island* (Hell-cats in knotted blouses, spoilt by poor production values).
10. *Human Experiments* (Another redneck pic, not to be confused with the *SS Experiment Camp* series).

It's amazing how often the same type recurs, the particular Blond. Outside of films, prison life soon washes the blond away. Mum was a semi-natural who kept the colour cold and bright with regular tint jobs and a string of personal stylists. Women's prisons are packed with trainee hairdressers. Any one of them would scratch out an eye for the chance to work on Mum's roots. Though after she transferred to Cookham Wood, scratching wouldn't have done them any good. Mum found her soul mate out there.

Aunty Jess was twenty-one when they met. She was an ex-tom from up Bradford way who turned round and killed a punter. No one ever found out why she'd done it, least of all the jury at her trial. She'd been through rapes and beatings but there was no evidence the guy she choked was a psycho. I guess he was just in the wrong place at the wrong time. Aunty Jess was dumb enough to use his credit cards and the prosecution argued her only motive was robbery. She was sixteen when she was given life. All long-term and lifers eventually end up in Cookham Wood so it was a cert that her and Mum would meet, but that doesn't mean it wasn't also fate.

Mum was transferred from Holloway in '80. She was lucky, there. The old prison was being refurbished so a quarter of Holloway went with her. She swept into Cookham Wood with a ready-built reputation and could have had any woman she wanted. But Aunty Jess meant more to her than a tint and a squeeze. They were inseparable for the six years they were together.

Mum's hair turned straw-dirty in the Summer of '87, soon after Aunty Jess got out on licence. This was the same year Mum told me how much she regretted the time we spent apart. I didn't want to hear her talk like that. Like some stranded old slag, hauled into life by weekly visits and a drip-feed of sentiment. I couldn't stomach the sentimentality and, really, I never believed her. She was a hopeless junkie by then, wrapped in self-pity and ready to say anything. It was even worse after Gran had a stroke because I was the one who brought Mum the drugs. I would have stopped if I could but it was a business so I had no choice.

With Aunty Jess on the outside, Mum started taking as much smack as she was dealing. It was a real touch-and-go scene for more than a year. Mum could never have dried out on her own but the long pleading letters Aunty Jess wrote did more harm than good. In the end, it was the Aunties inside who pulled her through. I owe them all but especially Aunty Myra. She never left Mum's side through the worst of her withdrawal.

I was scared to tell Gran just how much we owed Aunty Myra. I thought the news would kill her. Gran had been down on her from the moment she saw her in Cookham Wood. I remember asking why she was so freaked. She had said, 'You just keep away from her. Myra's done really nasty things to little kids.'

It didn't worry me then. I'd done plenty of nasty things to little kids, that's what I did at school. By 1987 I knew more about it but I still say Aunt Myra is okay. She did a lot for Mum and anyone who's ever been around Cookham Wood will say the same. I don't know what Gran says, I never understood a word she said since the stroke.

## IV

Gran doesn't come up to Cookham Wood at all anymore. It's a haul for her, all the way to Rochester, even with me doing the driving. Aunty Jess has moved to Walthamstow now, which is handy. I pick her up at her flat and we go see Mum together. We keep the conversation light, I talk about films and she promises to re-do my roots.

Mum's in her mid-forties. Considering where she is, she doesn't look bad. She still won't wear make-up, even foundation, so her skin's a weird colour but everything else is as sharp and bright as it ever was. The first thing she says is, How's your Gran? I tell her the home news and the conversation trips on.

'Are you looking after her?'

'Course I am. I left her a ton inside the gonk on the mantelpiece and there's a bloke coming round later to wheel her round the shops.'

'Where's she going this week?'

'I don't know. Whiteleys I think. The cinema's showing a reissue of *The Sound Of Music* and she always liked that.'

Mum said, 'Have you got anything for me?'

I picked up a re-issue of *Scrubbers* the other week but didn't get around to copying it. I gave Mum a video of *Shock Corridor* instead. It's set in a nut farm, not a prison, but it's a good laugh and she's not as bothered about prison flicks as me. I thought she'd go for the scene in the nympho ward and gave it ten minutes worth of scholarly introduction before I left her and Aunty Jess alone to catch up.

I spent maybe twenty minutes with Aunty Myra. When I got back, Mum had last Sunday's copy of *The People* spread out on the table in front of her. She was biting it back as she said, 'You didn't tell me about Derek and Charlie.'

I gave Aunty Jess a look but she only shrugged. I said, 'Yeah, well, it's only just got in the papers. I was chewing it over before I said anything.'

I was lying. The story hit the papers a month back. It started out as a page three filler. When it reached the centre spread, it was decked out with fuzzy surveillance pictures and an artist's impressions of the robbers. Mum had read the whole thing.

She said, 'It's them. Who else is it going to be? It's the exact same style and everything.'

I said, 'It's not both of them. Charlie Warren's got asbestosis. He's bought himself a council house and retired to Leeds.'

'Then it's Derek. He's out.'

I said, 'Do you know how long Derek Pease got?'

She shook her head, 'He was on the run so he didn't go to trial until after I was sent down. After a stunt like that, I assumed he'd get at least as long as me.'

'He got less than three years. He was out in eighteen months.'

She sat there with her mouth open, stunned. I said, 'You didn't know that, did you? Ain't it a shocker?'

I dropped Aunty Jess off on my way back to Willesden. We waved Bye close to Walthamstow Market and I told her I'd see her later. I got to the bank at 3.30pm and joined the queue. There were four people ahead of me, including a retired type who was trying to fill in a deposit form without his spectacles. As the line got shorter, he told me to take his place, 'I'm not ready yet, dear.'

I clicked past him with a thanks, the high heels were chafing and the carrier bag never got any lighter. As I stepped up to the window, Derek came charging through the door with a shotgun in his hand and a stocking over his face. The stockings were mine. He'd broken his nose sometime in the past fifteen years and the tight nylon mesh squeezed it flat. He would have frightened anyone, even without the gun. The whole bank froze.

It takes less than ten seconds for a counter-girl to get it together and reach for the panic button. I never give them the chance. I pulled my shotgun out of my bag and rammed it up against the window. Using my high, sweet voice I told her to keep still, 'The glass is no protection.'

There was a woman standing shaking behind the security door at the far end of the counter. I shouted down to her and told her to buzz my partner through. Derek took up his position in the doorway, swinging his shotgun between the customers and the staff at their desks.

There were three girls working the counter, including the one at my window. I pointed at two of them and said, 'Get away from the tills. Marcia, here...' I'd read her name tag by this time '...she's going to open them up and pass me the money.'

I filled my carrier bag with notes. At a glance, I'd say there was no more than five thousand pounds. As I finished, I smoothed down my skirt and coat and prepared to walk out. It's a habit I picked up from nowhere but it's always helped me to stay calm. I left holding the money in one hand and my shotgun in the other. Derek followed on behind, backing out to make sure no one moved.

He only turned around once he was safely out of the door. He was a professional, leaving it to the last moment before he looked to see if Aunty Jess was ready with the car. He expected to see me climbing inside. I wasn't. I was stood right behind him with the shotgun levelled at his head. I didn't really catch his expression before I blew him away.

As I trotted over to Jess's Sierra, she fired a smoke grenade over my head. I heard it whistle and explode behind me. We would drive out of a storm of smoke and blood. No one would ever follow us and there would never be a road block waiting ahead. Derek was the grass, so he got smoked.

# John Harvey

## *Notes*

When I sat down to write **Lonely Hearts**, *the first of the Charlie Resnick novels, it was with a clear sense of purpose: what I wanted to do was write a story which would simultaneously be English in its content and American in its influences. Its place and people would recognisably belong to the time and place in which I was living, but the means of presenting them would be closer to those of writers such as Elmore Leonard and Ross Thomas — which is to say the narrative would be character-based and dialogue-driven and that it would be possible for the tone to shift between the quirkily humourous and the highly dramatic. I was also impressed by the ways in which many American crime writers seemed able to convey a strong sense of a specific place and atmosphere in their work without resorting to the rather lengthy descriptive writing employed by some of their British counterparts.*

*My home was in Nottingham at the time — my second spell of living in that city — and I had previously used it as a setting for a television series called* **Hard Cases**, *which was a dramatic look at the work of probation officers and their clients, using a multi-strand narrative closely based upon that of* **Hill Street Blues**. *What these programmes tried to do was marry the realistic feel of location filming — in itself a strong characteristic of much British film and television — with the fast pace and off-the-wall humour that was so much a part of* **Hill Street Blues'** *success.*

*Once it became clear that the Resnick books were going to become an ongoing series — a sequence — I was confirmed in my intention of giving, through them, a picture of what living in a medium-sized, post-industrial British city was like in the post-Thatcher years. Most of the crimes I write about are ordinary and everyday; they are committed by ordinary, everyday people, and because I believe the roots of most crime is socio-economic it makes sense that I write in what is largely a 'realist' mode.*

*So while I'm tipping some kind of a stylistic hat at Leonard and Thomas and towards the writers of* Hill Street Blues *and their fore-runners — Joseph Wambaugh and Ed McBain — much of my roots lie in that school of English heightened social realism which harks back to Dickens and which, in Nottingham, means that it's difficult not to be aware of Alan Sillitoe and the early D H Lawrence breathing down your neck as you walk across the Old Market Square or enter Yates' Wine Lodge of a Friday night.*

*One of the things I enjoy doing in the few Resnick short stories I've written —* She Rote *is the third — is finding out a little more about characters who have appeared in previous novels. So, Ray-o and his Uncle Terry were in* Off Minor, *and now that I've got them here I have a feeling they'll move on into the next Resnick novel I'm set to write, which will be the ninth. As for the central element of the story — the young, unmarried mother — the genesis of that was in a poem I wrote during a poetry conference at the Squaw Valley Community of Writers in Northern California in the summer of 1995. A long way from Nottingham — or anywhere.*

# She Rote

## by John Harvey

She wrote Ray-O on her arm, scratching the letters with the blunted point of a compass she'd borrowed from one of the girls in Maths class. Scratched them and then gone over the outline in blue biro, painstakingly slow.

She wrote SARAH 4 RAY-O one hundred and twenty seven times in felt-tip on the inside of the toilet door. Only the persistence of two of the older girls, anxious to get in and light up, stopped her writing it one hundred and twenty eight, one hundred and twenty nine, one hundred and thirty.

She wrote a letter to the problem page of **Just Seventeen**: 'my boy frend wont use a condom he says theres no need cos I'm only 13. Please will you tell me if this is true. I need to no.'

But by then it was too late; by the end of the month she was bleeding but not enough, not the right kind.

Ray-o was nineteen, rising twenty. His real name was Raymond, Raymond Cooke, but everyone called him Ray-o. The longest job he'd held down before going with his Uncle Terry had been in the wholesale butchers, down by the abattoir on Cattle Market Road. Hefting carcasses from the hooks of the conveyor belt, emptying tubs of tripes and offal into the incinerator bins; blood under his fingernails, gristle in his hair; the smell of it insidious on his skin.

Terry had saved him from all that. 'How 'bout it, Ray-o? How d'you fancy working for me?' His uncle had taken a lease on a shop in Bobber's Mill, just to the north of the bridge. Second-hand stuff, that's what they'd be selling. Refrigerators, cookers, stereos, the odd bit of furniture — there was always a call.

'There's a couple of rooms over the top, an' all. Could live there if you want. Shan't charge you no more'n you're paying now. What d'you say? You and me, workin' together, eh?'

Raymond hadn't needed asking twice. A chance to get away from that poxy little room he had in Lenton, turn his back on all the shit and guts he'd been up to his elbows in. And besides, Terry, he was like a father to him really, more than his own father, that was sure; a father and a mate, both at the same time. Terry would take him out drinking, buy more than his fair share of pints, have a laugh about women, you know, doing it, having it away. 'Now then, Ray-o, how d'you fancy sinking your teeth into that lot? Need a pair of flippers and a bleedin' snorkel!'

And Terry knew what he was talking about — ever since that cow of a wife of his had left him, he had new girl friends all the time. Raymond didn't know how he did it: forty if he was a day. And that one he was going with now, Eileen, she couldn't have been much older than Raymond himself. Great looking, too. Really gorgeous. If ever she came round to the shop, Raymond couldn't look at her without blushing.

Off-duty, Mark Divine and Kevin Naylor were propping up the bar in the Mason's Arms, a little removed from their normal stalking grounds, but Divine had half a mind he might set eyes on one of his snouts who'd been avoiding him. Three pints and a couple of shorts down the road, so far he had had no luck.

'Another?' Naylor asked, hoisting a crisp new twenty in the barman's direction.

'Go on,' Divine said. 'Why not?'

Naylor's wife, Debbie, was off to her mum's, hatching plans for her sister's wedding; underskirts enough to bandage a battalion and more sequins than *Come Dancing*. Divine's on-again, off-again relationship with a staff nurse from the Queen's was decidedly off-again, and all he had to go home to was a video of *Baddiel and Skinner's Fantasy Football League* and the remains of last night's king prawn biriyani, adhering to its aluminium container in the fridge.

'This,' Divine said, at the end of a copious swallow, 'tastes like piss.'

'Yes,' Naylor said, licking the residue of froth from where he was considering growing a moustache. 'Agreed.'

Over to the far side of the room, in what would, before these democratic days, have been partitioned off as the public bar, a group of a dozen or so lads were in increasingly party mood. A good score of jokes, sexist, of course, ribald laughter, angry words, a bit of informal karaoke, spilt beer, a few choruses of *Happy Birthday*, a slight accident in the passageway outside when one of them didn't make it all the way to the bogs.

'Nice to see,' Divine said.

'How's that?'

'People enjoying themselves.'

Naylor nodded. He had personally felt the collars of at least two of them in the past eighteen months, one a suspected burglary, the other for being in possession of a controlled substance. Neither case had gone to court.

'Hey up!' Divine said, nudging Naylor in the ribs. 'Catch a look at that.'

The young woman who had come into the bar had long red hair, shading towards chestnut, and it hung loose past the collar of the oversize beige raincoat she was wearing. Aside from the hair, and the brightness of her lipsticked mouth, what marked her out most clearly was the policewoman's cap she wore at a jaunty angle on her head. A moment to take in the room and then she strode purposefully to where the lads were sitting.

'You don't think there's been a complaint?' Naylor said.

'Not yet.'

First the table, then the whole pub fell quiet.

'Which one of you is Darren Matthews?' the young woman asked, not a tremor in her voice.

A few shouts and jeers, pointed fingers and sniggering behind hands and the aforementioned made a passable attempt at getting to his feet, pale face and tie askew, speech slurred. 'Who wants to know?'

Before you could say Robert Peel, the woman had her raincoat unfastened and whisked away; she had obviously done this before. She was wearing police uniform skirt and tunic, black tights and three inch heels. 'Darren Matthews,' she said. 'You're nicked.'

In the resulting uproar, Divine caught the barman's attention and got in another couple of whiskies, doubles. Someone had switched on the pub stereo and Janet Jackson was breathing encouragement to the woman, as, on the table now, she danced and swayed in front of the birthday boy's face, removing her uniform piece by piece as she moved. With a semblance of unison, the others around the table clapped encouragement.

'Debbie do that for you this year, Kev?' he asked.

'Did she, heck as like. Set of socket wrenches and a pair of Paul Smith socks.'

The redhead stepped out of her skirt and revealed a pair of handcuffs tucked into the elastic of high-sided silk briefs with *Go to Jail* in tasteful red lettering over the crotch.

The object of her attentions did his best to make a bolt for it, but his mates grabbed him and pushed him back down.

'Only kind of arrest that poor sod's about to have,' Divine said, 'is of the cardiac variety.'

With a professionalism that many of Divine and Naylor's colleagues would have envied, the woman cuffed Matthews' wrists to the arms of the chair. So many were on their feet then, crowding round, it was difficult to see exactly what happened next, but what flew in the air above their heads was clearly Matthews' trousers.

'Jesus!' Divine exclaimed, shifting along the bar for a better view. 'She's only going to do the business.'

'She's never.'

'Want to bet?'

Naylor grabbed Divine by the arm. 'Then we're leaving.'

'You're bloody joking!' He could no longer see the swaying head of red hair and he guessed she must be down on her knees.

'You want to get in there and put a stop to it?' Naylor demanded.

'No, I bloody don't.'

Naylor pulled at the front of Divine's shirt. 'Then we're out of here. Now, Mark, now.'

Divine drove with almost exaggerated care; he didn't want to get pulled over and be ordered to blow into a plastic bag. 'What d'you reckon she gets for that?' he asked. 'Side from a nasty taste in the mouth.'

Naylor shrugged. Ever since leaving the pub, he'd been hoping against hope Debbie would be back from her mum's by the time he got in. 'Fifty, hundred.'

Divine whistled appreciatively. 'Only need to do that a few times, pull in more than you or me.'

'You fancy it then?'

'What? Spot of the old Chippendales? Why not? Might as well make some use of that old uniform, eh?' He laughed. 'You read about that bloke, did this act dressed as a copper, strip-o-gram, like. Poor bastard only got three years, didn't he? On account these women he stripped for complained how he'd — what was it? — humiliated and degraded them.'

'Maybe he had.'

'Yeh? Shame they hung around long enough for him to get his tackle out of his Y-fronts, then, might not've been so fucking degraded if they hadn't.'

Nodding, not really listening, Naylor glanced at his watch. He'd get Divine to drop him off at the Paki shop on the corner, pick up a bottle of that Chardonnay Debbie liked, glass or two to put her in the mood.

Terry was not quite asleep when he heard the key in the lock, a smile on his face as soon as he recognised Eileen's footsteps on the stairs.

'Hello, love. How'd it go?' Reaching up for her as she leaned across him, brushing the top of his head with a kiss.

'Fine. Yeh, it was fine.'

'Good tip?'

'Sixty. Not bad.'

Terry pulled her down towards him. 'Maybe we should celebrate.'

'Not now. I want to take a shower first, clean my teeth.'

'Okay, sweetheart. Whatever you say.'

But by the time she had come back again, Terry had begun to doze off, so that when she slipped under the covers beside him, what he did was slide himself against her gently, one arm covering hers, the pair of them slotted together like spoons. It was what he liked most: what he missed those nights she stayed away.

From her room along the landing, Sarah had heard Eileen come in too; had lain there listening to the litany of doors — bedroom, bedroom, bathroom, bathroom, finally the bedroom once more. Sometimes, if she tip-toed across the floor, opened her own door just a crack and listened long enough she would hear her dad cry out and know that they'd been doing it. The same sound that Ray-o made, she knew what it meant.

Ray-o. Sarah lifted the covers over her head and said the name out loud. Ray-o. Ray-o. Ray-o. Abruptly, she stopped, realising that she had been shouting and even muffled like that she might be heard, if not by her dad or Eileen, then by her grandmother in the room adjoining hers. Ray-o. If only they knew… She remembered the first time she'd gone with him, ages she'd been, deciding which skirt to wear, which top, using this article she'd torn from a magazine to get her make-up just right.

Ray-o had met her in the rec and they'd sat on a bench near the kids' swings, drinking cider and smoking Raymond's Silk Cut. After a bit, he'd said how it was getting cold and taken her up to his room. All his mates, the blokes he shared with, had been out. She remembered a smell of sour milk and something else which seemed to come from Raymond himself. When he kissed her he pushed his tongue so far into her mouth she almost choked.

'Wash that stuff off,' he said. 'Here.' Offering her a cloth.

'What stuff?'

'That muck you've got all over your face.'

When she'd finished, he took the cloth back from her and wet one corner of it with spittle, the way her mum had used to do when she was little; carefully, he wiped away the eye shadow that had smeared her cheek.

'Ray-o,' she said quietly.

'What?'

'Nothing.' She'd read somewhere it was a mistake to tell a boy you loved him too soon.

'That's all right then.' He started to take off his clothes and she thought that she should do the same.

When she was stretched back on the bed, one arm across her face to shield her eyes, she felt him touching her, her breasts and down between her legs. He hurt a little but not much.

'Here,' he said. 'Here.'

He was kneeling over her, his thing sticking out, hard and thin. His balls were tight in wrinkled skin. 'Here.' He took her hands and placed them on him, sliding them back and forth. After a while he closed his eyes, pushed her hands away and did it for himself. She didn't know what was more surprising, the way his stuff sprayed across her or the shout that was more of a scream. Concerned, she asked him if it hurt. He lifted the cloth coloured by her make-up from the floor and wiped himself then gave it to her to wipe the stickiness away.

'Ray-o,' she said.

'What?'

'I love you. Honest.' She couldn't help herself. After all, he hadn't done it to her the first time; that proved he respected her, right?

Without really wanting to, Sarah ran her hands gingerly over her stomach, the swell of her belly. She was larger each day now, she'd swear it, though when she was standing straight it wasn't as if she even showed. Her clothes she wore loose and shapeless, just in case. Careful to lock the bathroom door. Ray-o. She couldn't understand why her dad had flown off the handle when he'd seen Ray's name written on her arm. Crack! The back of his hand across her face so fast she'd scarcely seen it coming and the next thing she knew she'd been picking herself up from the floor. 'You stupid little cow! What d'you want to do a thing like that for?' And when she'd said it didn't mean anything, only that she liked him, he'd hauled her off the floor and shaken her until her eyes seemed to rattle in her head. 'Flesh and blood, you horny little cow! He's your own flesh and fucking blood!'

Well, he wasn't. He was only her cousin. In the bible, cousins did it all the time. She'd read it at primary school.

Through the wall Sarah could hear her gran's low, reverberating snore.

*

More months passed. The first frost caught Resnick by surprise. Opening the front door to retrieve the bottles (yes, still bottles) the milkman had left on the step, his feet nearly went from under him. Then he saw that the leaves that had collected in the lee of the wall were rimmed with white along their brittle edges; Dizzy's coat, when he ran his fingers along it, bristled cold and dampish to the touch.

Back in the kitchen, coffee ground and ready, he warmed the milk for all four cats before pouring it into their bowls. While the rye bread was toasting, he sliced Jarlsberg cheese and pulled the rind away from several rounds of Polish salami. The local weather forecaster was predicting a further drop in the temperature of five to ten degrees, but clear and sunny skies. One of the pullovers he had neglected to take to the cleaners had a bronze stain all down one side; the other was coming unravelled beneath the left arm. In the back of the drawer he found a sleeveless cardigan and he put this on over his pale blue shirt and beneath the brown tweed jacket he'd bought seven or eight years before, at a shop which now sold charity Christmas Cards and next year's calendars with twelve different picture of Madonna or Ryan Giggs.

The previous night he'd been listening to some Gerry Mulligan — the California Concerts from the early fifties — and he fancied hearing a handful of the tracks again, but there wasn't time. He had arranged for Graham Millington to give him a lift into the station, and, sure enough, there was the sergeant now, punctual as ever, sounding his horn.

'Cold enough to frighten brass monkeys,' Millington said, as Resnick climbed into the car.

'Happen we'll be busy, Graham. Take our mind off the weather.'

Millington stubbed his Lambert and Butler out in the ashtray between the seats and set the car in gear.

Busy wasn't the word for it. Aside from the ongoing investigations in which all the officers in Resnick's team were involved, the cold night had fostered a flurry of activity through the early hours. Amongst the items stolen from the good burghers of the city were seven fur coats, including two minks and one sable, two cases of five-star brandy, three electric blankets and a state-of-the-art gas fire with full three-dimensional coal effect, neatly removed from its marble fireplace home. And this was without the usual plethora of jewellery, CD collections and VCRs, most of which would, even now, be exchanging hands as part of the system on which the invisible economy depended. How else were people supposed to get pissed, book holidays in Spain, buy something decent for the kids, score weed, pay the tally man, eke out child support, place a bet or put a little aside for a rainy day? If they didn't win the lottery, that is.

'Then there's this, boss,' Divine said. They were sitting round the CID room, tea getting stewed, blue cigarette smoke frescoing the ceiling. 'British Telecom van broken into, two gross of new DF50 fax machines gone missing.'

'Soon be a lot of those around on discount, then,' mused Millington. 'Shouldn't mind one myself.'

'All right,' Resnick said, getting to his feet. 'Let's keep our eyes peeled. Known fences, second hand dealers, car boot sales, any of these fly-by-night merchants sailing along by the seats of their pants. Graham, we've got a list, let's parcel it out. And while Lynn's off on that course, you'd best put a few my way as well.'

For some reason, Raymond had caught himself thinking about Sara: not his cousin Sarah, Sarah with an *h*, but the Sara he used to go out with a couple of years before. The one who had been with him when... well, some of what had happened back then Raymond didn't like to remember. That little girl who'd gone missing and then all that business with the Paki copper as got knifed... but Sara, he didn't mind thinking about her. Nice, she was. Pretty and posh, sort of posh. Clever, too. Never able to understand what she'd seen in him, Raymond, and after a month or two, neither had Sara herself. She'd written him this letter, full of words he didn't properly understand — except he knew what they meant. She was dumping him, that was what. Raymond had tried to talk her out of it, get her to change her mind, but it hadn't been any good. 'I'm sorry, Ray, but I'm afraid my mind's quite made up.' And she'd walked off to where one of her customers was waiting to pay for a large bag of mixed soft-centres, head stuck in the air in that toffee-nosed way she had.

He hadn't been good enough for her, that's what it was. Of course, she hadn't come straight out and said it, Sara, not in so many words. She wasn't like that, better brought up. Whereas his cousin Sarah, she was pathetically grateful if you as much as looked at her, never mind anything else. Always hanging round though, that was the trouble. Wouldn't leave him alone. Not even indoors; in her house, his Uncle Terry's house. There they'd been, one day, Raymond feeling her up on the settee, thinking Terry was clear and instead he'd come breezing in, nearly caught them at it. 'I shouldn't like to think, Ray-o,' Terry said after Sarah had scarpered upstairs, 'that you were taking advantage of me.'

After that, of course, Raymond had backed off and told Sarah to do the same. Stop mooning after him, finding excuses to come to the shop, looking at him all the time like he was God's fucking gift — though from Sarah's point of view, most probably he was. Raymond couldn't see anyone else fancying it, scrawny little tart with a bony arse and tits like doorbells. Mind you, having said that, he thought she might have been putting on a bit of weight lately. All that ice cream and chocolate she was stuffing herself with, Raymond thought, making up for the fact that he wasn't giving her any. He was near the back of the shop, chuckling about that, when the street door opened and Detective Inspector Resnick walked in.

Raymond recognised him right off and the blood flew to his face. Half-turning a clumsy step away, he sent a clock radio crashing to the floor. The plastic top splintered clear across and the radio started playing Jarvis Cocker's *Underwear*.

'Raymond, isn't it?' Resnick said, letting the door swing to behind him. 'Raymond Cooke.'

Down on one knee, mis-hitting the control buttons and switching on the alarm instead, Raymond mumbled yes.

'So, what you up to these days?' Resnick asked, flicking idly through a shoebox of second-hand CDs. 'Keeping out of trouble?'

'Yes.'

'And you've got a job?'

'Yes, here. I work here. My uncle, he…'

'Uncle Terry?' Resnick asked. 'Terry Cooke?'

'Yeh.'

'His place, then?'

'Yes.'

'And you, you're what? Helping him out?'

'No, no, like I said, I'm here all the time. Live here, too. Upstairs.' Raymond pointed towards the ceiling, past a couple of slightly battered kiddies' mobiles and a string of plastic onions that could have done with a dust.

'Nice,' Resnick said. 'Handy.'

'Yeh.'

'Of course…' Resnick had taken one of the CDs from the box now and was studying the writing on the back. '…not so handy for the park, the rec, watching little girls on the swings.'

'I don't…' Breath caught high in Raymond's throat and for a moment he thought he wouldn't be able to breathe.

'Don't what, Raymond?'

'I'm not…'

'Yes?'

Raymond steadied himself against a tumble drier, cleared his throat, found a screwed-up tissue in his pocket and blew his nose. 'I've got a girl friend,' he said. 'Going steady.'

'That's nice, Raymond,' Resnick said pleasantly. 'Anyone I know?'

'No, no. Shouldn't think so, no.'

'You're not…' Resnick looked upwards. '…living together?'

Raymond shook his head. 'Thinking about it, you know.'

Resnick reached out suddenly with his free hand and, as Raymond flinched, flicked something from the shoulder of the youth's leather jacket. 'Treat her well, I hope, Raymond?'

'Yeh, yes, of course.'

Raymond gulped air and Resnick stepped back and glanced at the CD in his hand. 'How much?'

'Fiver.'

'Good condition is it? I mean I'm not going to get it home and find it doesn't play?'

Raymond shrugged. 'Far as I know it's okay.'

'You've not heard it then?'

'Jazz, isn't it?' He shook his head. 'Look, you can have it for four. Three-fifty.'

'You're sure? Only I wouldn't want to get you into trouble with Uncle Terry.'

'He doesn't mind. What I do in the shop here, it's up to me.'

'Responsibility.'

'Yeh.'

Smiling, Resnick gave him a five pound note and waited for his change. 'You wouldn't have anything in the way of fax machines, I suppose? You know, the kind with the telephone. Integral.'

Raymond's face brightened. 'Terry did say something, yes. I reckon we'll be getting some in, the next couple of days. You could always call back. You know, if you were passing.'

Resnick hesitated for a moment at the door. 'All right, Raymond, I might. Maybe you could even put one aside.'

Sarah had shut herself in the bathroom, the cabinet where her dad kept his aftershave and deodorant, his spare razor blades and his condoms, pulled over against the door. There were days — most days — when she could forget what was happening to her, happening to her inside, but this wasn't one of them. Sometimes the pain was so sudden and sharp, she had to bite her bottom lip to stop the screams; sometimes she almost went as far as thinking she would call her gran, ask her to help, but she knew she wouldn't do that. Not really. What she wanted — if she couldn't have Raymond — were friends to turn to, girl friends to ask for advice, but none of the girls at school would give her as much as the time of day.

After a while, she didn't know how long, she heard her gran going down the stairs, on her way to the early evening bingo. Her dad was already out, had been most of the day, she didn't know where. Squatting in the bath, Sarah bore down on the toothbrush she had placed across her mouth and bit it clean in half.

Millington was laughing as Mark Divine set down fresh pints between Resnick and himself. 'And that's what he said? Come back in a couple of days and I'll have one here ready?'

'More or less.'

'Daft twat!'

Resnick nodded. The more he thought about the way Raymond had reacted when he'd walked into the shop, the more he thought the lad might have something to hide, something he might like to ease off his chest. He doubted if it were anything as straightforward as a few BT fax machines.

'Turn him over, shall we?' Millington asked. 'What d'you think?'

Resnick set down his glass. 'Why not? Take Mark here and Kevin; pay them a call. Out of shop hours. But, Graham…'

'Yes?'

'This Cooke youth, Raymond, let's not drop him in it, not with the uncle. Let him stay clear.'

'Plans for him, have you?'

'Maybe.' He shrugged heavy shoulders. 'Stay on his good side for a while, that's all.'

Millington tapped the last Lambert and Butler from the packet; no sense in buying any more now till the morning, not with the wife how she was about him smoking. 'Just as you like.'

They went in with a warrant two days later; still not light. They had the door down before Raymond, deep asleep, could stumble down the stairs to let them in.

'Your uncle here?' Millington asked sharply.

Standing there in boxer shorts and an Oasis t-shirt, one hand cupped across his balls, Raymond just shook his head.

'Call him. Then get yourself back up there out of the way.'

The DF50s were in the store room on the first floor, below where Raymond slept. Two dozen, neatly boxed. All in all, they hauled away a van load of stuff, mostly electrical; nice job that would be for someone, checking them against the stolen goods inventory.

'Course,' Millington winked, 'you've got the paperwork on all this lot.'

Beside him on the pavement, hands deep in pockets, no time to grab a topcoat, freezing bloody cold, Terry Cooke didn't say a thing.

Sarah sat there in her room, curtains closed tight. She didn't know if it were day or night. Her eyes were open and then her eyes were closed. The pain came and then it went. Slowly, she reached from the side of the bed down into the drawer and lifted the baby with both hands. So small and light. So cold. Carefully, she unbuttoned her blouse and pressed him to her chest, the spongy top of his head soft against the nub of her breast.

Seeing it on the table where it had been left, poking out from the pages of last night's *Post*, Resnick realised he had never got around to playing his bargain price CD. *Charlie Parker: from*

*Dizzy to Miles*. Pouring himself a glass of the bison grass vodka he had won in a raffle at the Polish Club. he took the CD from its case, set on the machine and pressed play.

It began with two of the tracks Parker had recorded with Max Roach and Miles Davis in 1951, but through some quirk of programming, the third tune didn't appear till some way into the disc. One of those unison statements so beloved of boppers to begin and then Parker takes off in surprisingly light, long fluid phrases before giving way to the choppy sound of Miles' muted trumpet; a chorus of so-so piano which Parker can't wait to end before he's muscling back in, stronger now, more aggressive, grabbing the piece by the scruff of its neck and hurtling it into four bar exchanges with the drums. Three minutes and six seconds later, abruptly, it's over. *She Rote*.

Settled back in his chair, Resnick smiled: well worth three-pounds-fifty of anybody's money.

The grandmother found the baby the next morning, searching through Sarah's drawers for an old jumper to unpick for wool. He had been wrapped in several layers of clothing and set snug against the drawer's edge, buttons across his eyes.

Her dad found the note in the kitchen, propped up between the stacks of plates near the back door.

*Dear Dad,*
*I am riting to let you no you dont have to worry about me. I shall be OK. I'm sorry but I took the money from where you keep it in your room beside the bed and also from Grans bag. Im telling you this cos I didnt want you to blame Eileen or Ray-o.*
*Im sorry for what Iv done — and about the baby.*
*Love,*
*Sarah*
*xxxxx*

# Stella Duffy

## *Notes*

I became a writer by accident rather than intent. Although I have written for as long as I can remember and being a writer always seemed an 'interesting' thing to be and although I had written for five or six different theatre companies — it was not until I held a book with my name printed down the spine that I started to call myself a 'writer'.

My work has mostly been in performance, and in the last seven years primarily in comedy, specifically improvisation. The basis of impro is storytelling — the gagging and stand-up comedy routines are all very well, but a good impro show demands that the performers are also storytellers (albeit of the three minute variety), a bunch of one-liners is just not good enough. Five years of performing improvised plays once or twice a week taught me about structure, pace and, possibly most important, what to do when the audience is getting bored!

I didn't mean to write crime fiction either — as well as working in comedy, I'd also worked in physical theatre and was interested in putting that on the page — a passionate, juicy, physical girls' love story. Which is what I thought I'd done with my first book **Calendar Girl**. Unfortunately one of the girls was dead. So I needed a detective to find out why. Hence Serpent's Tail bought and sold it as a crime novel. Makes sense, but it wasn't what I intended. I knew nothing of the genre, had read next to no crime authors apart from a spate of Nancy Drew and Trixie Belden when I was eight, and didn't even know there was such a genre as 'lesbian crime'! (Although Nancy and Trixie may have grown up to understand the area better than me!)

*I come to crime writing from a position of knowing virtually nothing about my literary antecedents (though of course I've read lots now), my background is in comedy and theatre — political theatre, women's theatre, gay theatre... and always a longing to play Lady Macbeth at Stratford crossed with an alternate reality desire to marry the works of Steven Bochco.*

*I'm interested in telling stories — ideally two or three at a time. This year I was commissioned to write* **The Hand** *for Gay Sweatshop — a lesbian horror ballet (it's always sensible to start a new genre, at least you can be assured that yours is the world premiere!), which was a wonderful opportunity to explore a growing interest in sex, blood and violence.*

*I'm interested in the real world, the street, the dark, the fact that most things in life don't have happy endings, neat solutions — and I like my realism heightened.*

# Uncertainties and Small Surprises

## by Stella Duffy

'There are uncertainties,' he says, leaning over her in the near empty carriage, 'Uncertainties and small surprises to be had in an underground journey.'

He sits beside her. She smiles politely, buries her head deeper in her old copy of *Time Out*. Reads the letters page. Twice. It does no good. He starts again, smiling now.

'Take for example, the Northern Line train travelling south.'

She begins to wish she hadn't. The two gentlemen in the far corner shuffle their newspapers, glare at her and at the chattering man for disturbing them, say nothing. This man has a point to make, about trains and other matters. He goes on to make it.

'The noticeboard says "see front of train". The train, of course, says nothing. It is not after all, Thomas the Tank Engine. It does not have the luxury of a voice-over by Ringo Starr. Anyway, you decide to take your fate into your own hands. You board the train intending to travel to Victoria to meet your mother at the coach station and...' here he places his hand on hers for emphasis, her arm stiffens, she waits for his hand to move away. It goes nowhere. His grip is tight. He cares about his subject. The train takes a corner a little too quickly and he lurches once more into his discussion.

'And this is the good bit — it doesn't matter which line the train takes. Charing Cross or City Branch. It simply doesn't matter. You will not know what to do until you pass through the ghost of Mornington Crescent. Or not. Of course it is quicker to go to Euston on the Bank Line. You need only to cross the platform there. A few steps to the train you want. And those Victoria Line trains are so very regular.'

Far more regular than the beating of her heart which has gathered momentum in pace with his speech and is now racing at a speed of knots, charged up with adrenalin. Fearful adrenalin. And, if she is honest, which she always is, a tiny breath of excitement too.

Her arm loses its tension and she nods as if giving him permission to continue. He smiles.

'And that is where the small surprise lies. If you have plenty of time and can enjoy the fretful unease of at least six people in the carriage when they realise they are on the wrong side of the Northern Line — you can have a pleasant and enjoyable five minutes in what is usually described as one of the most nightmarish of underground journeys. You don't know what's coming but it doesn't matter. You will arrive at the same destination no matter what route you take. How often can you say that in life, eh? Of course, it only works if you're not in a hurry.'

She makes a leap of judgement and from observing becomes participant. 'Are you often not in a hurry?'

He looks at her, startled that she has joined him. This is new and unexpected. A small surprise.

'Well, no. Almost never. Still, I imagine it's good when it happens.'

She nods, folds the magazine in half and puts it back in her bag.

'Oh, it's always good when it happens.'

He moves his hand from her arm. He is not used to conversation. Does not invite conversation. He sits beside her and shuffles in his seat, his back sweaty against the dark stained covers. Dirty tunnel wind whips across his face and he looks at her, sideways through the cultivated lank fringe that flops over his left eye.

'I'm sorry. I don't think I understand. When what happens?'

'A surprise.'

The train slows. They have been though Euston, Kings Cross, the Angel. The men with neatly folded newspapers have left them alone. This is Old Street. She stands. Now she leans over him.

'This is my stop. Do you want to come?'

The train has shuddered itself into the station, the doors open.

'It's an uncertainty, isn't it? Do you want to come?'

She is more insistent. She likes this. Likes to lean over him. She can smell his hair, could kiss his forehead if the train jolted her forward only two centimetres. 'Quickly. Yes or no?'

Three lads roll into the carriage. They are drunk and loud. Louts. Young men frighten him. Even though he is a young man himself. There are no uncertainties with young men. He prefers to be surprised. Young men frighten her too. In packs. She knows how to take care of the singular. She puts her hand on his. 'Coming?'

He stands and they jump from the train as the doors begin to slam shut. She leads him quickly up stairs and through the empty passages and on to the escalator. They emerge into the open den entrance hall, rabbit warren alleyways leading out in circles to dark midnight. It was the last train south. He will not get home now. She runs up the escalator two moving steps at a time, he is out of breath trying to keep up. Her boots are DM's, shiny black patent leather. Small. She is small. Even in the running and out of breath, he acknowledges she would look silly with bigger feet. Like Minnie Mouse. This girl is small. He senses she is no mouse. This is an adventure. He is running up the steps like a man in a movie. He is tall and striding and she will take him home and make love to him and feed him and he will sleep in her caress and wake in a London that is not rain swept and winter dirty. He sees all this as they pass one after the other through the same ticket barrier. He looks over her little, narrow shoulders and sees all of this. He is seeing things.

Outside it is wet, cold after the suffocating recycled warmth of the tube. He shivers in the wind. She turns and laughs, grabs his hand again.

'Should have brought a coat, shouldn't you?'

Hers is red. Red wool he thinks, with black velvet collar and cuffs. It looks expensive. But she doesn't. There is something too sharp about her to look wealthy. And besides, she is leading him through alleyways, down dark streets. These houses are not tall white painted georgians. She is leading him to a council block. Up stairs, dark, lit by broken lights and reflected dirty puddles. She wouldn't live four floors up in a council block off Old Street if she was wearing a real wool coat. He thinks all this in the time it takes her to grab her keys from the bottom of her overfull bag and let them in. They walk down a short, blue painted passage. She shows him into the sitting room, turns on the light. It is normal. There is a view through the windows, she pulls the curtains against the distant lights of the city and the far more present tower block looming opposite. The room is small now and quiet, except for the remote thump of a too loud bass on a neighbour's stereo. There is a rug in front of the gas fire. A tiger skin rug. With head and staring, wide open eyes. The tail and ears are moth eaten.

'Like my cat?'

He laughs.

'It looks like it got a bit of a shock.'

'One of your small surprises?'

'Maybe. Do tigers deal in journeying uncertainties?'

She shrugs her shoulders.

'This one did.'

In the shrug, her autumn red hair lifts with the black velvet collar of her coat. He glances at the nape of her neck. Likes the look of it, her pale skin, and then looks back at the rug.

'It's cool, I suppose. But it's a bit old isn't it? A bit ravaged. You could pick up something nice from Camden Market. There's those great sun and moon rugs. Everyone's got them.'

Her smile is compassionate, knowing.

'Yes. They have. I'll see. I'll think about it. Turn on the fire. I'll make us a nice cup of tea.'

He had thought sex. At the least a quick snog, a fumble. But tea? He didn't think that women with tiger skin rugs drank tea. Even small women with narrow shoulders and wide hips. He frowns and looks at her.

'No beer?'

Her smile is still there.

'Leave it to me. It'll be a surprise.'

In the kitchen her hands are deft. The tea is to be ginger and honey. Warming with lots of soft brown sugar, lemon and a large

dash of whiskey. She is still unclear as to why she has brought
him here. Not sure what she means to do with him. Not sure
why she did it in the first place. She hears him walking around
her sitting room. He will be looking at the books, the pictures,
the photos. Her sister, her ex-lover. While the kettle boils she
removes her coat and boots. The kettle begins to whistle and in
its admiring glance she takes off her dress, tights, Marks and
Spencer's matching knickers and bra. A softer and babier pink
than she feels. She pours bubbling water into the pot, a drop
breaks out and splashes her naked stomach, she licks her finger
and smoothes the tiny burn with her own cool saliva. She
arranges the tray with heavy mugs and tea cosied pot, a plate of
tiny sweet Japanese biscuits and four thin slices of lemon. She
enters the sitting room with her offering.

He is on the floor by the fire. Going through her record collection. She has not yet graduated to CDs. He had expected to hear
her boots return and is surprised by padding feet. He looks up at
her. He is surprised.

'Oh. Yeah. I mean… wow! Great!'

In his exposition on the uncertainties of tube travel she had
thought him almost eloquent. It had helped her to take his
hand, offer herself. Now, in the face of her flesh, he has lost his
words. She hopes he will rediscover the power of speech. She
kneels on the rug, pours tea, adds lemon, a little more whiskey.
She hands him his drink. She waits for composure to return to
him. She had thought that making herself naked in her own
home would grant him some of the power he'd thrown away
as he came through the door. She had also thought that it might
just give her more power. She wasn't sure which would happen. You never can tell until the clothes are off. Another small
uncertainty.

She takes the Joni Mitchell album from him and they drink
hot tea with a free man in Paris. He is not sure if he is a free man
tonight but the tea has woken and refreshed him, it is whiskey
heavy and ginger invigorating like the whiskey macs his father
made him when they'd come in late from a cold night on the ter-
races. His mother clucked her disapproval. The young woman
in front of him smiles assent. He leans to kiss her and finds that
the soft peck on her mouth is biting back at his lips, cheek,
tongue. Their mouths taste of the same bitter sweet liquid. His

shirt, damp from tube sweat, rain-wet and nearly dried by the gas fire is damp again, sweat running from his armpits. He smells like travel and the beginnings of sex. Her nose wrinkles. She is still uncertain. Knows what to do next but not what to do after.

He is quickly naked. There is art in the removal of patent leather DM's, slowly drawing the shoelace through the silver eyelet holes. There is no art in the removal of thin wet shirt, old trainers, ripped jeans. They kneel opposite each other. The tea things to her left. Her narrow shoulders and wide hips swing towards him. He is not unaware that there is a certain ceremonial touch to all this, he just doesn't know what the ceremony is for.

In the hot moment of fucking, she looks down at him. His eyes shut tight beneath her kisses. She has done the next thing. The kissing. And done the next thing. The biting. And the next. The tracing of his collarbones under his thin blue veined skin. The kissing of his nipples, the kissing of his cock. They have been polite and quiet, taking it in turns to do the next thing and the next. They have maintained the order and the pattern that is expected even from a fuck picked up on the tube between Camden Town and Euston. And now they are here, in the fuck, the tiger is smiling at her and the young man's temples are throbbing above tightly shut eyes, all his energy, his life, pitched into doing that next thing. He would call out her name but he doesn't know it. She nods to the tiger, shakes her head clear of thought and joins this man in the moment of body where the only uncertainty is in when and the smallest surprise is the quiet 'oh' of after. Tired and finished he rolls himself into her and she strokes him to sleep.

He sleeps easy and fast.

She leaves him curled on the tiger rug and takes the tray back to the kitchen. On the draining board is the small paring knife she used to cut the lemon slices. The knife cuts sharply into his throat, his eyelids flutter as if they would wake and warn him but it is too late, he feels the acid of the lemon juice as he drowns in the gurgling blood and hiss of escaping air. She is glad she is naked, she would not want to stain the green velvet dress. The tiger is bloodied but that doesn't matter. The tiger is old. She has needed a new rug for some time. He said so, didn't he? She is finished in a couple of hours. Goes to the bathroom and showers with the plastic shower attachment. Her father had promised to put in a real shower but died before he had time. She could have done it herself, an easy enough job according to the cute boy in the hardware shop, but she'd never wanted to acknowledge to her father, even in death, that he was expendable. Besides, the shower attachment, in ugly grey plastic has a certain seventies, retro charm.

She goes to bed alone, Joni Mitchell in her head, his kiss on her breath.

In the morning she wakes bright and early. Climbs out of bed and pulls on her gym gear. She must do something to build up these narrow shoulders. Run more, swim more. Be more with her body. The morning is fine and clear, last night's rain has left a sharp clean city behind it. On her way out of the flat she peeks into the sitting room. He is lying in front of the fire, in a pool of pale winter sunshine. A man skin rug. With a look of surprise on his face.

# Russell James

## Notes

This was the first short story I ever had published. It was written in two days, following a tip-off that Maxim Jakubowski was short of material for a new anthology. He wanted harder edge, realistic stories from fresh young writers. So I lied about my age.

At that time I had had one book published (Underground) and was still recovering from the anticlimax of my first publication day: no reviews, no parties, not even a card. Reviews appeared eventually, varying from the surprisingly enthusiastic to the disdainful. Someone bought the film rights.

It was after my third book had come out and while I was working on my fourth (Slaughter Music) that I realised something no reviewer had picked up: practically nobody else in Britain was writing crime stories. They were writing detective stories, PI books, police procedurals. They were writing anti-crime stories — law enforcement novels. Why? Did they find policemen interesting?

My books are set among the low life of south east London. I write of punks and misfits, tough guys and shady dealers. I write of crime. Those who fight crime, police and detectives, hardly appear in my books at all; they are a peripheral presence.

To the criminal, the rules of conduct are set by their peers. Professional criminals (and here I exclude the many amateurs — street corner drug dealers, teenage burglars, motor freaks) are not the unpredictable, undisciplined vermin portrayed in the press — though they are social anarchists. Criminals do not share our homely values. They have not signed up to the same contract with society. They live by different rules.

And rules there are. One might almost say that in the UAPC (Unofficial Association of Professional Criminals) the guidelines and Code of Practice cover the same ground as in any recognised professional organisation, in which the one cardinal commandment is 'never betray a fellow member'.

In the supposedly non-criminal world outside, there are new examples every day of violence and betrayal: families evicted from their homes; small businesses closed down; people's jobs stolen from them. At the same time, rewards are handed out freely for fraud, deceit and abuse of power.

I am not saying that if Big Business cleaned up its act, crime elsewhere would disappear — though I would point out that more money is lost through white collar crime than through all other crime put together. I am saying that it is human nature to seize a chance. Think for a moment: if your forefathers had listened to pious exhortations to be content with their lot, you would not be reading this today. You would be huddling in a cave somewhere, wishing that some genius would invent fire.

So what does this have to do with the following story? Approach and attitude. This is not a story about the inherent tragedy of the human condition; it is a vignette, a pivotal evening in the lives of three people from the disregarded underclass. Though it does touch on professional practice, it is concerned more with personal respect. Whatever their backgrounds, people feel similarly — and despite what songwriters may tell you, it is not diamonds which are a girl's best friend, it is three little words.

# A Piece of Cake

## by Russell James

There was fresh blood on the tip of her first finger. She stared at it. Three times that cut had opened: each time she had stanched it with cold water, pressed a tissue against it, and held it there till the bleeding stopped. It was not a deep cut. It should not keep bleeding. A cut like that should not need a dressing.

If she could have found a bandage in the flat Terri would have used it. But there wasn't one. All she could find was a tin of sticking plasters in the cupboard in the bathroom — Jeg's ugly little medicine cupboard, cream painted, with a chip in the mirror. Presumably they were for when he cut himself shaving. But that wasn't why she didn't use them. Terri didn't like sticking plasters. She didn't like the way that when she ripped them off afterwards, they burnt her skin. She didn't like the way they made her flesh pucker — making it look shrivelled, pinky-white, like raw chicken. Terri had a thing about plasters.

So she used a tissue. Usually if she cut herself in the kitchen, a tissue would be enough. Hold it there five minutes until the bleeding stopped. As long as she took care not to bang her hand in the next few hours, it would be all right. It wouldn't bleed again. The cut would heal. No need for plaster.

What she should have done was use a J-cloth. Cut a piece off the end, maybe two inches long, moisten it at the sink, wrap that around her finger. Like a bandage. That's what she should have done. But it was too late now.

Terri forced herself to examine the cut. The blood had oozed out; it had not flowed. It was as if there was one last gob of phlegm that had to be coughed up to get things clear. A single last blob of red phlegm. It lay unmoving on her finger. Should she wipe it off?

Maybe if she left it there it would form a kind of skin not a scab exactly, but a natural protection manufactured by her blood system in place of the dressing that wasn't there. Bodies did that sort of thing, didn't they — healed themselves? That's what happened beneath a bandage. It wasn't lint that cured the bleeding; it was that the bandage let the blob of blood lie undisturbed until it curdled, like thick cream. Then thinner blood from inside her veins couldn't squeeze out, and the bleeding would slowly stop. Over the next day or so, the clean pink flesh would weld back together, like pastry dough.

If you thought about it like that, it was wonderful what the human body could do — on its own. But Terri didn't want to think about it like that. She didn't want to think about it at all. She hated blood.

Jeg put his hand inside the safe. 'Here we are.'

Wynne looked at him. He wondered why it was that though he cracked the combination, Jeg had to be first inside. Stuffing his big hand inside the door was the only contribution Jeg had made, apart from setting up the job. Setting it up? All Jeg had done was write down the address and time, and ring for Wynne. He hadn't had to plan anything. He just took orders from Mr Gottfleisch. Wynne did the work.

Wynne was the one who slipped the catch on the rear window, who disabled the infra-red, who came in first — all the relatively easy things that anyone could do. His skill should have been saved for the combination. That was his job. Jeg had done nothing. Outside, he had just stood in the shadow at the back of the shop with his hands in his pockets. Keeping watch, he said.

A 'born manager' was how Jeg saw himself, handling plans and organisation. Wynne shook his head. Who was Jeg kidding?

All the detail came from Gottfleisch. Most of the profit would go there too. Wynne and Jeg were just the errand boys. Gottfleisch employed Jeg because he was big, tough and unintelligent. An ideal worker. He'd do his job, take his wages, ask no questions.

And what makes you so different, Wynne asked himself? You are doing the job, you will take your wages, you won't ask awkward questions. Even if you wanted to, Jeg wouldn't let you. He thinks he owns you.

For now though, Jeg's thoughts were on the jewellery. As he scooped the pieces into his canvas bag he wondered if Gottfleisch knew exactly what was there. Jeg thought he would. Knowing Gottfleisch, he'd have each one listed. Anyway, Jeg wouldn't cross him. He knew the kind of things that happened if you tried to cross Mr Gottfleisch.

Another man might have considered it. Over any one of those smaller pieces of jewellery, another man's fingers might have hesitated. A little bracelet like that would be handy for the wife. But not Jeg. He would not be tempted. Even if he had had a wife, work would come first.

Terri washed her hands. Carefully. She watched the blob of blood loosen and then fall away. When she brought her hand out from the tepid water, the cut seemed to have healed. A flap of pale skin, curved like an idiot's smile, sat on the ball of her finger. She looked away. Then looked back again. Terri looked around the kitchen for distraction. The cut was horrible. It made her nauseous. She wouldn't look at it again.

Terri clutched at the rim of the sink and breathed in, deeply. Her eyes were wide. An attack of giddiness filled her with alarm. If she left the sink now to find a chair she might be sick. But if she didn't sit down soon she might faint.

She would count to ten.

Slowly in her throat the taste of vomit rose like warm water in a drain. And like warm water it found a level. It lingered there. Her face grew cold.

Being sick in the kitchen-sink brought relief. She felt detached from that shivering blonde woman who leant there retching. She used her right hand to turn on the water, and watched with clinical curiosity as the soup of half digested food swirled around the plug-hole. Whenever larger pieces of vegetable — perfectly recognisable — became stuck in the grille, Terri prodded them through with one of the fingers of her good right hand. Each spasm in her stomach now had become mechanical. She could cope with this.

Walking through the street, Jeg began to swagger. The cool night air was telling him he was free.

'It was a piece of cake,' he said. 'Like always, didn't I tell yer?'

'Like always,' Wynne agreed, two steps behind.

'So what's your plan now?' Jeg asked. 'You got something tasty lined up at home?'

Wynne did not reply. He continued walking the dark street, watching the nape of big Jeg's neck. Wynne decided that the reason Jeg was walking fast was that he wouldn't wear a topcoat. He strode along the pavement in pullover and jeans as if he'd just stepped out the house to fetch his car. The little canvas bag was stuffed inside his pullover, and he looked as ordinary a bloke as you could meet.

You had to give him that, Wynne conceded. Jeg was the sort of guy could walk up to a copper right this moment, the bag of jewellery stuffed inside his pullover, could ask the time and not get caught. Jeg would do it, if a cop appeared.

One didn't.

Wynne's car was parked in a quiet alley, three streets away from the shop that they had burgled. Wynne unlocked the car doors and they slipped inside.

'Don't hang about,' Jeg said, smirking through the window. 'It's time for all good people to be in bed.'

As she pulled on a pair of yellow rubber gloves, Terri wrinkled her tiny nose. In a sense, the gloves would act as a dressing. Except that the way the clammy rubber dragged against her skin made it possible the cut might re-open. Any blood, though, would remain inside.

Wearing gloves meant she was able to function more normally. She rinsed crockery at the sink, finished a glass of whisky she had poured because she needed it, rinsed that as well. She wiped the table.

With the J-cloth in her hand, Terri drifted around Jeg's flat, cleaning surfaces. She liked to keep things respectable and clean.

Jeg's flat was typical of a man who lived on his own: untidy, uncared for, grimy in the corners. For the last hour, Terri had had the window open, refreshing the stale air. But she knew she had better close it now, before Jeg got home.

Terri took some magazines off the side table and placed them on a shelf. She cleaned the table. Then she returned to the kitchen to fetch the crockery. The plates and cups and saucers looked pretty, she thought, on the newly cleaned table. She fetched some sugar, and a jug of milk.

Then Terri brought in the cake.

'A piece of cake,' Jeg remarked.

Wynne concentrated on his driving. In the lonely streets at this time of night there was almost no traffic. But he kept his speed below thirty and took no chances at the lights.

'Makes you feel good, though, dunnit?' Jeg continued. 'Gets your pecker up. Do the job right, no problems, back to bed. Round things off with a bit of nookie. Bloody perfect.'

Wynne smiled, uneasily.

'You ain't saying much, Wynne. You gone to sleep?'

'No, it's late. You know — driving.'

'Well, remember this, sunbeam, you're working nights tonight. Gotta stay awake.'

Wynne wondered what they could talk about. He could think of nothing except to ask, 'You got some nookie, then, have you — lined up waiting?'

'Well, you know, just Terri. Got her staying round my place for the night.'

'Oh yeah, Terri. Nice kid, that.'

'Nice kid? D'you fancy her yourself?'

'No.' Wynne grimaced through the windscreen. 'No, not much.'

'Don't like my taste?'

'Not if your taste lingers. No, she's not my type.'

'I thought you fancied her.'

Wynne let out a chuckle, to dismiss it. But he didn't say anything. That could be risky. After what had happened that afternoon, he should not have continued this conversation. He should have left the subject well alone. He had called at the flat that afternoon to find Jeg out. Terri was in. When she opened the door Wynne saw that she had a pink bruise on her cheek and had been crying. She stood at the door holding a drying-up cloth in her hands and wringing it out as if it was full of water. He couldn't leave.

He had stepped inside, said something soothing, and the next thing he knew she was in his arms. She burst out crying. She covered his neck with tears and told him that Jeg had beaten her again. Not badly, not like he sometimes had, not like when she'd had to stay curled up in bed till the marks had faded. This time he had just back-handed her and gone off to the pub.

Wynne should have joined him.

'Are yer coming up for a drink?'

'What?' For the past two minutes, Wynne had driven on auto-pilot. He had hardly realised they'd arrived.

'I said come on up and have a drink.'

Wynne felt his stomach tightening. He didn't want to go up to the flat.

'Well — '

'Turn the car off, Wynne. You'll wake the bloody neighbours.'

'Maybe I'll just get home to bed.'

'What's wrong with you tonight? Like a bloody zombie.'

Wynne felt weak. His hands were sweating. 'No, it's just that I'm feeling tired.' He couldn't rely on Terri to be sensible. Sometimes she didn't seem to be all there. 'I'll shoot off home.'

'What are yer — a fuckin' minicab driver? Come in and have a drink.'

Wynne switched off the car. There was no way he could avoid Terri now.

She heard the engine throbbing in the quiet night street. She reheated water in the kettle. She made the tea.

When Wynne and Jeg came through the door, Terri was stooping over the small side table like a vicar's wife. She still wore the apron and rubber gloves. On the table, amid a ring of teacups and plates, they saw the pot of tea and the bowl of sugar and a jug of milk snuggled against a large white-crusted sponge. Each little plate had on it a side-knife and a paper napkin. There was a big knife for the cake. There were teaspoons in the saucers. There was another teaspoon in the sugar bowl.

'The fuck is this?'

'I made some tea.'

'I can fucking see that. What's the idea?'

'You know, Jeg, a celebration.'

'With cups of tea? Oh, do grow up.'

Terri's shoulders sagged. She sat down on a wooden chair beside the table. 'I thought you'd like it.'

'What you dressed up like a maid for? Think it turns me on?'

Jeg looked across at Wynne for a reaction. He didn't get one. Terri stayed on her chair, plucking at her fingers.

'You been moving round my things?'

Jeg glared at Terri. She wouldn't look at him when she spoke. 'I just cleaned up a bit — tidied things away.'

'Well, fucking don't.' He turned to Wynne. 'She thinks she's moving in, that's what it is.'

Wynne glanced at Terri, sitting silent and alone at the side table. 'I wouldn't mind a cup of tea,' he said.

Jeg snorted. 'Not you as well. Let's have a beer.'

He strode towards the kitchen.

'I don't want a beer.'

The room went silent. Jeg frowned at him. Wynne struggled on. 'I mean, it's one o'clock. I'll be up peeing half the night.'

'On a glass of beer? Wotcher saying — don't you piss if you drink tea?'

Terri rose from her chair. 'We can have the cake with beer instead of tea.' She smiled brightly at them.

Jeg ambled back toward the table. 'You keep your stupid trap shut. What's with you, Wynne?'

Across Jeg's shoulder, Wynne saw Terri watching him. He licked his lips, but said nothing.

Jeg inhaled angrily. 'You lost your voice?'

'No, I —'

'You been behaving like a prat the whole night long.'

Terri stared into Wynne's downcast eyes, asking a silent, urgent question. But he didn't look at her. He knew what she was asking. but he didn't have a reply. He said: 'I'll have a beer.'

'What — you're doing me a favour?'

Wynne shook his head. 'I don't care,' he said. 'Beer, cup of tea, or I'll just go home. You invited me up here.'

For a moment the two men stared in each other's eyes.

Wynne was the first to look away.

Terri said, 'I'll cut the cake.'

'You stay out of this!' Jeg swung his fist, back-handed, without looking where she was. But he missed her. She had been caught that way before.

'You cut the cake,' she said. 'I'll get the beer.'

This time Jeg did turn towards her. The scowl on his face obliterated any trace of the dark good looks that had once attracted her. He jabbed his finger, pointing at her face. 'Just keep your trap shut, girl. I told yer once.'

She let her face freeze.

The silence was embarrassing. Jeg found that he was stuck in a clumsy statuesque position with both the others watching him. He pulled his arm back.

'What's with this fucking cake, anyway?'

Terri shrugged. 'I'll fetch the beer. You both sit down.'

She kept an armchair between them as she walked towards the kitchen. The men breathed out.

'Oh, sit down,' said Jeg.

As Wynne eased himself onto the edge of a wooden seat, he glanced towards the kitchen. She was watching him. Motionless in the doorway she stood erect. She raised an eyebrow. Frail as Terri was, Wynne recognised her strength.

She tilted her head and mouthed across the room at him: 'Well?'

'I'll cut the cake,' he saïd.

Terri stood at Jeg's sink with her eyes closed. She felt very tense. She gripped the rim of the sink so tightly that it made the end of her cut finger ache again. She could feel it throbbing through the glove. Slowly, she breathed in and out.

In the next room the two men talked uneasily. They each ate a slice of the bought sponge cake, and they drank a beer. When Jeg opened a second bottle, Wynne declined. He said he was only halfway through his first.

Terri shook her head. Wynne was spineless. The weakling and the bully, that's who they were. This afternoon, when she had sagged unexpectedly into Wynne's arms, she had hoped he would be different. She knew he wanted her. It was obvious. He had wanted her for weeks. Now he had finally plucked up the courage to come to the flat when Jeg was out, she made it easy for him. But he had funked it.

Wynne had said, 'Why don't I come round to your place, private like?'

'When Jeg's not there?'

'Yeah.'

'Jeg's not here, is he?'

'Yeah. But... Where d'you live, Terri?'

'D'you love me, Wynne?'

That threw the man. That was the question that threw every man.

'D'you love me. Jeg?'

'What?'

'Do you love me?'

Jeg stood with his back to her, looking down from the window as Wynne got into his car. Jeg said, 'What a prat that Wynnie is.'

'Forget him now.'

'Yeah, you're right.' Jeg turned from the window. He grinned at her.

She said, 'Did your job go all right?'

'Oh yeah.' Jeg seemed eager to talk of it. 'A piece of cake. Straight in, straight out. In the morning I take the jewels round to Gottfleisch. You know him: never likes yer going straight from a job to his place. You might be followed. But if the Old Bill don't nick you in the night, they ain't got a lead on yer, have they? So we wait till morning.'

'Gottfleisch will be fast asleep now.'

'I expect you're right. Doesn't sound such a bad idea, neither.' Jeg grinned again. 'Come on, girl, get your clothes off. I'm in the mood.'

'Oh, that's nice. That's really romantic.'

'I'm always in the mood after a job. D'you know you still got those stupid gloves on?'

'I hurt my finger.'

'Oh, poor girl.'

Terri hesitated in the middle of the room. 'But do you love me, Jeg?'

'What is this?'

'You know — do you?'

He laughed shortly, looking quickly round the room as if for an audience. 'Come on, Terri, leave it out.'

'Don't you love me, then?'

When Terri put that plaintive expression on her face, Jeg never could resist her. Every time she did it, Jeg wanted to punch her, hurt her, assert his masculinity on her. She knew he did.

'Love yer? Of course I love yer. I fucks yer, don't I?'

Jeg laughed coarsely as he marched across the room. He opened his big arms to her. 'Give yer man a kiss! What d'yer say?'

Terri slid into his arms, and rammed the carving knife into his guts. The heavy blade slipped behind his ribs and pierced his heart. Jeg hesitated, just a moment, leaning towards her on the balls of his feet, before he fell. The expression on his face was as if he had just forgotten something important — which he had: something vital. He had forgotten it completely.

She did not touch the knife again. She left it deep inside his body. As she unpeeled her rubber gloves she remembered with satisfaction that it had been Wynne who sliced the cake. He had used the carving knife. And that rackety old car of his: maybe someone had seen him leave. It didn't matter. The police had his fingerprints.

Terri took the jewels from Jeg's canvas bag. While she transferred them to her own black handbag she critically examined every piece. There was a brooch she thought especially ugly — an Alexandrine perhaps. She tossed it across the room so that it rolled beside an armchair. It would give a motive.

Terri didn't need to check the flat again. Nothing of hers remained. There was nothing she wanted there.

# Maxim Jakubowski

## Notes

I cheated. I read all the other stories in this collection before I wrote mine. Editorial advantage and all that.

But I don't think it made any difference.

I had just completed a new book, a cycle of intimately-linked short stories, some crime, some not, and was beginning to think of new imaginative horizons between looming non-fiction deadlines. So I thought writing a good clear-cut modern crime story with a realistic background would be an interesting exercise. Little did I know that once again I would prove incapable of driving down a traditional path and that my obsessions and bad habits would force their way with insolent ease into the new story. And some of the characters from the book. Will they ever leave me, I wonder?

I knew it had to be set in London. So many of my other tales have taken place in America; a fantasy America constructed from small touches of places I have seen and visited and, even more, of the America of my mind, so a British setting was necessary for the touch of realism required. And all I really know well is London, since I was brought up abroad and my British travels have been woefully incurious.

Sadly, I'm too much of a detached (cynical?) observer of the social and political scene to inject credible comment on the state of the nation. I have my views, sure, but it's people, emotions that matter so much more to me.

*There had to be violence. Crude. Even shocking. I remembered all the fuss some years back when Bret Easton Ellis' American Psycho appeared and the prospect of having a stab, so to speak, at An American Psycho In London was appealing. But then I think the central character is in fact English, so I suppose it spoils the joke slightly…*

*All the earlier stories were dripping with sex, so this time around I wanted that element to be less direct but still pervasive overall. I think I will never tire of describing women, bodies, faces and why should I deprive myself? My philosophy is, if you have an itch, scratch it until it bleeds and beyond. No limits. No censorship. And damn it if some people are shocked. So the pieces slowly came together in my mind and the story wrote itself quite rapidly during an intense period of travel between London, Paris, Cognac and Courmayeur in the winter of 1995.*

*My sympathies naturally lean toward the realist school of crime fiction. It's a dark, noir world out there and I believe writers should reflect this, and remind readers of how grim and cold it can be outside, while all along not forgetting to tell a damn good story in the process. In my usual oblique way, my aim is the same whenever I visit the mystery genre. It's just that the form is less traditional. Blame post-modernism. And by the way, all those other stories full of sex and fury appear in* Life In The World Of Women, *from this publisher any day now. Go on, indulge in your baser nature…*

# Blood and Guts, Goodge Street

## by Maxim Jakubowski

H *er body, like a landscape, stretching out, in softer shades of white across the darker hues of the bed cover, the colours of the sky outside falling over the calm expanse of her skin, her flesh, like a sacrament, filtered through the glass of the window pane.*

I exited at Goodge Street, off the Northern Line going south, ambled along the grey corridors and reached the elevators. There were only six other passengers getting off the train. We all waited for one of the twin elevators to arrive. Three men, three women. Once inside the lift, the gate closed rapidly. One of the women looked at me. She was rather pretty, upturned nose, auburn hair, shapely under her winter coat from what I could see or guess. Or maybe she wasn't looking at me, but past me, lost in idle contemplation and thoughts. No matter. I looked away. Two of the men had receding chins. The lift came to a halt at street level. Outside the station the newsagent was building a display wall of the latest *Time Out*. It was Tuesday morning. I walked past the Scientologists' window. It was still too early for them to be recruiting on the sidewalk. Good for them, today I would have been fucking rude. More than usual. I turned off Tottenham Court Road and in to Goodge Street proper. First left, down Whitfield Street past the small park where I had once lurked early one morning shielding the pathetic bouquet of flowers I'd got for her birthday. Finally Windmill Street, another left turn and road and a further hundred yards or so to the building she worked in.

I stopped a dozen steps or so beyond the door. Collected my thoughts. Took an assortment of deep breaths. I was reaching the point of no return. The gun felt heavy in the pocket of my leather jacket. Illegal of course. Johnny Angelo, who knew everyone normal folk don't want to know in Tulse Hill in south London had obtained it. He owed me some favours. Never asked me any questions. Hand deep in pocket, I gripped the weapon's handle. Warm steel. It was always too hot on London Underground. It felt solid. Real.

Hand out of pocket now, I turned. Back. Just a few steps. A white porch, with the company's name and its old-fashioned logo above. The letter-box through which I had deposited so many letters full of anger, self-pity and despair.

In.

Reception area. A young girl with dark hair and a pony-tail. No doubt the one who always sounded dead stupid on the phone, 'Who's calling, please?'. She was reading some fashion magazine and looked up toward me with unfeigned annoyance. Behind her, a glass partition leading through to the ground floor open-plan offices. Just a couple of people at desks. The usual clutter of a publishing house. Files, piles of papers everywhere, the flickering screen of a computer.

'Is Kay Cambridge in today?' I asked the girl.

'Yes, she is. Do you have an appointment? Who wishes to see her?' she blurted out mechanically.

I looked her in the eyes. Held my gaze. No reaction. I could just as well have been invisible to her. She twisted her lips, indicating thus she was still expecting me to respond. The telephone on her desk rang. Still looking past me, she picked the receiver up. '*Mumble mumble* Books… yes, who's calling, please? Connecting you… Diane, it's for you. Roddy Smith from WH Smith…' She put the phone down, still looking at me.

'Yes?'

Still silent, I smiled.

'Your name?'

Didn't even call me 'sir'. No manners. Kids today.

I pulled the gun out of my pocket and levelled it at her.

The look on her face. She didn't know whether to laugh or scream. Mind you, I suppose it's not the sort of thing they warn you about in secretarial training.

Her turn to be silent. She slowly raised her hands. Good, she'd seen all the right movies.

'Stand up,' I ordered her.

She did.

'Don't move. How does the front door lock?'

'There's a latch,' she whispered. The phone rang again.

'Don't answer it.'

It didn't keep ringing for long before someone in the offices picked up. Not on the ground floor. I could see the other two from where I was standing, still at their desks, with their backs to the receptionist and me.

I calmly explained to her what we were going to do. First, call the ground floor denizens over on some pretext or other.

'You've got a basement, haven't you?' I asked.

I knew that was where the fax machine and the old editorial files were kept.

'Yes,' she nodded, indicating a door next to the entrance hallway, to her left.

'Good,' I said.

One by one, the front door to the building now locked, safe from unwelcome visitors or further intrusions, following a quick descent into the basement where I tore away from their sockets the wires connecting the telephone and the fax machine, the receptionist summoned all the staff in house. Except for Kay. Who must have been too busy answering the calls reception was no longer intercepting to notice the gradual exodus of her workmates.

There was a corner in the basement which was being used for packing books, and there was enough rope there to tie them all up. Some of them were very pale; a couple of the men were almost shitting their pants. Amazing how a pointed gun affects folks.

Finally, the job was complete. Only Kay, on the first floor where she usually worked, away from the window, at the old wooden desk on which she regularly bruised her thighs, and myself were left. Today's full complement of lousy publishers were securely bound and locked up in the basement, with no contact with the outside world, their feeble shouts shielded by solid brick walls and two thick doors onto the street.

I slowly walked up the stairs. Nervously brushed my hair back into place. Replaced the gun in my pocket. Her head was down, features obscured by the crazy tangle of her hair. Typing away at a computer keyboard.

'Hello, Kay,' I said very quietly.

*Her body in sweet repose, an altar for his adoration, from pale neck to hot cunt to cold toes, a subtle geography of his all-conquering desire interrupted here and there by scattered, minor imperfections: moles, discolourations of the skin or minute birth marks.*

Two Hours Earlier:

'No, I can't discuss it over the phone,' I had told him.

'I understand,' he said.

I'd arranged the meeting by the small pond I remembered from my childhood days in Epping Forest. Isolated, and hopefully very quiet at this time of day. All so easy. A phone call to the studio, asked for his name at the Business and Economics Unit. Stuff about some huge institutional mortgage scam amongst the larger building societies. On his patch. He was hooked. Fast. Ready to come running. Smelling the proverbial scoop like an eager puppy.

Dawn. Thin morning mist rising from the dirty waters of the pond. Bare autumn trees. The distant noise of heavy traffic near Whipps Cross Corner. I didn't know where he had parked his Vauxhall, but it didn't matter, I knew I wasn't pursuing the perfect crime this time around. Had I ever?

He walked over toward me. At first, he appeared surprised. I wasn't what he was expecting. Neither City-like or criminal in my appearance, I suppose. He was carrying a heavy-duty tape recorder in a shoulder bag.

'No tape,' I said, when we reached the edge of the water.

'Fine,' he answered. 'But can I take notes?'

'I don't think it will be necessary.'

'Are you sure?'

'Very.'

Even though this was the first time we had actually met in the flesh, I knew him inside out already. From Kay's stories, the photographs, his journalistic work. A bit bulkier, I suppose. The skin a touch ruddy, spotty. A big man, as she had once warned me. Had he played rugby at college? Certainly had the size and shape. Not a man who would age gracefully. Yes, she did deserve better.

'So, Mark,' I said.

'Tell me all about it,' he said solicitously.

'I know your wife, were you aware of that?' I enquired.

'Ah, so was it her who suggested you get in touch with me with the story? She sometimes gets good contacts working as she does in book publishing.'

'I know your wife,' I repeated, my fingers gripping the gun now.

'I see.'

'I know your wife,' I told him. 'She has a small beauty spot just above the tip of her left breast, and another darker one, a mole, just below her right buttock. And when she gives head, she's very good, you never feel her teeth.'

'What the hell?' he roared, anger rising in his eyes. Then realised.

'You're him? The bloody bastard who made her so unhappy.'

'Look who's talking, Mark.'

I pulled the gun out.

He looked down at it. Frowned. Looked up at me again. Uncomprehending.

'Yes, it's me.'

'You've got a bloody nerve.'

'Have I?'

'You won't get away with this, you know.'

'Indeed, but getting away with it is the last thing on my mind,' I told him.

'So what is this all about?' he asked.

'It's about anger, it's about pain, Mark. It's about if you've somehow pressured her into not seeing or speaking to me again, then I don't want you to have her any longer. It's about how you took her for granted too long and wasted her best years, and then loomed like a malevolent shadow over her when the two of us had a chance of happiness, of tenderness. It's about how she used to undress me and slide her fingers through the hair on my chest and my arms and made me tingle like no other woman had done before, about the way she moaned, writhed and exhaled when I touched her in all the places you couldn't satisfy. It's about Kay, Mark. It's about me.'

'You're crazy,' he said.

'Don't I know it?' I answered with a smile. 'But there are worse conditions. Your present one, for instance.' I waved the gun menacingly toward his nose.

'So what are you going to do,' he asked. 'Rub my face again in all the sheer filth she and you got up to. You make me sick, you do.'

'Mistake, Mark, for you the flesh might be filth, but it never was for us. A very bad mistake. Yes. Now, turn round, turn your back to me.'

'Why?'

'Do it.'

'Come on, I'm sure we can talk, put all this behind us…'

'Do it.'

Mark turned, facing the pond.

'Don't move one single inch.'

Make him squirm a bit, I knew it was petty, but it was also cruel fun. What was he thinking right then? That I was going to tell him to count to a thousand and fade away like a bad dream? No chance.

The surrounding silence assaulted us. The lorries, the far traffic on the North Circular Road, all gone, we were in a different world.

Swinging the gun with all the force I could muster, I brought it down on his skull. He collapsed to the ground, just like in the movies. I looked all around. Behind the surrounding trees, the other side of the pond, no one, no witnesses. I picked his tape recorder up and threw it in the water. That should confuse them a little. Eliminate theft. I rolled Mark over onto his back. It was almost as if he were sleeping, there on the dark ground, sprawled out like a baby octopus, in his boring brown outside broadcast-suit and nondescript shirt and tie, his hair ruffled, thinning at the top, the beginning of a beer belly pushing against his trouser belt. He was still breathing. Of course. You don't kill people so easily. I extracted the Stanley knife with the metal grey handle from the inside pocket of my leather jacket. Clicked it open and slit his throat. Tougher than I expected, or maybe the blade wasn't sharp enough. Very careful not to stain myself with his blood. When I first cut into the skin, he moved a bit, the pain percolating through his unconsciousness, then squirmed, the heaving movement gliding down his body from throat to chest to midriff to legs. But it only lasted a few seconds. Not enough to worry me. Quickly over. Most of the blood was absorbed by his shirt collar. Dead. I stood up, looked down at the fucker. See, you bastard. You fucking bloody bastard, now you've ruined my life twice. I kicked him in the ribs. And again. Bastard. Bastard. Kneeled, watched the blood trickling slowly out of the aperture I had created onto the ground. His face was growing paler all the time. Broke his fucking nose with my fist. Sliced his left ear lobe off. Like butter now, the knife miraculously sharpened by the initial slash. Began laughing. Homage to Quentin Tarantino. Yeah, Mark, all over now, you're not going to screw her any more, your wife, my Kay, in the doggie position, as she preferred it, hey? A few more kicks for the road. Then an afterthought. *American Psycho in London*. Why not? Loosened the belt at his waist and pulled the trousers down to his knees. Striped boxer shorts. Rather incongruous. The corpse wore boxer shorts, good title that. A small damp patch at the front of the shorts. You dirty bastard. Tugged at them, unveiling his shrivelled cock, greyish, off colour, uncircumcised. Look how tiny it is now, Mark, you fucker. Out for the count, mate, no more conjugal visits, no more soiling her, thrusting in her like a pig, pawing her white skin as if you owned it. The knife. Took the inert penis by its soft shaft and cut. Like gristle. Tough. Cut. Cut. Cut. Shit, the blood spurting from the severed stem all over his legs and my hands. Pry his mouth open and stuff the useless piece of meat inside. Used to read how Algerian terrorists would do that to the bodies of French soldiers during the colonial war then. Caught my imagination. More recently in the old Yugoslavia. Eat that, you cunt. Too messy to do his balls, his pitiful scrotal sack, no, no need for that. It would be in bad taste to bring Kay his balls wrapped in a handkerchief. Didn't have a handkerchief with me anyway. My head clearing, the sound of birds over the clearing. I walked away from my crime scene.

*Her body, indelibly etched alive like a computer screen saver on the backdrop of his unforgiving memory. Naked. Sacred. Her breasts gentle hills, her rump a daunting elevation, the gash of her vaginal lips a by-*

*way into unforetold treasures. Her mouth a subliminal echo of her now-forgotten voice.*

Back in Real-Time:

'Hello, Kay,' I said very quietly.

She looked away from her blue screen.

'What the hell are you doing here? Who showed you upstairs?' she asked, then looked around the room. 'Where are all the others? What is this?'

I kept on smiling at her.

'It's been a long time, Kay,'

'Yes.'

'Nearly two and a half years.'

'I know. And are you going to bore me again with the sad news you've been thinking of me every single day since? You're pathetic.'

'I suppose so.'

She composed herself, stood up, faced me resolutely.

'So what are you up to now? Mischief, no doubt. You just like to hurt people, don't you? Could you never take "no" for an answer? Couldn't take rejection? Coming up to beg me for one last time, one last fuck, are you? Well, the answer is no. You had your chance. You blew it.'

I could see the anger rising, like a strong wind, Chandler's Santa Ana red wind which blinds the mind and the emotions.

'Oh, Kay…'

'Don't "Kay" me,' she spat at me with undisguised contempt. Sad how affection can so easily turn to hate. Not fair. Not fair at all.

'Do you know where your husband is?' I asked her.

'On some journalistic goose-chase in East London. Why?'

'An assignment in Epping Forest, maybe?'

'Yes. But how do… It was you who phoned, wasn't it? You've met him. You vile bastard, you promised you would never contact him. Never. You promised.'

'I've killed him.'

'I don't believe you, you haven't got the guts. My god, you're quite crazy.'

'I did.'

'Oh, come on, at worst you spiked his car tank with sugar, that's the extent of your perception of evil.'

'I did. Do you want the details?'

Her look wavered as she inspected me, searching for invisible answers in my posture, my clothes. She blinked.

It's then, I think, she finally understood I was quite serious. She held my gaze, but her shoulders slumped, the anger left her as quickly as it had taken hold. She was wearing a tight white sweater with a wide open neck, her knee-length grey skirt and a brown suede waistcoat. Her legs went on for ever.

'Why?' she then asked, calmly resigning herself to the fact.

'Because I hated him. I was jealous. Envious that he had you and I didn't,' I answered. 'As simple as that.'

'I always knew you were too dangerous.'

'Yeah,' I answered. 'As the gangster said to the contracts manager, you shouldn't have messed with me.'

She leaned back against her desk, her body in need of support as the news registered at a deeper level.

'What now? What do you plan to do with me? Do you think that now that you're rid of Mark, I might come running back to you? Never. If that was your plan, it was a bad one. I'd rather die.'

'Maybe you deserve to after what you did to me.'

'What I did to you? What sort of joke is that?' she protested.

She hastily picked up the phone. The line was dead. The situation sunk in. Alone with a crazed ex-lover who claimed to have murdered her husband.

'So what should I do, Kay?' I asked her.

'Whatever you want,' she answered, almost whispering.

I took the gun from my pocket. Set it down on the nearest desk surface. Her eyes widened. She almost said something, but then her lips closed quickly again, as she changed her mind.

'I no longer know what I should do,' I admitted.

She took a step towards me, with a furtive glance at the gun on the nearby desk.

Her dark eyes pleaded with me.

'I know, Kay, I know it can never be like before again. I'm not that crazy that I can't recognise reality, the finality of it. But what should I do? I still lust for you with the passion of the first day. I still feel my heart beat faster whenever I drive through south London even if I'm miles away from where you live; my fingers shake when my tube stops at Goodge Street twice a day and I imagine you on the other platform; in shops I recognise with a sigh of despair every book you've ever worked on and your publicity people twist the knife in my gut each time they advertise one of your company's titles on posters plastered all over town, in places I can't avoid. I've tried to get you out of my life, but nothing works. You are my only reason for living.'

'Please…'

'No, don't interrupt me. A thousand times I've dreamed, imagined myself with you here, in this office, among all the people who see you daily, speak with you, joke with you, the women who share the loo with you and see you putting your make-up back on or adjust a stocking or your tights at the end of the working day, the men who catch a surreptitious glimpse of your thigh when your split skirt opens wide, or a vision of your cleavage when you bend over to pick something up. And how I hated them for stealing those visions. I would have wonderful things to say. I would speak with class, wit and elegance and watch your smile widen and the birth of a laugh. I dreamed, I thought of you on foreign beaches away from all the mediocrity of this everyday life that surrounds us, and the way your skin would feel when I would finally touch it again, after this eternal drought of longing in sheer darkness. To feel you again, to see you again, how foolish I was to kid myself I would then find the right words to say. Now, right here, I am mute, I have nothing to say to you. The anger and the bitterness have robbed me of my poetry, of my words. It comes down to this, Kay, I have killed for you…'

She bit her lower lip.

'And once killers begin their spree, doesn't pulp tradition decree that they continue, until they are caught or blown up to high heavens? Isn't it? Isn't this the time and place, Kay, when the jilted lover orders you to strip and then plunges his knife into your soft, pliant flesh?'

I pulled the knife from my jacket pocket. I had cleaned it since Mark, but I was sure his blood was still visible on the blade. Kay shivered.

'Wouldn't killing you banish you forever from my life? I just can't see any other way.'

'No.'

'Don't plead. Please. It cheapens you. And do not evoke the days when we were together as a way of softening me up. It would only make me more angry. And after I've dug the knife into your heart, you wouldn't want me to make a bid for the tabloid press by carving you up, would you? As I did your husband.'

She stood still. Paler than ever.

'How would I do it? Would I start by inserting the blade into your vagina and sharply pulling downward towards your arse until there is only one bloody opening. Would I slash your stomach until your guts are pouring out? Should I carve your nipples off with precision and delicacy? Maybe. But I wouldn't touch your face, Kay, I promise. And after I've done my worst, I would dress you again, I would. Don't want complete strangers, cops, medics, seeing you so nude and vulnerable. No, I would want to be the last to feast my eyes on your opulent nudity. If there is a razor blade in the bathroom, I might even shave your cunt and paint your lower lips scarlet with your own lipstick before I slip my cock inside your mouth one final time, before saying goodbye. What sort of crazed serial killer would I make, hey?'

'Not a very good one,' she said feebly.

'Remember all the obscene stories I would whisper in your ear when we made love, and how it turned you on so much?' I asked her.

'Yes, I do and it did,' she answered calmly. 'But that was another time and another place, and right now you're allowing your imagination to run riot.'

'I want to touch you, Kay. With so much tenderness.'

I moved a step nearer to her.

'Don't,' she said.

I dropped the knife to the floor, behind my back, in a gesture of appeasement.

Right then, there was a massive commotion downstairs. The other staff of the publishing house must have broken the basement door down and freed themselves.

Kay took advantage of the situation and jumped sideways towards the other desk. Making for the gun. I had to react and leapt ahead of her, blocking her path. She bumped into me. The first contact between our bodies in so long. Her hand on my outstretched arm. The other pushing against my shoulder. Shouting suddenly: 'Help, help!' A voice downstairs: 'He's got Kay. He's still here. Get the police.'

We struggled clumsily against each other for a moment. My chin nestled against her neck. Smelling her perfume. Her fear. I felt the gun against my hand as she still tried to push me aside, scattering files across the floor in the process. As I strengthened my grip on the weapon's handle, she grabbed my hand, reaching for the weapon. She was tall, but anger sapped her energy. It must almost have looked as if we were dancing, in close embrace, as for a minute or so we waltzed between the desks, fighting for control of the gun. Neither of us said a word.

She furiously tried to twist my wrist. I resisted as best I could, my whole body angling in the opposite direction. I slipped on a manuscript page, and had to loosen my grip on Johnny Angelo's illicit gun. Kay sensed my temporary weakness and attempted to trip me. She only half succeeded as I allowed my left knee to graze the floor. She kicked wildly ahead of her, aiming for my groin but only caught the side of my thigh. It was enough to unbalance me and I oscillated sideways as her other hand reached again for the weapon I was still holding.

The gun went off. Too many fingers interfering with it. I held my breath. So did Kay. A look of surprise in our eyes. Then, ever so slowly, she slumped down to the floor. A bloodstain appeared on her white sweater, right where her heart was I reckoned, expanded, a dark flower blooming in no man's land.

'My God!' voices downstairs. 'That was a gun shot. The guy has shot Kay.'

Another voice, female, shrill. 'Lock the front door. Until the police get here. So he can't get out.'

Kay was still alive. Her eyes were clouding over.

'Jesus, Jesus,' she said. Then closed her eyes.

Gently, I laid her out on the floor, on a bed of manuscripts, straightened out her clothes, ruffled her hair, her million and one blonde curls with my hand and delicately kissed the light scar on her right cheek.

'Sleep tight, my love.'

And waited.

*Her tangled hair once a battleground for his fingers and hardy explorations, her eyes accusing, dark, questioning, deep pools of coldness. He bitterly sweeps the images away, whispers her name quietly in the silence of the bedroom 'Oh K, oh K, oh K' and then, mindful of Conrad 'the pain, the pain, the pain!'*

A loudhailer.

'This is the police. Throw your weapon out of the window and please come peacefully. If you do, no harm will come of you.'

A repetitive shuffle of feet in the street outside. Sirens. Cars parking in the distance. The whole road no doubt being cordoned off.

'Is your hostage alive?'

So this is what it comes to, is it? Gunfight at the Goodge Street Coral. Dog Day Afternoon WC1-style.

There are five bullets in my cartridge. I intend to use every one of them.

If they want me that bad, then I won't give them the satisfaction of getting me alive. London is such a boring place. This will put a bit of life in the old place, I reckon.

This guy is going out all fucking guns blazing.

'Top of the world, Kay. Top of the world.'

I move to the window and aim the gun ahead of me.

# Mark Timlin

## *Notes*

This pretty much sums up to me what a modern, realistic crime fiction short story should be all about. It's modern, it's short, it's got a story. It's got a hero who even makes a moral choice, ambiguous though it may be. It's based on a true incident that took place in south-west London some time ago, and I wondered what was happening in the gunman's head as he was chased by armed police. I can't guarantee I've got it right, but I've tried. It's also got guns, a car chase, blood and a helicopter. But is it real? Probably not, but it's a bit of a laugh. So why isn't anyone else writing stories like this that I can start to read one where I don't know how it's going to end? Because no one is. At least no one I can find in my local bookstore. And there's plenty of people who want to. I meet them all the time. They just can't hack it. And I guarantee you that even most of the other stories in this volume won't really ring true. Hard as they try most crime writers just don't know what the little girls understand. If it don't make you wet, it ain't worth a fuck.

# Nowhere To Run

## by Mark Timlin

When the shooting stopped, the street was terribly still and quiet except for the ringing in my ears from the gunshots. The sun seemed to stop in the perfect blue sky that curved in an arc over London, and the few people who had witnessed the incident were frozen as if by staying perfectly still they'd become invisible and we wouldn't turn our guns on them.

Our car was on the pavement, halfway through the wall it had demolished, and hot water was still dripping from its ruptured radiator and steaming as it hit the ground. The police car was slewed across the road with both front doors wide open. The driver was lying curled up in the gutter, blood pouring from the shotgun wound in his gut. The other was kneeling behind the passenger door, his hand raised as if it could stop a bullet. The back nearside window had been punched out by the second shotgun blast, and the metal of the door and the roof was pockmarked with pellet holes.

Kenny was standing next to me with a nine millimetre automatic in his hand and Johnno covered the kneeling copper with his twelve gauge Remington semi-auto shotgun, the barrel sawn off just in front of the pump and the stock carved into a pistol grip, with the used cartridge cases from his shots still rolling across the tarmac where they'd been ejected.

It had all happened that quickly.

The copper with his guts spilling all over the street, coughed once, almost apologetically, spat out a big mouthful of blood, and died.

That's torn it, I thought.

Kenny and Johnno had done the building society, with me sitting outside in the Sierra Cosworth I'd nicked from a used car dealer the previous day. I'd taken it out for a test run with the yuppied-up salesman sitting next to me, chewing gum, smoking a Silk Cut, and fondling his portable phone like a hard on.

I took the motor out onto the Kingston bypass and got it up to a ton-thirty before he started to tell me to slow down. I slammed on the anchors and the four wheel drive and ABS held it in a straight line as it stopped with smoke blowing up from its tyres. I took the Colt .38 two-incher out of my pocket and stuck it in his face, nicked his wallet and his phone, slung him out just by the Robin Hood Roundabout, and was home in time for tea with the Cossie garaged up sweet as a nut in Johnno's lock-up in Catford.

We done the place just after dinner time. Johnno reckoned there'd be nine or ten grand up on offer, which wasn't bad wages for a few hours work, including casing the gaff, me nicking the wheels, and us doing the job itself.

But it started to go wrong right off. Since we'd given the place the once over, they'd fitted those screens that shoot up over the counters as soon as one of the cashiers presses a button, and Old Bill was on our tail in a second.

And it kept going from bad to worse.

The building society was in Streatham, and after it all went on top, and the boys were back in the motor without as much as a ten-pence-piece to show for all our hard work, I headed down the High Road in the direction of Brixton with a police Rover on my tail, when I saw another set of blue lights heading towards us. I cut across the dual carriageway and bounced the motor up one of those avenues opposite the old Locarno. The Cossie stuck to the road like glue, but I gave it too much gas at the top of the hill, and four-wheel-drive and ABS or not, the bastard thing spun out on me, did a full circle and smashed into the wall.

'You silly cunt,' said Johnno, who by now was well pissed off, understandably like, and we all bailed out of the motor, just as the Rover came round the corner behind us and skidded to a halt.

Then the shit really hit the fan.

The two Old Bill jumped out of the car eager as you please. Stupid thing to do really when the three of us were standing there loaded down with ordnance, and not exactly ready to come quietly down to the nick for a little chat, and Johnno puts up the Remington and blows the driver's guts out.

That was when the second copper hit the deck and where we all came in.

'Split,' shouts Johnno, and heads towards a little alley that dog- legged to the left and God knows where, but at least would get us out of sight.

But when things start to go wrong, it's my experience that they keep going wrong, and they did.

As we reached the dog-leg, Johnno in front, Kenny next, and me last, I heard from round the corner a voice shout: 'ARMED POLICE! THROW DOWN YOUR WEAPONS.'

See what I mean about things going wrong? It was just the way our luck was running for an ARV to be in the area. Johnno and Kenny stopped, Kenny dropped his pistol sharpish, but Johnno brought up the shotgun again and he just exploded. I heard Christ knows how many shots all together, so that they just sounded like one, and he was thrown back against the wall as the back of his shirt blew out, as at least three bullets went clean through him, and his blood and flash spattered the brick work.

I skidded to a halt, turned and ran back the way I'd come to the street again, where the second copper was pulling himself to his feet.

I showed him my Colt and he knelt down again sharpish.

And then with a noise like a building being demolished, a police helicopter came over the tops of the houses, so low that I could almost see where the geezer peering out at me through the side window had cut himself shaving that morning.

I lifted the Colt and popped off a couple of rounds at the chopper. Now when Big Arnie or Bruce Willis or Kee-ar-noo fuckin' Reeves does that at the pictures, what happens? What happens is the bloody thing explodes in a big ball of fire and drops like a stone. What happened when I did it? Sweet FA, that's what. But at least the driver, or pilot, or whatever you call him veered it away so the noise of the engine didn't do my head in so bad.

I knew that armed police would be after me sharpish, and I could hear a load of sirens in the distance, and I also knew that on shanksies I'd be fucked in a minute, so I showed the live copper the gun again and told him to fuck off, which he did, walking slowly backwards, and never taking his eyes off me for a second. Then I jumped into the driving seat of the Rover, found the keys in the ignition, fired up the engine and took off so fast that the passenger door slammed shut.

There were a load of extra switches on the dashboard, so I hit the lot and the blue lights on top came on, and the screamer started with a yelp, and even though I was nearly shitting myself at what had happened, I couldn't help but laugh out loud. Look at me, mum, I thought. I made it to driving a cop car at last.

But I wasn't laughing for long. As the motor shot over the mini roundabout at the next corner, a panda car turned off the South Circ' in front of me heading in my direction.

I done a hand brake turn, nearly losing that motor too, but managed to keep it on even keel, headed back the way I came, and did a left at the roundabout towards Tulse Hill.

No go there, either. A police van was blocking the road in front of the lights so I had to do a sharp right into another street and the bottom of it was blocked by one of those gates the council put up to stop drivers using side streets as rat runs.

I was well fucked, and broadsided the motor, jumped out and took it on my toes.

The sounds of sirens was louder now, and the chopper that had been following me all along was buzzing up and down, well out of range of the peashooter I was carrying, telling all the Bill exactly were I was and what I was doing.

I felt like crying, I don't mind telling you.

Now's the time to get into a hostage situation, I thought. Make a name for myself on the six o'clock news, and maybe get interviewed on *London Tonight* by the tart with the blonde barnet. So I ran up the path of the next house I passed and hammered on the door.

I saw some movement through one of the frosted panes that were set in the top half of the door, but no one opened it, so I hammered again, louder this time, so the door shook on its hinges. The movement got closer and the door opened on a chain as the sound of the sirens got louder still, coming from all directions.

I saw a woman's face in the gap and said 'Police,' but I could tell she didn't believe me and she tried to slam the door shut, as another Rover jam sandwich came tearing round the corner, and I put me shoulder to the door. I'd've got it open too, if a couple of coppers hadn't jumped out of the squad car and come tearing along the pavement towards me, and I hadn't had to pin them down with another shot. But as I turned to do it, she managed to bang the door on me, and I heard bolts slam shut, and knew it was over.

More cop cars were arriving at every second, and the chopper was right above me, and one of the geezers in it was telling me to surrender through the big loudspeaker mounted on the bottom, and I knew I was facing at least twenty years of being banged-up every night and slopping out every morning, no matter what they say about getting every prisoner his own personal toilet. And I knew I couldn't face that, so I just slid down in the porch with my back to the door, pulled back the hammer on the Colt and stuck the barrel, which was still hot from the last firing, and stunk of old gunpowder, into my mouth and hooked my thumb round the trigger. And my last thought wasn't about my mum, or how much I was going to miss going to footie on Saturday afternoons, but that the lady who wouldn't open up for me was going to have to get her door repainted.

And even with the hot metal in me gob, it was all I could do not to laugh before I pulled the trigger…

# Ian Rankin

## *Notes*

Is Natural Selection *a 'realistic' crime story? Well, there's realism and then, standing a long way off, there's reality. To my mind, a story is realistic if it makes the reader think they're part of the narrative: a sci-fi fantasy novel can still be realistic. Realism is a state of mind, a series of tricks played by the author to suck (or sucker) the reader in. Novelists have been here before — Zola's 'naturalism', Robbe-Grillet's* nouveau roman *— but the problem is, the harder you try to make a fiction look like a slice of real world pie, the more artful and false it can seem.*

Natural Selection *does not even take place in a real pub, but in an amalgam of all the bad pubs in west-central Fife. I used to spend seemingly interminable Friday and Saturday nights in these places, waiting for something to happen. It invariably did: I'd get drunk, then hit the local Chinese for a Chicken Maryland. I was working weekdays in a chicken hatchery, not a bad job except for gassing all the males. Oh, and I got meningitis — revenge of the gas-chamber chicks.*

*That was a while back, but it's part of the inspiration behind the story. I write short stories between novels: they're like a dose of salts. They're also a way to experiment with narrative voice.* Natural Selection *is an experiment: how much can I get these characters to tell us without the narrator having to do the work? In other words, what can dialogue do? I had a lot of examples in my mind when I started writing: James Joyce's pub scenes in* Ulysses; *Derek Raymond's dialogue: and more than his fair share of Jim Kelman.*

*Beneath the apparent realism of the dialogue (dutifully artful, like Kelman's),* Natural Selection *is, of course, open to wider interpretation. Are these villains really in a pub, or are they in hell, or maybe somewhere just north of? How do the story's Biblical resonances interact with the apparent Darwinism of the title? How much does the story owe to Huis Clos, or to any of those novels, plays and films where the characters don't know they're already dead? Are these people really dead, or just spiritually so? Mmm, tough ones, and I'm damned if I know the answers. I only just thought of the questions.*

*In the end, is a story like* Natural Selection *so different from the 'classical' whodunit? Well, my story doesn't have a tidy ending: we don't know 'what happens', and to me that doesn't matter in the slightest. Throughout, there has been tension — hopefully, otherwise the reader will have lost interest — and all crime stories share that common thread. In the end, I prefer to read (and write) 'realistic' stories because I like to deal with the world I know, a world of bad pubs, blasted lives and subcutaneous despair. Happy shiny people? Not today, thanks.*

# *Natural Selection*

## by Ian Rankin

'Hellish about Anthony.'

'Christ, isn't it? Six years.'

'Six is a long one.'

'The longest,' Thomas agreed. 'I've only ever done two and a half.'

'Three, me,' said Paul. 'My shout then.'

'No, Paul, it's mine,' Philip said.

'Your money's no good today, Philip,' Paul said. 'Hi, Matthew, give us two spesh, a dark rum, and a vodka.'

Paul was buying. Paul, for a change, had plenty money,

'Cheers, Paul.'

'Aye, all the best, Paolo.'

'You're quiet, Leonard,' Paul said.

'Eh?'

'Quiet.'

Leonard shrugged. He wasn't usually quiet. But then it wasn't a normal day. 'Just thinking about Anthony.'

'Six years,' said Philip, exhaling.

'Hellish,' said Paul. 'Here, Leonard, have a —'

'No, I'll take it neat.'

'You always have a skoosh of Irn-Bru in your vodka.'

'Not today.'

'What's wrong, Leonardo?'

'Christ, nothing, I just don't... look, okay, give me the Irn-Bru.'

'Not if you don't want it.'

'I want it.'

'You've changed your mind?'

'Just give the bottle here.'

'Touchy today, isn't he, Thomasino?'

'A bit, Paul, I'd have to agree with you there.'

'Hell, all I said was...'

'Okay, Leonard, no problemo, big man. You take your vodka any way you want your vodka. No big deal. Okay?'

'It's only vodka.'

'A metaphysical statement indeed. So get it down you. Hey, Philip, how's your spesh?'

'Nothing special.'

Paul laughed. 'Says the same thing every time. Dependable, Philip, that's you. Not like these two.'

'What?'

'Look at you,' Paul told them. 'Leonard usually going twenty to the dozen, Thomas like a deaf mute in a sensory deprivation tank. Roles reversed today, eh?'

'What's a sensory deprivation tank?'

'Well,' said Philip, 'here's to Anthony.'

'Anthony.'

'Cheers.'

'All the best.'

'So... a wee skoosh of Irn-Bru after all, eh, Leonard?'

'I thought we weren't going to —'

'You are not wrong, I was out of turn. Sorry, Leonard.'

'Leonard's all right.'

'Why shouldn't I be?'

'One for yourself, Matthew?'

The barman was still waiting to be paid. 'Thanks, Paul, I'll stick one aside for later.' He walked back to his till with the cash.

'Matthew's all right,' Paul said, tucking his wallet back into his pocket.

'Not bad.'

'Keeps himself to himself.'

'Wise in a place like this,' said Thomas, wiping foam from his top lip, 'full of people like us. I'll tell you something, Paul, if I wasn't me, *I* wouldn't drink in here.'

'Where else is there?'

'There's the Last Drop or the World's End.'

'No chance.'

'Well, it's a hell-hole all the same.'

'Ach, you get used to it. I've been drinking here thirty years, man and boy. Come on, Leonard, no slacking.'

'I'm pacing myself.'

'Philip's finished his spesh already, by the way.'

'Thirsty,' Philip explained.

'Whose shout?'

'I mean,' Paul went on, 'this is a big night, a kind of wake. No night to be pacing yourself. Six years: we're drinking for Anthony tonight.'

'That judge…'

'And the jury.'

'Ach, it was the evidence though,' said Philip. 'If they've got the evidence, what can you do?'

'You can't scare off every jury.'

'They knew everything.'

'Who did?' Leonard asked.

'Those two cops. How did they know all that?'

'Another vodka, Leonard'?'

'Go on then.'

'What do you say, Leonard?'

'Huh?'

'You're the one with the brains. How did those two cops know?'

'Guesswork? I don't know.'

'Maybe they got lucky,' Philip suggested.

'They can't all be as thick as the ones we know,' Thomas added.

'Or as scared.'

'Anthony'll be all right,' said Paul. 'Whichever nick he goes to, he'll end up running the place.'

'Very true,' said Philip. 'All the same, six years. He'll be out in what? Three? Three years locked up, no fresh air…'

'When did that ever bother Anthony?'

'How do you mean, Leonard?'

'Or any of us, come to that,' Leonard went on. 'I mean, at least the screws will make him go for a walk around the yard. That's more fresh air than he ever got sitting in here.'

'You're a cheery bugger,' said Thomas.

'He's probably got a cell bigger than this… and better decorated.'

'Leonard, Leonard, where would we be without you, eh? Always joking.'

'Am I?'

'You know you are,' Paul said, lighting a cigarette and passing the pack on. 'We're all gutted, it's a natural reaction.'

'What is?'

'Eh? Good man, Matthew. Put them down there, and chalk up another for yourself' Paul reached into his pocket for the wallet.

'Where did all that cash come from, by the way?' Leonard asked.

'Never you mind.' Paul winked and handed Matthew another ten. Matthew went back to the till.

'You know,' Paul said quietly, 'I sometimes wonder how much Matthew hears.'

'You mean how much he listens?'

'Yes.'

'Matthew's all right.'

'Well, he knows everything we talk about in here.'

'We never talk jobs.'

'Don't get me wrong, I'm not saying he'd… you know.'

'What's going on?' Thomas asked, appearing not to follow things at all.

'Just a natural reaction,' said Philip. He was watching Paul hand out the drinks. 'We're all… something like this, it guts you, doesn't it?'

'All right, Thomas,' Paul said, 'get this down you, leave all your troubles behind. Leonard, another wee vodka. There's the Irn-Bru, your decision, okay? You're a free agent. All right there, Thomasino? Cough it up. Good man, now get that down you. Philip, one pint of delicious foaming spesh. Enough to quench the fire, eh?'

'It's never enough.'

'Cheers, Paul.'

'No, but it's only natural, isn't it'?' Paul said, not touching his own Black Heart. 'I mean, natural to wonder, to ask yourself how the cops knew. It's a reaction, we'll get over it. Having trouble with that bottle-top, Leonard?'

'You always screw the fucking thing back on too tight.'

'Give it here.'

'No, I can —'

'Here, I'll —'

'*I can do it!*'

'Whoa there, Leonardo.' Brakes on, pal, no need for this. Look, there it is, the top's off. Amazing how strong you can get when you're angry. Right then, everybody, good health.'

'Cheers.'

'All the best.'

'Aye.'

'Hey, Matthew,' Thomas called, 'can you no' open a window? It's like a furnace in here.' He turned to Paul. 'Windows, they paint over them, you can't open the things. Never would have happened in the old days. Sloppy these days, decorators. I mean, hot's fine in the winter, but this isn't winter.'

'Hellish hot,' Leonard agreed, calm again. 'It's always too hot in here.'

'You could heat pies without a microwave.'

'One of those ceiling fans would be nice,' Paul said. 'There used to be one, didn't there?'

'Did there?'

'This was before your time, Leonard, before you came here. Up there it was, a big white electric fan.'

'White electric?'

'I mean painted white, run on electric.'

'Right.'

'I don't know how you can put Irn-Bru in that.'

'You want me to drink it neat?'

'Christ, don't be so… look, just do what —'

'I like Irn-Bru.'

'Me too,' said Philip.

'Ach, everyone likes Irn-Bru… but with vodka?'

'I used to drink it that way at school,' Leonard said. 'I'd steal some voddy from the drinks cabinet and mix it in an Irn-Bru bottle.'

'Drinks cabinet, eh? Your family had class, Leonard.'

'Didn't stop him turning into a criminal at an early age.'

'I was born a criminal.'

'Isn't everybody?' Philip said, deep into his drink.

'No,' said Leonard, 'some people have to learn. Anthony wasn't a born criminal.'

'You don't think so?'

'He told me so. He ran with his big brother's gang. He was okay till he started running with them.'

'His brother Donny?'

'That's the one.'

'You don't see him in here.'

'He's gone away,' said Thomas. 'Been away a while.'

'There's a lot you don't see in here any more.'

'Well, we're here,' said Paul, 'and that's all that matters.'

'Aye, we're always here.'

'For ever and ever, amen.'

'Where *did* you get that money though, Paul?'

Paul winked again. 'Is it bothering you, Leonard?'

'Was it the gee-gees?' Thomas guessed. 'Lottery? Dogs? Pools? I'll bet it was a betting thing.'

'You'd lose your money. Now either stop asking, or stop taking drinks off me.'

Thomas laughed. 'Nobody'd be that daft.'

'No? What about you, Leonard?'

'What about me?'

'Nothing,' said Paul.

'No,' Leonard persisted, 'what is it? Something's stuck up your arse and I'd like to know what it is.'

Paul looked amazed. 'Me? There's nothing bothering *me*, pal. What about you, Leonardo?'

'Here we go again,' said Philip. 'Just cool it, compadres.'

'You're right, Philip,' said Paul, 'as ever. How come you're always right? You never lose your rag, do you'? You're the calm sort, controlled. Isn't he, lads?' Paul tapped his own brow. There was a sheen of sweat on it. 'But we know there's a lot going on in that head of his.'

'It's the quiet ones you have to watch,' said Thomas.

'Thomas, you'll never say a truer word. Out of the mouths of babes, as they say. Jesus, Philip, are you finished already?'

'It's hot,' Philip said.

'A furnace.'

'This thirst,' Philip added,' 'I can't seem to shake it.'

'Christ, Matthew,' Paul called, 'do something, will you?'

'Like what?'

'Open the fridge door or something. Start putting ice in the drinks. *Something.*'

'We're out of ice.'

'You'll be out of a job if we take our custom elsewhere.'

Matthew smiled. 'You four aren't going anywhere.'

'No talking back to the customers. Matthew,' Paul said, pointing a finger. 'Leonard, ready for another?'

'I've two in front of me.'

'Apply yourself to the task. We'll have the same again, Matthew.'

'Not for me,' said Leonard.

'Play the game, Leonardo. Give him another, Matthew.'

The barman walked back to the optics.

'You're wasting your money, Paul.'

'It's my money.'

'You'll be skint again tomorrow.'

'Who cares about tomorrow?'

'Suit yourself.'

'I always do.'

'This is very pleasant,' said Philip.

'It's not meant to be pleasant,' Paul said. 'It's a wake, remember?'

'How can I forget?'

'Levity ill becomes you, Filipi.'

'What's levity?' Thomas asked.

'Lightness,' Leonard explained.

Thomas nodded. 'Like being light in the head?'

'Lot of levity about here,' Paul said, winking.

'Maybe I'm ill,' said Philip, loosening his collar. 'My mouth's parched all day.'

'Could be a lot of reasons for that,' Paul said. 'Could be nerves.'

'Nerves?'

'I saw something yesterday,' Thomas said, 'on the telly. It was about these insects that eat each other. Or maybe it was their babies they ate.'

Paul and Philip looked at one another, the way they did when Thomas said this sort of thing.

'That's not so rare,' Leonard told Thomas, his eyes on Paul.

'You're a smart one, aren't you?' said Paul.

Leonard shook his head, drained one of his vodkas. 'It's all relative,' he said. Then he slipped off his barstool.

'First one tonight.' said Paul, smiling. 'And as usual it's Leonard. Three shorts he's put away, but he's bursting for a piss. You need a bladder transplant, Leonardo.'

Leonard stopped in front of Paul. 'Maybe it's just nerves, Paul,' he said.

Nobody said anything as he left the bar.

The toilet was reeking. There was the constant hiss of a broken ballcock, and names scratched into the paint on the dark red wall. The urinal was a stainless steel trough. It was cooler in here though, damp and cool. Leonard lit a cigarette for himself. He reckoned if it weren't for the smell, this place would be a preferable alternative to the bar itself. Freezing in winter, though. Bloody awful pub altogether, why didn't they just leave? Well, as somebody had said, where else was there?

The door creaked open and Matthew came in.

'Matthew.'

'Leonard.'

The barman went to the urinal and unzipped himself loudly. His stare was high up the wall when he spoke.

'They're out for your blood.'

'What?'

'Those three. Well, Paul specifically, but he'll carry the other two. He's buying, after all.'

'What have I done?'

'Come on, Leonard. Paul thinks you shopped Anthony.'

'Then how come he's the one with the money?'

'If it was a cop payoff, he wouldn't be flashing it about. Get out, right now. Just run for it.'

'I've never run in my life.'

'It's up to you.' Matthew zipped himself up. 'But if I was in your shoes, I'd be offski.'

'Where would I go?'

'I don't know.' There was another creak as the door opened. Paul came in first. Philip and Thomas were right behind him. The door closed quietly after them.

'What's that you're saying, Matthew?'

'Nothing, Paul.'

'You're a great one for talking, aren't you?'

'No.'

'A gossip, a right wee sweetie-wife. Talking's in your blood.'

'No.'

'No? This had the look of a snitches' convention when I walked in. Guilty looks all round.'

Matthew tried shaking his head.

'Easy to confuse guilt with fear,' Leonard said quietly.

'Know where that money came from?' Paul said. He wasn't speaking to any one of them in particular. His eyes were on his shoes, examining the toes. 'I'll tell you, it came from Anthony.'

'Anthony?' Thomas said. 'Why did he give you that much money? I mean, he's usually tight… I mean, careful. He,'s canny with his money.' Thomas's voice died away.

Paul half-turned his head and gave Thomas a smile full of sympathy.

'You aren't half going on tonight, Thomasino. Not like you at all. It's not like him at all, is it, Philip?'

Philip was wiping his face with the roller-towel. 'No, it's not,' he said.

'He's usually quiet, isn't he?'

'Quiet as the grave,' Philip agreed.

'And even someone as thick as you sometimes appear to be, Thomas, has got to have an inkling why Anthony would give me a load of cash.' He paused. 'Don't *you* want to know, Philip?'

Philip shrugged. 'You'll tell us when you're ready.'

Paul was smiling. 'You never change, Philip. Always the same face, the same voice. Nothing out of place. I bet you could do away with your granny and we'd never know about it, not by looking at you.' He paused again. 'Except tonight you're sweating. Why is that?'

'I think I'm coming down with something.'

'Well, we'll see to it you get a doctor when this is over.' Matthew started to open the door. '*Shut it!*' Paul smiled. 'Don't want to let the heat in, do we?' He turned to Leonard. 'Anthony gave me the money because he wants someone taken care of. Someone in particular. He told me once I was sure in my mind, I was to start earning the cash. That's what Anthony told me.'

'In other words, he doesn't know?'

'That's right, Leonard.'

'Funny he asked you.'

'He trusts me.'

'But what if he's wrong, Paolo? What if he's wrong about that?' Leonard looked to the other men in the cramped space — Matthew, Philip, Thomas. 'What if *you* grassed him up, and *we* found out?' They'd all been looking nervous; now they were looking interested. 'What would we do?'

'Yes,' Thomas said quietly, getting it, 'what would we do?'

Philip was nodding slowly, and Matthew straightened his back, adding an inch to his height.

'There's only one guilty party here, Leonard,' Paul was saying.

'You really believe that?'

'I'm not saying it's you.' Paul was staring into Leonard's eyes. He saw red paint reflected from the walls.

'You're saying it's one of us, Paul. The rest of us don't like that.'

Leonard took a step forwards. Paul's hand went to his jacket pocket. Philip was behind him, his arms stretching. Thomas's hands were fists. Matthew leaned against the door, keeping it closed.

Outside it was dark, no streetlight, no traffic. You would bet that it couldn't get any darker, but you'd be wrong. People most often are.

# Derek Raymond

*Notes*

*R*obin Cook, who wrote as Derek Raymond, died in 1995. A
prominent exponent of a particular form of British noir writing,
he was adopted by many younger British realist crime writers
as a father-figure during the course of his last years back in London.

*His deeply pessimistic but humane Factory novels will no doubt
prove to be his main legacy to the genre, and will hopefully be as much
of a cult in English as they already are in the rest of Europe.*

*Any collection of cutting edge contemporary British crime fiction
would feel somewhat hollow without Robin's presence. Which is why we
are particularly proud to be able to feature unpublished material by him.
Ironically, it is not set down mean British streets, but in Paris. Nevertheless, his unique voice and empathy for the downtrodden remains
prominent. British critic and writer John Williams explains how this
piece — previously unpublished in English — came to light. (MJ)*

*

*S*hortly before Robin died he made me his literary executor, a job I
gladly accepted without having much of a clue what it meant.
Well, apart from trying to make sense of Robin's mildly chaotic
business affairs, the most intriguing part of the job so far has been the

search for unpublished material. I have both of Robin's computers in my care: the Amstrad on which he wrote Dora Suarez, The Hidden Files and Dead Man Upright; the Mac Classic on which he wrote Not Till The Red Fog Rises. And lurking amid the Hidden Files are all manner of other strange files containing notes, odd glosses on the fiction, putative titles — Snout, Botherboots — some poems and the odd short story. All fascinating stuff but sadly no undiscovered long fiction.

Which left me with the problem of the two French novels that have never appeared in the English language. Robin never wanted to see the first, Le Soleil Qui S'Eteint (English title: Sick Transit), published here; he regarded it as a pot-boiler that had simply eased him back into writing after his long layoff during the seventies. The other, Cauchemar Dans La Rue (English Title: Nightmare In The Street) was another matter. A policier set in Paris, it was a book Robin remained fond of. The only problem was that he appeared to have lost the English manuscript. The British and French publishers couldn't find one, nor could the agent, but then Robin's daughter Zoe searched through his papers at his house in France, and turned up what appeared to be two partial manuscripts. One used the working title Death In E Major, the other he called Correspondence Sebastopol. All may not have been lost, but at least half seemed to be. Then Maxim Jakubowski called to ask for a piece for this anthology and, by some strange alchemy, I took one more look at the material and was able to assemble a complete manuscript.

So, here is the opening chapter from the great lost Robin Cook novel...

# Nightmare In The Street

## by Derek Raymond

I'm a plain-clothes copper, my name is Kleber; I don't like the sunshine or the daylight, and never have. I don't like bright parties, dull people, flash-bulbs, cakes and music that sends me to sleep, family photograph albums and the fakery that accompanies three or four kisses on the cheeks and the purse tight shut — I never have liked these things and never will; I am tuned to the noises that the dark brings.

I do have a passion for love, and for people in it. What I can't stand is coldness and that egoism which opens the barrier to terror and evil. Evil is well-armed; I know all about that.

I look like any ordinary copper, but I'm not. I'm only hard-boiled over criminals, but I cry over what they've done and swear to get them. I have my reasons for behaving the way I do: I'm in love myself, adoring my wife Elenya, who is all I have, and all I shall ever need to have. I have heard her described as what she was until the time when I met her — a little Polish whore on the streets. But I have only heard that as gossip; no-one, and I mean no-one, has dared to say it to my face. I had it repeated to me at times, and for a short time, after we married. But when I reacted in a direct manner, not as a policeman but behind walls, one man to another, on dark ground in the night, all that stopped. For what I battled for was the right to equality of spirit for each one of us, and I always won.

It wasn't Elenya's fault that she was a whore. If you like, it was her face's fault: she was too beautiful, too well-made for the quarter she grew up in, the concrete block whose walls sweated (I've been there), the despair, the unemployment, the collapse in the relations between neighbours under the pressures of having no work and no money except for that undignified cheque from Social Security which underlines the fact that you have no money, no work, and no prospect or hope of ever repairing those two holes in your personal wall for the foreseeable future. But Elenya was beautiful, and well-developed for her age. So her father raped her at that age: it began as a good-night cuddle when he came into her room one Saturday night, drunk. He liked to tell them down at the bar that he was a self-educated and well-educated man — but he was full of shit. He was a clerk in an electronics factory who had been fired for his absurd fussiness, telling too many people what to do when he was in fact at the bottom of the ladder there. So they called him in one Friday night and gave him his cards and his money and told him to get lost, and after that he never got a job again. And no wonder — he was already forty-five and looked older. He liked to look mysterious and above it all in his sitting-room and blag on, which wasn't difficult: he had no competition except from his wife, and she was always talking to the wall about curtains, eiderdowns and the value of things (the monetary value, that is) and whether they oughtn't to save for a new telly.

Yes, the mother was a great gabbler, and stupid with it; as long as she could go on talking without interruption she neither knew nor cared what was going on. She had a great long, loose mouth the shape of a broad river, part of it, loops and twists seen from the air, and any old rubbish would come pouring out of it: from counting pennies to bargains she had read about (those lips moving soundlessly as she read) in the junk mail that got poked through her door. Also, she was so busy talking that she would never let her husband have it, shrugging him off in bed, preferring to go on talking, if necessary even in her sleep, something that drove her neighbours crazy, since her face was against the partition wall in the high-rise block they lived in, which the municipal authorities, in order to save money on the blocks so that they could put it into their own pockets, had built pretty thin.

And so, one night, Dad came into his daughter's room, none too sober, to say goodnight, and by the time the child realised what was really going on, it was too late.

The other trouble was that Mother caught him at it — even she wasn't quite that stupid — hearing the cries. But as she couldn't have hoped to get her new telly without her husband's monthly cheque from the Social Security, and as she managed to persuade herself that the child had led him on, it was Elenya that had to go.

And so she did go, in a state of shock, into the clubs, into the pubs, onto the streets. She soon learned to drink and be unhappy, and she soon found out that, at fifteen, hundreds of men wanted to get into where her father had been. She found out about drugs, too, and started to get into that, discovering at the same time that, if you didn't let men do what they wanted, the supply dried up and that everyone, the other girls in the game included, started to treat you like dirt and that you were back where you started. So on the whole she let people do it to her, and they did it to her while she was in a dream — the dream being her adolescent dreams, anyone's dreams at that age: and so she was mercifully protected, despite being surrounded by evil, from the whole of her life becoming a bad dream.

She started to do her nightly batter in the centre of the city and then, of course, because of her looks, a major pimp got onto her and gave her her stretch of street (taking seventy-per-cent of what she made off her, of course) and that was where I came in one night as I happened to pass, off duty, to find him beating her up in a doorway and trying to snatch her bag off her.

I kicked him where he didn't care for it and nearly killed the cunt, and that was where Elenya and I began, because I put her into a taxi and took her home and put her in the spare room I had, and on the third day she did me the honour of telling me, as I was waiting for her to get lunch ready (it was a Sunday) that I was the first decent human being she had ever known.

She said she was afraid now to go back where I had met her (it was where she liked to do her shopping), but I told her not to be afraid; she ran no risk at all. I got a list out and went to see a mate of mine on the Vice Squad, and her troubles were very swiftly looked after.

After a while, she took me to her home (home?) to see her parents, and listened quite silently while each of them gabbled towards me in their different directions. I knew their story from Elenya, of course — but they didn't know mine, and somehow I just didn't take the trouble to tell them. The mother I dismissed at once as just a fat, well-made fool; but Dad I didn't like at all. Not only because I knew what he had done to his daughter, but because, as a copper, to me he had all the makings of a grass or even worse — though, apart from a killer, there isn't anything much worse in my vocabulary. The swollen ego busting like liver through a stomach wound was the image I got of him as he started, in the face of what he took to be my stupid silence, to tell me what I ought to do next. I told him I was a cab-driver — I had to tell him something — and he began telling me how I could really improve myself in life if I worked hard at it. I thought of the things he himself had worked hard at. His eyes were set too close to his nose, which was long, and foam rattled as he spoke between his split teeth. He was as neatly dressed as if he were going off to work somewhere in the morning, and was extremely careful with the ash at the end of the occasional cigarette he smoked. His eyes darted constantly to see how far the level had gone down in the bottle of Scotch that Elenya and I had brought; I went out of my way to help myself liberally to it. He was very keen on politics until I said: 'Your vote'll make no more difference than mine will. Our opinions don't matter a damn, Mr Kucharski, you and I are just the little people.'

'I'd have you know I've spent my whole life educating myself,' he stormed.

There was a pretty long silence from him after that, broken only by his wife gabbling at Elenya behind the shut door of the kitchen until Kucharski said: 'What do you want with my daughter, then?'

'I want to marry her,' I said, and added: 'I want to be with her where no man's ever been before. As a father, you must appreciate that.'

'You'll find her a difficult girl.'

'Really?' I said, 'I wonder why? I don't find her difficult at all.'

'She errs in her ways.'

'Perhaps she's a lost sheep,' I said, 'though I've no means of knowing whose fault that might be, if she is.'

'Are you trying to be clever or something?' Kucharski said.

'I don't have to try in order to be clever,' I said, 'in my opinion any fool can be clever, Mr Kucharski. What we all have to try and do is to understand other people, which isn't the same. Like I'm trying to do with your daughter.'

'You love her, do you?'

'I certainly do.'

'Do you know what love is?'

'Do you?' I said. 'Does your wife? Do any of us?'

He pursed his wet little lips and shook his head slowly. 'I don't know about you and our girl,' he said. 'My mind's not satisfied about you yet. No, I'm not at all sure.'

'Never mind,' I said. I stood up. 'I'm perfectly sure, and so is Elenya. You ask her.'

But he didn't have to because, as I spoke, she burst in through the kitchen door and stood on the yellow carpet of the sitting-room with her closed hands on her hips and said: 'I love him, and that's all any of you need to worry about, except your-selves.'

Her mother, who had followed her into the room, was stopped by this remark in the middle of a speech about new carpet-sweepers. She stood there, gaping.

'She's very young to be married,' said Kucharski in the end, feebly.

'Better than being too old,' I said. I looked at my watch and said to Elenya: 'We'd better get going, love.'

'Coming,' she said, and got her coat off the hook behind the front door.

'You can say goodnight to the future Mrs Kleber,' I said, and they did say it — in unison, without moving.

I had been taken off a murder case I had already solved: it was a matter of a girl who had lead popped into her head by one of her boyfriends, and it had been my job to find out which one had pulled the trigger on her. I had found him all right through my usual patient questioning. After asking and asking him why he had split her head into about five pieces with number five shot at point-blank range he had told me simply that it was from despair, because she had been two-timing him with his best friend who had gone on playing darts with him and going to Saturday matches with him and the mob. Because I never use violence with a suspect I wanted, as I always do, to disentangle the threads of so final a situation delicately and quietly, and he had said he had only gone and got the gun, and even then only finally pulled the trigger on her when she had repeatedly laughed in his face and told him he wasn't a man. After he had killed her he had wiped everything clean at her place, which was where he had done it, and fled.

'But the fact you brought the gun round to her place —'

'I left it in the car, then went and got it —'

'Proves,' I said, 'that you had the idea to kill her beforehand, and a judge hates that.'

'It's true I was very angry with her,' he said, 'there'd been lots of scenes. I knew by some instinct she was screwing with someone else.'

'Did it ever occur to you that it might have been this mate of yours, Henri?'

'I did think of it. I didn't really believe it could have been him really, though.'

'And did she tell you it was him?'

'She told me Henri was more of a man than I was, but no more than that. It was me she was getting at really. She said she was sick of me hanging around her like a wet water-lily the whole time. If only you knew how it gets at you being in love when she doesn't love you back,' he said seriously, 'I can't tell you what a state you get into, you hardly know what you're doing in the end, what with no sleep, no peace, no hope of things turning out right and you end up one night, with a few drinks inside you like I had that night, and you've no idea what you're going to do next except that you must put an end to it all somehow, make things somehow move on.' And he added: 'And what's more, when you're in that state, you don't much care how you do it, either — you're not really yourself any more, it's as if you were someone else, and then afterwards you seem to come back into the person you thought you were, but then by that time it's been done. You know. It was that sick jealousy made me do it, that, and she would keep telling me how dull I was compared to all her other lays. I'm not dull,' he declared, 'anyway I used not to be. After what's happened, perhaps I am now. Well I don't care. What's the point in caring about anything now? She's dead and I killed her, what more do you want?'

I imagined the shallow little person the girl must have been as I took the boy down with me to be charged; I didn't think the boy was dull at all, just mortally overruled by his heart that one time.

We got down to the station, and in came the inspector I most hated.

'Got there at last, have you?' he sneered. 'Going to actually charge the cunt, are you?'

'That's what we're here for.'

'What are you pinning on him?'

'Manslaughter,' I said, 'with mitigating circumstances, and what the fuck has it got to do with you? It's my case.'

This cunt started to roar with laughter. 'Manslaughter!' he grinned, 'you want to make me piss in my pants laughing? Murder! Do him for murder! What mitigating circumstances? I saw the photos of what he did to her, he blew her head practically off!'

'I know what you'd have done if you'd have found your wife in bed with another man,' I said, 'you'd just have broken down and cried, you pathetic little man, now get out of this room, nobody ordered you.'

'Don't you dare talk to your superiors like that.'

I stood between this idiot and the boy. 'Get out,' I said. 'Never interfere with my cases, I've told you before, I've warned you. Now fuck off.'

'I'll take this over now,' the Inspector said. 'I'll just have ten minutes alone with this idiot boy.'

'It'll be over your dead body,' I said, 'not mine. Now I'm very definitely telling you.'

'Are you threatening me, Sergeant?'

'No,' I said, 'I'm doing it to you.' Whereupon I stepped up to him and hit him so hard that I broke his nose and knocked four of his front teeth out. After that I picked up the phone in my office and told them to come up and clear what was left of him away.

And that was why I was having trouble at work. It wouldn't teach an egoist any love for people, but it might teach him respect for them. A stupid gesture, really, but one I couldn't help any more than the boy could help blowing his girl-friend's head off, an impulse stronger than the rest of me, and there was my career on the cooker now.

Yes, you could call that kind of an event trouble at work, certainly you could call it that.

I was sorry for that bemused boy, because I could see so clearly why he had done it. Don't the mildest of us finally act out of despair, with death just a step away?

'If I could take it back,' he had said to me on our way down, 'if I'd been in my right mind I'd have just waved to her, said OK and goodbye. But I'd been through the mill over her for months and the pain just ate me away so in the end, over her, I couldn't think straight any more.'

It was my view that the Inspector whose nose I'd just broken wasn't in his right mind or anyone else's — I went downstairs wondering how much violence it needed to finally prove to us that human instinct can never be controlled by force, and that men like my Inspector are best penned up where they can do less harm; it was hospital for a week or two in his case.

While I was waiting to be called up in front of the Chief, I charged the boy myself in front of two other officers as if nothing had happened. I saw to it myself that it was quite quiet, almost informal, there were no ringing tones or any self-satisfaction in the scene. I went down with him myself afterwards to the cell where he would spend the night before being taken next morning before the magistrate and then away on remand and sat with him for a while.

'Am I really a murderer?' he said.

'Well, you've killed someone.'

'I know,' he said, 'yet I can still hardly believe it.'

'What's the effect?' I said.

'It's made me afraid of myself all right,' he said. 'I was always told I was so mild. My mum and dad told me I was. I told myself I was. Sandra my girl told me I was too mild. They said I was mild at school; the others used to take the piss out of me over it.'

'The gun, then,' I said, 'but we know where the gun came from.'

'Yes, I stole it from my father,' he said, 'I told you that. I did it in a kind of dream, as if I was drunk, or drugged. Of course I knew I was taking it and that then I was going round to see her, but I did it in a kind of dream. The lights in the sitting-room were too bright, it seemed to me, when I got there — everything was too brilliant and concentrated, I could just see the dark oak cupboard where I knew the gun was and myself taking it out and loading it and then putting it in the car, and then starting the car and going round to her place, and that was all clear in my mind and to my eyes, the road, everything, and outside of what I was doing it was all a blur, like a fog.'

'You didn't think you were mad or anything when you did it?'

'Not at all,' he said, 'not except mad with love, I suppose you could say. And she had been getting at me so. On and on about how weak I was, weak as a man I mean. And I can't tell you how terrible it was for me, having lain in her arms for months and making love, and then when I begged for us to be able to please do it again, her just standing there laughing at me and her saying what? With *you*? Oh, well then I got in despair because I saw there was no hope, I remember looking at her face and seeing no hope for me or us there, or in her eyes, so then I just quietly went down out into the street to the car and got the gun and came back up with it.'

'Some of the less perceptive minds among us here thought your best friend had done it,' I said. 'Henri.'

'Henri?' he said. 'But why should he have done it? Henri was already sleeping with her.'

Yes, what a silly little girl she must have been, I thought, and added to myself, well, it cost her her life.

'Tell me honestly,' he said, 'do you think I'm mad?'

'No I don't,' I said, and added to myself, and a jury won't either, and that's why you'll go to jail, not to a nice comfy asylum, and what a mess it all is.

'It's funny now to think I was training to be a surveyor,' he mused. 'My mum and dad aren't badly off, and what with the job I'd have got I could have promised her a good life, kids, a nice house, a car, the lot. Amazing to think there won't be any of that now, isn't it?' He paused, then said: 'I wonder if any of us really want all of that, in these days? It's like a 1932 movie when you think of it, isn't it? Completely out-of-date.' He paused, looking at the cell floor as he sat on the edge of his thin bed with the army blankets on it, then looked up at me and said: 'What happens to people like me, do you think? I mean, like afterwards, when I come out?'

I didn't answer because I couldn't, I didn't know how to, and he said: 'You know, when everything was going so well between the two of us, everything seemed so beautiful, so magical, at least to me it did.' He added: 'But perhaps we fell into too much of a routine, meeting too punctually every night after work at the same time, same place, always seeing the same people, and she must have got bored. I see how I loved her now,' he added, 'but never understood her. Perhaps if I'd had a sister,' he said slowly, 'I might have understood her better. But I was an only child.'

I knew that if he got the wrong judge, the wrong counsel and the wrong jury he would draw ten years because he was so bloody sane, intelligent and kind and had acted for reasons beyond his control and I didn't think I could stand any more. So I stood up and said: 'I'd better be going now.'

'Will you be all right over that inspector you hit?'

'Don't let that bother you.'

'You shouldn't have done it on my account.'

'Don't we all get carried away at times?' I said. 'He'd been asking for it for a long time. I don't like being interfered with in my work, I'd told him often.'

'In a way it's like her and me,' he said, 'I imagine.' He too stood up.

I found that I hated what I had done to him, putting him in this place.

I went to the door and banged on it to be let out and he said: 'I'm sorry you've got to go, it means I'll be alone with my memories, and there were lots of things we could have —'

'I've got to go, I shouldn't even be here.'

'Well, it's been ever so nice to talk to you,' he said, 'and I feel nothing against you, if that means anything, and I hope one day we might meet again.'

'I hope so too,' I said, and so I left the grave young face framed in the collar of a shirt that had so recently been white, but was already greying.

I went out into the street wishing that I could hit that fucking Inspector all over again, make him pay for everyone in the world who was anything like him. I squinted into the terrible sunlight against my eyes; it was sunny but cold. I thought: we must never lose hope, even though despair's the fashion.

I think of the man I have just left, of the girl he had, and then of Elenya. I feel as if my own affairs are threatening to come to a crisis, quite apart from my future in the police. I don't give a damn about that. I joined the police to contribute to human justice, not to respect people like the man whose nose I had broken.

The instant I think about Elenya I go over to a pub, The Painted Ocean, and call her. I find she is quite all right, taking things out of the washing machine, and feel immediately as if I were home in the known world. Looking out of the window of the pub, I see there is a light frost on the roofs opposite, shining brightly under the sun in its red and yellow sky, so stained with grey morning clouds, and feel as if I had come up after a very deep dive in the sea, as if I had come back to familiar things, marvellous in their simplicity, after having returned from a long way off.

I do the sensible thing in such a state and drink a double whisky with ice.

I feel as if I were one of the few to have escaped from some abominable war that hasn't finished yet — I have just been sent back for a moment to rest. But such rest is putative. The face of the dead girl I had seen in the morgue, rises to meet me even in the pub, nearly deserted at ten past eleven, in spite of the sunshine glittering cheerfully on the brass handles of the beer-pumps and the bar smelling cleanly of polish. I see the face, already carved into by grief, of the young man I have just left in the police cell across the street and wonder what I and the rest of us all owe the dead, and the dead in life.

I can't help it, I'm just like that. Every case I have, for whatever reason, I end it feeling charged with a sadness beyond words I can express: I think perhaps because I can't bear to see another human being lost, whose right to the air is equal to mine and who, having lost it, diminishes the value of my own existence in too many ways for me to describe.

They say that I am too cheeky and independent, but I see nothing in my contract with the police, or with my fellow men for that matter, that prevents me from feeling like a human being if I care enough. It's paradoxical that my violent love for the world makes me break the noses of brutes and fools.

I'm a good detective because I can enter the mind of a killer so well, so easily — a bad one because I sweep so clean and neat that, with the quarter of a twist of the wheel, I might very nearly be a killer myself, the only difference being that I hate all that is false and evil.

# Joe Canzius

## Notes

The idea for No Strings Attached *came to me while I was talking
with a couple of black youths in a caff in Tottenham. This was
shortly after the Metropolitan Police had launched one of their
many clean-up operations, which coincided with the news that a
Jamaican gangster, imported by the police to inform on a Jamaican
gang, had severely embarrassed the police by embarking on a one man
crime wave.*

*The youths were pitiless in their condemnation of informers, but as
the conversation went on, what struck me was the fact that they were
describing an intimate relationship between the police and the world of
petty crime. After all, they said, all this stuff about fingerprints, DNA,
psychological profiling and the rest of it is just window dressing to
impress the judges and the juries. These things were usually useless in
the business of finding out who actually did a burglary or a murder or a
rape, and the streets were full of people who'd got away with it, because
the police usually had no idea until someone told them. This was why
informants were so important to the police.*

*Over the next hour they talked about the various ways that the
police tricked or coerced people into working for them. By the same
token, policemen themselves had to be active in setting up and manipu-
lating various criminal enterprises. At this point they told me the story*

*of Snapper and Chesney, and when I came to write it down, it seemed to illustrate the sense in which the traditional narrative of cops 'n' robbers shooting at each other across a moral divide, had become a sort of fairy story. To Snapper, Chesney and the policemen who controlled them, personal morality was irrelevant to the world in which they conducted their activities. Like stockbrokers or race horse owners, they went out and did the business, leaving the morality for their victims to consider.*

# No Strings Attached

## by Joe Canzius

The smell in the caff was a combination of frying bacon slices, sausages, ten thousand eggs, marinaded lamb kebabs, aged beefburgers, dead fish in batter, stale milk, rancid yoghurt, a whiff of black pudding, and the stinking puffs from a generation of vapourous assholes.

Chesney came in through the door, and paused, holding his breath. About twenty, short, his head clean shaven all over, anorak and jeans, he looked like one of the hard black youths who hung out on the common nearby dealing small packets to a drifting mob of white grungies, which was exactly what he'd been doing until a quarter of an hour before he walked into the caff.

He let his breath out and stood motionless, ignoring Spyros, who took a good look at him, then went back to scraping beefburgers off the range behind the counter. In the same moment Chesney saw the boy he was looking for sitting by himself at a table up the back. Light-skinned, tall and thin, an oval patch dyed blond on top of his head and alongside it three straight lines razored into each side. This had to be Snapper.

Chesney walked over and sat down, but Snapper didn't look up. Instead, he opened the packet of Marlborough Lights in front of him, and put one in his mouth. Then he pushed the fags over towards Chesney.

'Take one,' he advised. 'Fill your lungs with smoke. Save you from breathing in this shit.'

Chesney didn't bother to smile. Having a laugh was the last thing on his mind.

'What did they tell you?' he asked.

'You tell me,' Snapper replied. 'All I know is some shavehead guy name of Chesney was going to meet me. That's you.'

Chesney nodded. He didn't let it show on his face, but he'd recognised Snapper as soon as he'd opened his mouth. They'd been to the same school, although Snapper was younger, and a couple of years behind. In fact, Chesney had been expelled and banned from the premises for more than a year before Snapper got into serious trouble. He'd only been fourteen but he was already a noted troublemaker, and one day he'd waylaid Miss Jackson in the stairwell leading to the gym. She was a sprauncy-looking trainee teacher, who'd been giving him earache about his reading, and Snapper had pushed her head through the stair railings, and looped his belt round her neck, so that she couldn't move without choking. Then he'd sliced her tights and knickers off with his knife and he was just about to impale her with his throbbing horn, when Mr Watson, the gym teacher, and the only black man on the staff, came up from behind, grabbed him and threw him against the wall. Snapper was unlucky there, because Mr Watson took the black kids' behaviour personally. So he gave Snapper a good beating, then without allowing him to pull his trousers up, he dragged him, with his pants flapping round his ankles and all his dickaments hanging out, up the stairs, down the corridors and through the mobs of giggling schoolkids, to the headmaster's office, where they waited for the police to arrive. They'd sent Snapper away, but when he was sixteen they'd let him back home, an event which he celebrated by trying to hold up a newsagent with a water pistol. He'd taken another beating, and this time they sent him away for real. That was the last Chesney had seen of the guy, but he'd been hearing his name around the area for a good year now, and by the look of him he'd grown up and turned hard.

'You know what it's about,' Chesney said. 'What have you got?'

Snapper leaned forward and lowered his voice.

'Listen guy,' he said. 'This ain't like standing on the green, you're handing out pieces of rock, you see Babylon coming and you drop it on the floor and rub your foot over it. Finito. This is serious.'

'I know that, dun I,' Chesney told him, without disguising his irritation. 'If you don't want to do business I'll piss off.'

Snapper leaned a little closer. He put his hand on the table between them, the fingers spread.

'Look at that.'

Chesney looked. The top of Spanner's middle finger was missing. It had been cut square across halfway down the nail, leaving it with a curiously blunt look.

'So?'

'So I got this through trusting a man. Black man, locks down to here, and everything. We came out the Scrubs same time, so I join him up with a firm. They go to do a job, and Babylon waiting for them. Everyone else was solid y'know, only this guy. They knew he was the informer and he was down to me. My life was on the line and I had to pay. I got off easy, but this finger is my satellite warning. So don't fuck with me.'

'What happened to the other guy?'

Snapper sat up abruptly. He rolled his eyes as if to show it was a stupid question.

'I didn't ask no stupid questions you know. You work that one out for yourself.'

'So what you telling me?' Chesney asked. 'You don't want to do this thing?'

'I'm telling you I'll do it my way'

Chesney nodded. He was beginning to get a feel for the vibes. The guy was suspicious, but he had every intention of doing the business and all this was just a bit of foreplay before they got down to it.

'Aright,' he said. 'So what you want me to do? You want to see my gold card or some shit?'

Snapper grinned.

'You ain't got no gold card.'

Chesney felt in his pocket, took out the gold card and put it on the table between them. In the gloom of the caff it had a dull shine, like real gold. Chesney had got it in a deal the night before from a youth who'd got it off another youth who'd taken it that afternoon from a geezer down Camden Town. It was pure coincidence that Chesney had it on him because he was planning to get rid of it in the next half an hour, but he couldn't resist using to show Snapper up.

Snapper reached for the card, but Chesney put his finger on it and drew it back towards him.

'You want to do business now?' he asked.

But Snapper wasn't finished yet. He leaned forward again and stared into Chesney's eyes. This was serious eyeballing. The stare of confrontation which looked into the other man's heart to see what was there, hard man or wanker. It was a stare which said that if you didn't have the heart to die you would have to submit. It was a stare to set the pulse racing and the blood rushing through the veins. It was the stare Chesney had learned coming out the school gates when he was twelve.

Snapper gave it a few seconds longer, then he pulled on his fag and let the smoke drift away into Chesney's face. Chesney didn't react. He knew this was the way to win. Snapper had done all the talking, probing and jerking around, while Chesney had stayed immobile and expressionless. Deep down he knew that Snapper couldn't move him, and that Snapper knew it too. So far he was on top.

'What you want?' Snapper asked.

'Nine millimetre,' Chesney said. 'Police gun. Them big thing. They look at that they know it's a gun, not some fucking water pistol. You know how I mean?'

Snapper didn't move a muscle but Chesney could tell he didn't like that at all. For a moment his forehead wrinkled and he started to put on the stare of confrontation, but then he changed his mind, and got down to business.

'Use a shotgun then. Fucking big enough for you.'

Chesney didn't like shotguns, which was why he'd come to Snapper in the first place and Snapper knew that.

'Fuck shotguns,' Chesney told him. 'I can pick up one of them out a public toilet in Kilburn. Just tell me what you got.'

'Something special,' Snapper said. 'You won't get this in fucking Kilburn I can tell you that. Nine mil Centurion. Same as the Beretta. US army and police. Eight inches long. Automatic or single shot. Fifteen shots in the magazine. Pull the trigger and the fucker will blow a hole through that wall before you can open your hand.'

They spent the next quarter of an hour haggling about the

price, then Chesney slid out of his seat and walked out without looking behind him. As he walked round the corner into Green Lanes he took out his mobile phone and dialled. When he heard the brief squawk from the other end he spoke one word, shut the instrument and put it in his pocket.

In another few minutes he reached the park gates, went in and walked down to the football pitch where he stood leaning against the railings. It was the middle of a weekday and the pitch was deserted, but Chesney kept thinking about playing there with his firm on Sunday morning. They hadn't played for a couple of years, because two of the boys were dead, five had been sent down and the rest were too busy doing business on Saturday night to get up in time to play football of a Sunday.

Chesney was so occupied dreaming about this that he didn't hear Fisher coming up behind him, but when he heard the voice he was too much in control to jump, the way he suspected that Fisher wanted him to.

'Yo,' Fisher said. 'Wha de blood claat yah dream bout?'

Chesney didn't answer or turn around, because he didn't want Fisher to have the satisfaction of seeing how much he'd pissed him off, even though he had the uneasy feeling that Fisher already knew.

'So wha' appen,' Fisher went on. 'Answer I and I nah man.'

Chesney knew he was only doing it to annoy but it still got to him. A white man like Fisher talking Jam down was more than insulting. Fisher was telling him that there was no escape, not even in the words that formed a bond with his friends, not even inside the language that kept his thoughts private, and not even behind the mask which hid his true face from the faces he met on the street.

'Aright,' Chesney said reluctantly.

Fisher leaned on the railings watching him silently, a little smile on his face. The smile said that he knew what Chesney was thinking and he didn't give a shit. It was the same smile Chesney had seen the first time he met Fisher. This was in Brixton, when they brought him up to see his lawyer, they said. The screw had pushed him into the little interview room then slammed the door behind him, and this tall thin white man had turned round from where he was sitting on the edge of the big table and given him a big smile.

Chesney had an idea about what he wanted from the moment he saw him stood there in a pinstripe grey suit, his long brown hair brushing his shining white collar at the back, and the big smile on his face. It was a good deal, especially if you were fronting up better than five years for dealing crack, with no remission on top of that. Fisher said he could get the charges reduced to possession and get the judge to take into consideration the time he'd spent on remand. He'd be out in a couple of months. All he had to do was give up a few names.

Chesney struggled, but in the end he did what Fisher wanted. He knew the risks, which were that he'd wind up crippled or dead if the brothers whose names he was spouting ever found out, but the truth was that he was only one of several small dealers who did business with these guys. If anybody heavy got nicked they'd have a few dozen options as to who did the dirty on them, and when Chesney weighed that chance up against the five years he was looking at, it was no contest. Besides, on the street, informing was the biggest sin you could commit, but everyone knew that the only reason the police ever worked out who did what was because somebody told them. Sooner or later everybody talked.

So he said yes to Fisher, and he was out in a couple of months, and he reckoned that was the end of it, until one day soon after he was walking down the street towards the Seven-Eleven when a car pulled up beside him and Fisher looked out of the driver's window.

'Get in the car,' Fisher said.

'Fuck off,' Chesney told him.

Fisher smiled that smile.

'Look in your pocket big boy.'

He felt in his jacket pocket and took out a card which hadn't been there when he left the house. It was a plain white card, like some kind of filing card, with words written on it.

'I'll tell you what it says,' Fisher said. 'It says: this is how easy it is.'

Chesney read the words at same time as he heard them and right then he knew he was working for Fisher.

The funny thing about it was that Fisher never told him what kind of cop he was or what he really wanted. He wasn't from the local station, Chesney knew that.

He knew all the detectives there and Fisher wasn't one of them. He wasn't an ordinary detective, either, because he didn't seem interested in drugs or nicking anyone for rock. Mostly, he just asked stupid questions like who was running this firm or that firm, or what was Top Cat's real name? The other thing he wanted to know was about guns, and this was why Chesney had been told to contact Snapper and make a deal with him that morning.

'So how was it?' Fisher asked eventually. 'Done it?'

Chesney didn't turn around. It was as if he could preserve something of himself by refusing to look at Fisher while he told him the details of the deal he'd fixed with Snapper and when and where they were going to meet.

'You done good, boy,' Fisher said when he'd finished. He tapped on Chesney's arm with a bulky envelope. 'Here's the dosh. I want you to buy the gun, then tell him you're setting up something big, like a bank, and you need a dozen weapons for your firm. You need some big vicious looking shit, like the army carries. Automatic rifles. Something you fire at the ceiling and it falls down. You got that?'

'Where's he going to get the stuff?' Chesney asked.

'That's exactly what I want to know,' Fisher told him. 'Tell him if you're going to spend that much you need to meet the guy who's supplying them. You can't take a chance getting ripped off. You know what to say.'

Chesney would have pulled out there and then if he could have, but he knew he couldn't, so he sleepwalked through the afternoon and most of the evening until he found himself going down the High Street towards the address that Snapper had given him. It was in a dimly-lit little cul-de-sac which curved round in a crescent shape, and was lined by fire escapes running up the backs of deserted shops and offices. Near the end of it was the building which might once have been a shopfront or something, but now it was so thickly plastered with posters that you couldn't tell.

He rapped twice on the door the way Snapper had said, then twice again, completing the signal. The door opened abruptly and Snapper stuck his head out and looked past him up and down the alley. Then he pulled Chesney inside and slammed the door shut behind him.

It was a big empty room with twists of newspaper lying around and a few packing cases scattered near the wall. The only light came from a lamp balanced on one of the packing cases with a long cord dangling off it.

Chesney's eyes swivelled around the room, taking it all in, then he turned and saw the gun pointing directly at his head from a couple of inches away. He held his breath, and Snapper satisfied by the look on Chesney's face, laughed and reversing the pistol in one fast motion held it out butt first. Chesney took it without comment, although what he really wanted was to smash it across Snapper's sneering mouth. It felt lighter than he'd expected but when he hefted it in his hand, feeling its weight, Snapper produced the magazine and gave it to him.

'Let me show you how to break it down,' Snapper said. In the silence of the room his voice seemed unnecessarily loud.

'I know that,' Chesney told him. 'Forget about that. I have another deal for you.'

'I leave it unloaded then,' Snapper said.

Chesney shrugged. The place made him nervous, and his instinct was to do the business quick and get out. So he started on the story Fisher had instructed him to tell. Snapper's expression grew more and more incredulous as he listened.

'What?' he said loudly when Chesney finished. 'You want twelve big guns? Automatics? What you going to do? Invade the United States?'

Chesney grinned at that, not because he thought it was funny, more because he wanted to keep Snapper relaxed.

'So what?' he asked. 'I talking serious money.'

'Gimme a minute,' Snapper said.

Chesney wondered what he had to think about, and he was just about to say so, when there was a huge bang on the door which made the room seem to vibrate, and at the same time a brilliant bluish white light went on outside.

'You inside,' an amplified voice shouted. 'This is the police. Open up.'

Chesney looked around wildly. For the first time it struck him that there was no way out. He swung back to look at Snapper, whose complexion had turned livid in the glare, and who was staring at him, his face twisted with rage.

'Informer,' Snapper shouted. 'Informer. You bring them here.'

Chesney opened his mouth to scream a denial, but before he could get the words out Snapper was on him. A sideways kick to the thigh flung him back against the wall, and he scooted back along it, fumbling in his pocket for the knife. It came out smoothly and when he pressed the button as he brought it up to arm's length, six inches of steel sprang out of the curved bone handle. Seeing it, Snapper froze in mid-air.

'Come on, you rass claat fuck,' Chesney said.

Snapper fell back a pace, then crouched down, his own knife out and pointing. The youths circled slowly, but neither of them had time to make a move, because at that moment the door flew in and crashed in the middle of the floor, immediately followed by a mob of policemen.

'Drop it,' someone shouted, and when Chesney turned his head, he saw a cop dressed in a blue boiler-suit and a peaked hat pointing a rifle straight at him. He dropped the knife.

Later on he couldn't remember much about the arrest. He hardly remembered anything except a confused jumble of lights and sounds, and being handcuffed and pushed into the van. The thought which filled his head was that Fisher had done this to him. Why, he kept wondering? Why?

At the station they took him straight into the interview room on the second floor, and a minute later Ronald McDonald came in. Chesney didn't know his real name, but some of the youths called him that because of his red hair and the fact that he was always clowning around.

'Chesney, Chesney, Chesney,' Ronald said, looking down and shaking his head as if he gave a shit. 'I thought you were a respectable dope dealer. Now you get involved in this. Bang to rights. A knife. A gun. An envelope full of notes.' He paused and drew his breath in sharply. 'The judge won't like that. Then there's conspiracy to commit armed robbery. This is five years my son.'

It was always five years, Chesney thought.

'I want a lawyer,' he told Ronald.

'Don't get ideas above your station,' Ronald said. Then he roared with laughter. 'Above your station. Get it?'

Chesney didn't bother to look at him.

'I want a lawyer,' he repeated.

Ronald sat opposite him and leaned forward.

'Don't be in too much of a hurry, son,' he advised. 'We haven't charged you yet. There's a way out of this.'

'What you on about?'

'I'm glad you asked,' Ronald said, putting on a funny voice. 'All you have to do is tell us about your firm, where the job you're going to do is, and when you're going to do it. We'll get you out of here, you go on the job, and you walk free as a bird when we pull your mates in.' He paused. 'I know you, Ches. You're a decent kid. Do something to help yourself.'

Chesney laughed. This was the first thing to strike him as really funny during the whole of the day.

'That's how I got here,' Chesney said.

'What you on about?' Ronald said roughly. 'Don't mess me about.'

'I'm not,' Chesney told him. 'I'm working with one of your lot. How'd you think I got that money?'

Without pausing he told Ronald about Fisher, how he'd come to see him in Brixton, how he'd sent him to buy the gun and all the rest of it. At the end of the story Ronald wasn't smiling anymore. He pointed a threatening finger at Chesney's face.

'If you're making this up Chesney, you're finished. You know what I mean? You're going down.'

'Check Brixton,' Chesney told him. 'They've got to know about him.'

'Ballocks,' Ronald said. 'There's people in and out of there like a dog's dick.'

That was when Chesney gave him the one piece of information he'd memorised and had been saving up for an emergency like this. The number of Fisher's BMW. Ronald wrote it down and got up in a hurry.

'Don't go anywhere,' he said.

Chesney sat where he was, thinking it over. He wondered how and why Fisher had done it, and who he really was. Then he gave that up and thought about his mum. The last time he'd seen her she'd been standing on the street corner opposite the shopping mall with a dozen other women singing hymns. He'd watched her for a while from the bus stop, then went on his way because he couldn't think what to say to her. He wondered also whether his father was dead or alive and where he could have been all these years. One thing was true: with a mum like that, he couldn't blame his dad for taking off, because he'd done the same thing himself as soon as he could.

It was well over an hour before Ronald came back, and when he did he didn't sit down or try to start psyching Chesney out. Instead he left the door open and dumped the stuff they'd taken from his pockets on the desk. The knife wasn't there, but Chesney didn't want to push his luck by asking.

'You can go,' Ronald said.

Chesney packed his pockets quickly and walked out ahead of Ronald. He felt like laughing and shouting. Free at last. He hurried through the lobby of the station without looking at anyone and through the double doors into the night. By now it was early in the morning, the street deserted. It had rained sometime in the night and he could hear the cars making splashing sounds as they went by. He walked at a fast pace, almost running down the High Street, not knowing and not caring where he was going, and he'd turned the first corner before the car cut into the kerb beside him and he heard Fisher's voice.

'Get in the car.'

'Fuck off,' Chesney said.

The BMW speeded up, moved ahead of him, and stopped. Light flared as Fisher got out and stood waiting for him to approach.

'Don't fuck with me, Ches,' Fisher said. 'I can put you back where you came from before you get fifty yards down the road.' He paused. 'And worse.'

Chesney got in the back of the car. Fisher got back in the driver's seat and shut the door.

'It was all a cock-up,' Fisher said. 'But you shouldn't have used my name. Don't ever do that again. I would have found a way to get you out. Quietly. But our relationship is private. You get me?'

He had that little smile again, and now Chesney couldn't hold it in.

'Fuck you,' he shouted. 'Why didn't you tell me they were going to raid the place? You could have done it after I left, or before I got there. You wanted Snapper, you could have had him any time.'

Fisher watched him, smiling, till he'd stopped and turned away to stare out of the window.

'I didn't want Snapper,' Fisher said. 'I'm not interested in Snapper any more. As a matter of fact I passed Snapper going down that club down the road an hour ago and I didn't say a word to him. Snapper's okay.'

Chesney's first reaction was a tightening in his throat and gut. If Snapper was out he'd be spreading the word that Chesney had done him up and got him nicked.

'He got bail?' Chesney asked. 'That quick?'

Fisher's smile got broader.

'He didn't need bail. I told you it was all a cock-up. I thought Snapper would lead you to a source for those nice new army guns that your mates have been buying lately. The local filth thought that you would lead them to a firm that was using the guns. We were both wrong.'

Then it hit Chesney. It was Snapper, and while they were dancing around suspecting each other, they were both working for the law.

'Snapper set me up.'

Fisher grinned openly.

'If I were you, I'd keep away from that boy. He's trouble.'

Chesney thought it over. If that was how things were, Snapper wouldn't say anything about what had happened, but he still might make trouble for Chesney with the police or with some of the rock-heads hanging out on the common.

'I might take a trip,' he told Fisher.

In fact he'd been thinking about it for a while. Joy and the baby had moved back to Bristol the previous year and sometimes he'd thought about going to see her. This would be as good a time as any, and maybe he could get some kind of a job down there.

'You do that,' Fisher said. 'Do you good. But you'll be back.'

'Maybe not,' Chesney said. He looked Fisher straight in the eye for the first time since they'd met. 'Do what you like. You can't stop me.'

Fisher laughed.

'Stop you? Why would I want to do that? You're a free agent, man.' He held his hands up and opened them wide as if to show there was nothing in them. 'Don't worry Ches. I'll ask you to do the odd job now and again, but apart from that you're free to do what you like. No strings attached.'

# John B Spencer

## Notes

**W**hile I would defend anybody's right to protest what they consider to be a just cause, it, nevertheless, afforded some small amusement to observe the reaction of the Animal Rights activists to the policing of their recent demonstrations. They complained of excessive use of force and — and this is the clincher — impertinence.

Ah, the middle classes.

An incredulous brush with reality.

After all, none of their number had ever died in police custody, or in the back of a police Transit as a result of resisting arrest.

Go tell it to the people of Stockwell Park or Stoke Newington…

Unless unfortunate enough to be involved in a major car accident, or some other random catastrophe, the middle class experience of violence is framed within the carefully choreographed scenarios of the television or the cinema screen. They rarely, with the telling exception of the domestic arena, experience the extremis that allows violence to be perceived as the solution rather than the problem. The world of Cracker or Scorsese's Taxi Driver is not their world. Even war comes clean… the carnage of an open market square in Sarajevo after a mortar attack, the indiscriminate slaughter of men, women and children in a Baghdad housing project after one of our blue-eyed flyers has computed *his vectors, released his missile — these realities are kept from them, lie rejected on the cutting room floor.*

*They are protected.*

*Cosseted.*

*Cocooned in a 'Child On-Board' fantasy.*

*As each of my sons, in turn, becomes old enough to drive, I warn him, 'Don't get involved in any fracas on the road, you never know what kind of nutter you're likely to meet up with.'*

**Harry's Down** *is a short story adapted from a novel in progress which, I hope, will offer the same salutary advice.*

# *Harry's Down*

## by John B Spencer

'So, who was the stud?'
Harry already knowing the answer, Ross having briefed him on the drive in from Gatwick, the last leg, up through St. John's Wood, traffic almost at a fucking stand-still.

'You're weird, you know that, don't you, Harry?'

Harry standing there in a towelling bath robe, bare feet, just had a long hot soak, bath salts, the works, now feeling a whole lot better, remembering Ross, face like a wet week, waiting in the arrivals lounge, Harry saying to him, 'That time of month, again, is it, Ross?'

'I've been stuck here since eight-thirty, Harry.'

'You should be so fucking lucky.'

Not bothering to explain.

Cab straight to Kennedy from Nestor's club on the South Side, no sleep, stuck there four hours waiting for the fog to lift — what the fuck did they have instruments for? Up there three hours, then the captain's announcement, like some fucking big kid, turbulence is expected. A thousand foot drop in the time it took to blink. Harry not sure if he had screamed or not...

Smiling now, looking at Celeste down on her hands and knees doing one of those jigsaws she was so fond of, in her housecoat, still not dressed, large gin and tonic, ice cubes and a twist, having difficulty slotting the pieces together because of the thick pile of the carpet, not giving an even surface. The jigsaw complete enough for Harry to make out a wooden ship with a tall single funnel, belching smoke, a larger sailing ship behind it, ghostlike, didn't look finished, so why the fuck should anybody want to waste good money on a picture didn't look finished?

'Turner,' Celeste said, not looking up, '*The Fighting Temeraire.*'

'Since when did you know anything about paintings?'

'I may not know much about art, Harry, but I can read what it says on a box. "*The Fighting Temeraire Tugged to her Last Berth*, JMW Turner".' Tossing the jigsaw box lid in his direction, Harry bending to pick it up, the bigger older ship still not looking any more finished in the painting reproduced on the lid. Harry went over to the sofa, sat down, the way a big man who knows it does, legs splayed, arms spread-eagled along the top of the headrest, still holding the jigsaw box lid.

'Pass it back, will you, Harry, I can't do it without that.'

Celeste, draining the gin and tonic, stood up, gave Harry a look, went over to the bar to fix another drink. Harry noticed she was walking steady, checked his watch, still only eleven-thirty.

Early enough.

'While you're there, build me a scotch and coke, would you?'

'You're home now, Harry. You build bridges, drinks you mix.'

Celeste poured a small measure of single malt, Isle of Jura, picked it from the shelf because she liked the shape of the bottle, splash of coke, no ice... Harry didn't like ice with his spirits, 'liquor' — Harry would say. 'The idea is it's supposed to burn, why drown it in cold water, for Christ's sake?'

'One of these days you're going to come up with the bright idea of inviting me along with you on one of your trips.'

'You wouldn't like it, stuck on your own all the time, you think I spend my time sight-seeing?'

Celeste handing him his drink, taking the jigsaw lid, waving it like a fan, 'Harry, I have no idea what you spend your time doing.'

Sipping from her drink.

Taking it easy, now.

Knowing the question wasn't going to go away...

*So, who was the stud?*

'Tingo Maria.'

'What?'

'Ten days time, you wouldn't like it.'

'Sounds like a drink people don't drink have at Christmas.'

'It's in Peru — you want to tell me about this fuckhead you've been screwing senseless while I was away?'

'I don't screw around, you know that.'

'I do know that, Celeste, and I don't care. Only, this time it's different.'

'You're weirder than I thought.'

'I don't see it that way. You're happy, I'm happy. That such a bad deal?'

'Plenty I know would beg to differ.'

'You with the prosecution or the defence?'

'Sounds to me I'm in the dock, welcome home, Harry.'

Raising her glass.

Knowing it was a dangerous thing to do.

Harry sensing her fear, not wanting to be the predator — not with Celeste — sitting forward on the sofa, elbows on his knees, scotch and coke held two-fisted, swirling the glass — one thing about no ice cubes, you didn't get that tinkerbell sound when you swirled the glass. 'The fucker's a journalist, you didn't know that?'

'You think I checked his CV?'

Coming back strong.

Maybe, too strong.

'You bring him back here?'

'What do you think — we did it in the back of his car?'

Remembering the invite sat there on the mantlepiece, press preview, new film by that old goat, Max Duncan — Christ! Celeste couldn't stand the sight of him — made porno movies, black and white, young street-cred journalists all of a sudden conjuring up crap like *Erotica As Art On A Shoestring*. Porno movies backed by Harry's money. Harry laughing, that was rare, but, showing her those clippings just before he flew off to New York, he cracked up. Come the night, Harry still three thousand five hundred miles away, invite still sat there on the mantlepiece, she thought, 'Why the fuck not?' Up till then, Celeste had thought ICA was something to do with a soap powder.

'So, what did you think?'

Rick talking to her across the rim of a wine glass.

Celeste's first impression:

Thinking, not saying...

Shouldn't you be home finishing off some homework?

Christ! They let them out of school early these days.

Not even interested, but then, wanting to make a point to the adolescent bitch with the crew cut and ankle boots. Let her know, woman to woman, that competition was more than just a big mouth and a *you can fuck me if you're lucky* attitude.

Rick was parked in a slip-road off The Mall. Shadow of the Pall Mall Club building rising high to the right, beyond the trees. Lamps throwing pools of orange light, turning the leaves and grass grey. The car was a Morris Minor, would have fitted in the boot of Harry's Roller, no trouble.

'This is a car?'

'Vintage fifty-eight. Classic small family saloon. Run for ever just so long as you check the steering pinions on a regular basis.'

'You lost me, Rick.'

Steering pinions?

What the fuck!

'Basic design fault. Front wheel collapses, you cartwheel down the motorway. You either love them or you hate them.'

Celeste: 'Read my lips.'

Rick had to push the front seat forward so they could get in the back, Celeste noticing for the first time the lights of Buckingham Palace further down The Mall. Rick seeing where she was looking, saying, 'What happens if the Queen comes out, decides to take the corgis for their constitutional?'

Nervous as shit.

The kid's idea of a joke.

'Won't she be surprised.'

'You don't want to go somewhere?'

'We are somewhere.'

'I mean —'

'You mean I don't seem the type?'

'I mean, I'm easy if you are.'

'Try me.'

There on the back seat, the warm surprise as he entered her, that moment always a surprise, the gasp she could never help, forced between clenched teeth, Celeste's knee painful against the metal ashtray, palms flat against the roof of the car, pushing hard. Just like the first time ever? You were supposed to always remember the first time ever. Celeste didn't. Wondering why she didn't. Coming down. *Erotica As Art On A Shoestring* — too fucking right!

Lighting a cigarette.

Rick didn't complain about her smoking, not that first time.

'You didn't call out your wife's name. Things not too good on the home front?'

'What makes you think I'm married?'

'You must be joking.'

Adjusting clothing.

Dampness growing cold.

'I'd have called out yours, only I don't know it.'

'Smooth talking bastard.'

Remembering Harry, one time, singing, to the tune of *All of Me*, Christ! Harry had a lousy voice, 'I took the best, I took Celeste.' Harry, now, saying: 'Celeste, do me a favour, I *know* you did it in the back of his car.'

Celeste coming back with, 'You know so much, you know I brought him back here.'

'A fucking journalist nosing around in my house!'

Not:

'Screwing my wife!'

No, not Harry.

'My house!'

Saying it again.

The house that Harry built.

Celeste still had the estate agent's spec-sheet tucked away in a drawer somewhere upstairs. Just before Christmas, seven years back. They'd been shopping in Knightsbridge and Harry had suggested an early supper in Mr Chow's. Celeste had been trying to make sense of the menu, saying, 'Crab Butterfly, Harry? What the fuck is a Crab Butterfly? Couldn't we just get a take-away?' Harry had slid the spec-sheet across the table to her, Celeste noticing first the embossed letterhead: *Sackville Rose, South Audley Street*. Harry saying, 'Happy Christmas.'

Big grin on his face.

Celeste reading through the spec-sheet.

'"Gazebo!" We going to have wild animals running around,

Harry?'

'It's a summer house, Celeste, comes with the garden.'

'Joke, Harry. You think I don't know what a gazebo is?'

Harry worried that he might have offended. Spoilt the surprise. Celeste reaching across and touching his hand, wanting to say, had wanted to say ever since, that that cold December night, with the sleet coming down and the traffic piling up along the Brompton Road, cars misting up, wipers going, fog lights on, that spec-sheet had seemed like the most beautiful poem she had ever read.

House of dreams.

Hampstead Lane.

Overlooking the Heath. Overlooking the whole of London. On a clear day you could see Shooter's Hill, Blackheath. Watch the passenger jets, all in a line, following the Thames into Heathrow... Concorde, five-thirty every afternoon, you could set your watch by it. Two hundred and five thousand pounds, seven years ago, you have to remember... How the fuck did Harry get his hands on that kind of money?

The dumb question they always asked.

That Rick had finally got round to asking.

Celeste saying, now, 'You want it straight, Harry, we were too busy screwing for him to have time to be nosing around the house.'

Harry trying not to give her the look.

That look.

'I need to be certain.'

'So how will you manage that?'

'Piece of piss — I'll ask him.'

Celeste struggling to take it all in. Needing to get into some clothes. Go upstairs, take a shower, put on her face, be more prepared for Harry in this kind of mood. What the fuck did he care Rick was a journalist?

'I need to go dress, Harry.'

Jeans.

T-shirt.

Nothing fancy.

Harry, not reading her mind, just knowing her well enough, saying: 'Do me a favour, Celeste, put on something nice... that black number you picked up in Italy, you haven't worn that in a while.'

'Italy? That was five years ago, Harry.'

Harry hated jeans. Never wore them himself. Could never work out what was the big attraction, that old pair Celeste was so fond of, frayed pockets, gone at the knees, why the fuck, money he gave her for clothes? Women in jeans reminded Harry of those scrubbers down the Mile End Road, waiting for the overnight lorry drivers, hanging around outside McDonalds, after the pubs had turned out, hair down to their arses…

Harry holding it right there.

That wasn't Celeste…

Not in a million years.

'Just a thought.'

Celeste kicked out at the jigsaw, scattering the pieces, a section of the ghost ship left there on the carpet, making no sense whatever without it's outline, grey, like a storm cloud, nobody knew how to paint the edges.

'Promise me you don't ever see him again.'

Thinking, that was not going to be a problem after Ross was through with him.

After Harry made the call.

'Fuck you, Harry, what is this?'

Harry not sure he could explain, even if he had wanted to. A safe pair of hands, he had always prided himself on that. The Tingo Maria connection on the telephone, long distance, a bunch of greasers now seeing him as a loose cannon. Fuck knows what the kid might have dug up, Celeste sleeping off a session, World War Three wouldn't wake her. Imagining the conversation, Nestor or Ramon saying: 'We got the London editions here, Harry, it don't look good.' Harry on the defensive, 'No sweat, nothing I can't handle.' 'Maybe now is not such a good time. No disrespect, Harry, but we should wait till this blows over.' Harry knowing this was a crock of shit. That they would never get back to him. Ever. Thinking he should ring Bertram right now, have him come over, go through the paperwork, check how much of it could be incriminating, see if anything was missing, find out what exactly the kid could have worked out given Celeste hadn't fucked out *all* his brain cells.

The scotch kicking in.

Jet lag.

Empty stomach.

Harry laughing.

Thinking:

Ease off, Harry. Who the fuck needed Bertram round here going through the books, first morning back with Celeste?

Saying:

'When was it, Celeste?'

'When was what?'

Knowing what he meant.

That look on Harry's face, sat there on the sofa.

Who needed hard to get?

'Eight days, two hours,' glance at her watch, 'twenty-seven minutes. Right after Ross packed your cases in the boot, sat out there waiting, with the engine running.'

Not sure about the minutes, but knowing it would please Harry.

'So, what's new?'

'He was twenty-six, Harry. You think he would know something you don't?'

'Kids today, who knows?'

Astride Harry's lap, Celeste's knees deep into the sofa, working on getting Harry uncomfortable, then her hand guiding him to the one place it wouldn't hurt. Harry sighing, then losing it. Celeste, her hand in Harry's mouth, offering him her fingers one by one, Harry biting each one just enough to hurt, knowing she liked that, watching her head down between his legs, dressing gown open, thinking about Nestor and Ramon, the South Side club, night before he flew home, business settled, 'Let's have ourselves a good time, Harry.'

Nestor saying, 'In the normal way of things, Harry, this would not be such a good movie. The guy, he's in too much of a hurry, doesn't let her see it coming, you know what I mean?'

Snuff movie.

Ramon adding, 'She don't see it coming, what's the fucking point?'

Woman in her early twenties, white bridal gown, white veil, bunch of red roses, coming down the aisle, priest stood there waiting with a bible open in his hands. 'This sister, she never did anything like this before, old man up for armed robbery, murder one on two counts, got a sick kid and a habit to support, not expensive, but now more than she can afford... guy says he can maybe help her out she does him this small favour, fuckin' incredible!' The priest has his pecker out, the bride is now on her knees, takes it into her mouth, working on it. 'Now this is where the script changes, only the sister, she don't know that.' The priest: '...in sickness and in health.... to love, honour and obey...' Taking a thirty-eight Cobra out from underneath his cassock, pointing it down at the top of the woman's head, she hasn't seen a thing, too busy still working on his pecker... 'Catch this, Harry. This is what makes this such a great movie... man, you any idea how much copies of this change hands for?' Pulls the trigger as he comes. The woman's head explodes, white wedding dress and red roses, you can't now tell them apart, wedding dress crumpled on the floor as if there was nobody in it, the priest quick-stepping backwards in a Michael Jackson dance routine, screaming, clutching himself, pumping blood... Nestor, Ramon, everybody laughing hysterically, 'You dig that, man,' Ramon saying...' Dumb fucker just blew away his own pecker.'

*Let's have ourselves a good time, Harry.*

Harry wanting to throw up.

Celeste, given up trying, looking up into Harry's face.

'What is it, Harry?'

Reaching up, putting her arms round him, her face close to his.

Holding Harry tight.

'Stay like that, will you, Celeste?'

'Long as you want, Harry,' Celeste said.

# Denise Danks

## Notes

Georgina Powers started out as a development of Enid Blyton's George, one of *The Famous Five*, the fictional children's characters of the Fifties and Sixties. I wondered what would happen to an independent tomboy, an only child with just a dog for company, insufferable male cousins, too pretty and sensible by half female cousin, a domineering, self-centred, bad-tempered father, an appeasing mother, and a penchant for hanging about with gypsy boys. I got Georgina Powers, cynical freelance computer journalist, stubborn as a mule, tough, vulnerable, smart, dumb, divorced, smoker, drinker, an East End flat, West End habits, no pets, and a penchant for hanging out, and having sex with some very bad guys. Her milieu is the computer industry with all its fast moving twists and turns, its nerds and ne'er do wells, its chip wizards and corporation cowboys. Life for Georgina is a sort of David Mamet Video Game with no cheat sheet. In Phreak, the fifth novel in the series, Georgina sets out to expose a phone scam which leads her into a whole mess of trouble with phone phreakers, Internet lonely hearts and Bengali protection gangs. Trouble is, that whereas with the first four, Georgina was well ahead of her time: Baring-type financial derivatives and market manipulation (The Pizza House Crash), rock star deaths (Better Off Dead), virtual sex, virtual murder, and multi-user Porno games to bet on (Frame Grabber), chip theft (Wink a Hopeful Eye), with Phreak, the plot seems to be unfolding daily in the pages of the national press as I write. I wake up and can't wait to compare notes. Hey, maybe someone's hacking into my system...

# Phreak

## by Denise Danks

Little Stevie Wonder lay at the bottom of the huge metal drum among the rubbish bags. His head was twisted this way and his body that. I held on to the metal rim ten foot off the ground and looked down at him. My heart was beating like a hummingbird's wing.

Next to me, Chronic Delaney was holding tight to the rim too and staring down into the shadows at the body that'd fallen, probably, from just where we were hanging on. The smell coming up on the night air from the depths of the bin was sweet and sickly. It was a mix of interminable decay: wet plastic, damp paper, the rotting remnants of quick lunches. I let go and slid to the ground. Chronic waited for a moment before he followed.

'What do you think?' he said.

'I think he's dead,' I replied.

'No point in calling an ambulance then.'

'We should call the police and an ambulance. He looks dead but what do we know? We can hardly see him.'

We stood in the narrow road behind the flat, square British Telecom building. I looked up at the dull stonework and blank windows.

'Think they've got a phone?'

Chronic looked up too, pushing his lank fringe from his eyes.

'You got to get your stomach onto the rim and lean down to get the bags. He could've fallen,' he said.

'Gimme the torch.'

He unzipped an outside pocket of his black parka with shaky hands and gave me the rubberised flashlight without a word. I switched it on and the shadows leapt up our faces. He bent down, cupping his nicotined hands in a cradle for my booted foot, and heaved so that I could lever myself up high enough to rest my elbows on the steel edge of the bin. I pointed the beam downward. The circle of light shuddered as he hoisted himself up beside me.

We looked down like two curious children in a tree might stare down at some strange human activity occurring in the dark bushes below, round-eyed at the tantalisingly adult enterprise that had been rumoured but never actually seen in the flesh. We watched for signs of life and learned that death is very different. It was Abdul Malik all right. There he was lying chest down on a bed of yellow plastic bags and old McDonald cartons. We could make out the University of Santa Cruz Banana Slug T-shirt that he liked to wear in honour of his favourite movie. His baggy jeaned legs were twisted to the right as if he were running. He still had his clean white Nike trainers on. His brown arms were outstretched: one hand clutching the neck of a large bag, the other holding one to his side like a favourite toy. His face looked backwards, unnaturally twisted more than one hundred and eighty degrees over his left shoulder. His stunned mouth gaped and his dull eyes stared beyond the light into the darkness like the blind gaze of an heroic mask, his hair a fixed halo of black rays, and on his shirt, a smudge of deepest red. We observed the still detail of his marble face in silence and disappointment until a fluorescent striplight coming on in one of the offices above startled us. Chronic slid quickly down the dump bin, leaning against its cold metal for cover. He caught my swinging legs, helped me down and nervously lit us both a cigarette. I took at least two deep drags before I spoke.

'You know what the problem with that corpse is?' I said, puffing and blowing.

'It ain't dead?'

'I wouldn't say that not being dead was a problem, Chronic.'

'What then? What's the fucking problem that is more than this fucking problem, fuck it?'

'It has my lipstick on its collar, Chronic, that's what.'

He took a couple of swift inhales and moved anxiously from one foot to the other. I pulled my cigarette from my mouth and inspected the tell-tale red wax on the filter. The image of my mouth was stuck to it like a fingerprint. My hand was shaking as I smeared my lips roughly against it.

'God damn it.'

The whooping sound of sirens spliced into the even hum of background city traffic and Chronic closed his eyes and whirled away, turning silently before me in the twilight. His shoulders jolted with the imaginary force of a recoiling machine gun. Long red flares of burning tobacco streamed out behind him like the tails of a night kite. His body jerked and danced, his lank hair flicked back and forth across his face. He turned to me, finally raising his no-show Kalashnikov aloft, his crazy eyes lost and confused and then he legged it, leaving me alone by the dump bin with the dead body of Abdul Malik, formerly known to his friends as Little Stevie Wonder, the boy who played with phones.

Jesus, I wanted to run too.

Richard was pretty good about cooking me something when I got in. I said I didn't need it, couldn't face it, but he got going with a frying pan, little button mushrooms softened in olive oil and stung with lemon juice, a couple of slices of smoked best-back bacon and a corner of soft white ciabatta to dip in the juices. He sat me down at the kitchen table and opened up a bottle of beer.

'Glass?'

'Leave it, thanks, Richard.'

He put the bottle by my plate and sat opposite me to watch. People who cook like to watch people eat their food, like parents like to watch their kids win races on sports day. He sat anticipating my next mouthful like a dog eyeing a ball. I didn't disappoint him. I was surprised that I was so hungry. Death can ruin the appetite. I'd heard some coppers throw up. Not that the hard man that took my statement would. No way. His insides were firmly anchored to his steely heart. He was the sort that thought solicitors were an impediment to justice and that reporting for newspapers should be an arrestable offence. The way he had looked at me suggested that I had very little future in my game. I think he knew my statement was missing something. They get a feel for that sort of thing. I told him what I did and what I saw. I didn't tell him about my brand of lipstick.

'I'm going to run the story,' Richard said.

I wiped my mouth on a piece of floral kitchen roll and took a drink of my beer.

'How long?'

'A short, about a hundred and fifty, two hundred words.'

'OK. There's more though. I know it.'

'We've still got to run a brief about the kid's death, and keep in touch with the police on this. We don't know how it's going to pan out, could be, you know…'

'I know. Someone could have pushed the poor bastard then we have to find out why.'

Richard had been trying to be sensitive, not something he was particularly skilled at, and he was excited about this. He was a news editor after all. If he hadn't been excited he might as well have turned his hand to delivering milk. That's why he'd stayed up with me. First, he wanted to make sure I wasn't going to dig into my scotch or, if I failed to find any left, his brandy. Second, he wanted to be briefed well enough to write it himself if I happened to stumble across either. It was Press Day at *Technology Week* the next day and Abdul had timed his final exit just right from the point of view of a front page down page filler.

'I don't want anyone else sniffing around just yet. It's my story,' I said.

'This won't keep, Georgina.'

I chewed on the bacon. I loved the taste of salt and oil. I loved the doughiness of the bread. I couldn't understand why people wanted to fuck when faced with death when eating like this was a possibility. I'd take the last supper any time.

'Whatever you think you're onto, you're still a jump ahead. That's all you usually need,' he said.

It was a see-through compliment but I let him get away with it. I took another drink of cold beer, pushed the empty plate away and tore the wrapping off a fresh packet of cigarettes. I patted my jacket that was hanging over the back of my chair for a light.

'Mary safely tucked up in bed?' I enquired, holding up the unlit cigarette. Richard pushed an ashtray towards me.

'She moving in or what?' I said.

Richard wasn't answering.

'Don't you find it a bit boring working with someone all day, every day and sleeping with them all night, every night? Don't you fancy a break, don't you want to be alone for a change or at least with a fresh face once in a while?'

'It's not every night.'

'Every night, Richard. She's going to start paying rent soon.'

'It's my house.'

The way he said it was the clue.

'She's moving in, isn't she?'

He didn't answer. He looked uncomfortable. He ran his chunky nail-bitten fingers through his hair that was thinning quite rapidly from the front. Richard had taken to wearing a ponytail of the long curly hair that he had left, just when the world was phasing them out in favour of goatees. I'd told him about it, but he thought it looked cool. Like he thought his Guatemalan mules looked cool with baggy military shorts. Personally, I blame Mary's vegetarianism for bringing out the Oxfam in him. Richard cleared his throat.

'She doesn't mind the cigarettes as much as she does the smell of dope.'

I lit my cigarette and stared at him.

'I really didn't think you'd want me to knock on the bedroom door and pass it around.'

'It's illegal, George...'

The taste of my cigarette had started me thinking about a joint.

'...And a bit retro.'

'You've been reading those style magazines again, haven't you?'

Through the smoke I could see that it wouldn't take much to push him right over the line. He probably hadn't had any since Glastonbury '83, when it was way out of fashion.

'NATO's experiments on arachnids show that it does affect the efficient spinning of spiders' webs; on the other hand, there is an enormous amount of anecdotal evidence that, in humans, it can have an aphrodisiac effect on the highly sexed.'

He mulled this over, for about a nanosecond. The pictures in his mind seemed to project onto the ceiling. 'Don't mind if I do,' was what he said.

An hour later Richard and I were slouched in the front room. We talked about Glastonbury '83 — correction, he talked about it, and he talked about it, until I asked him very slowly and carefully: 'Do you know John Delaney?'

'Who?'

'John Delaney. Chronic.'

'Is he? What does he do, play for Arsenal?'

I started to laugh. I laughed more than Richard's weedy unintentional joke called for. I laughed so loudly and infectiously that Richard started. He didn't know what he was laughing at. He was laughing because I was and he hadn't laughed in such a long while and it was all hilarious. It was even funnier when Mary opened the door and stood there in a long, green, polyester nightdress with a cream lace trim. Richard's critical mistake was that he laughed even louder than I did. She wasn't laughing. She told us it was two-thirty in the morning and asked what the hell did we think we were doing?

'Laughing. We're laughing, laughing, laughing,' I said in the unsophisticated maniacal manner of a complete blockhead.

How Richard laughed at that. But Mary had a frown on her that would have disconcerted a Sumo wrestler and gradually she directed the pissy look on her face from Richard to concentrate on me, the evil corrupter of her man-baby. When our infantile amusement had subsided and silence returned to the smoke-filled room, she turned to Richard.

'I'm going to bed. Coming?'

It was a command thinly disguised as an invitation. The inane grin on Richard's face collapsed like a torn pocket. He sighed and stood up slowly and clumsily, almost to attention. I watched the door close behind him and wagered with my conscience that the aphrodisiac quality of the drug was going to go to complete waste. As for me, I slumped backwards on the sofa and tried to remember what I had told that steely-eyed policeman, Detective Sergeant Duggan.

I could see Abdul's kohl-black mischievous and deceptive eyes hovering slightly above Duggan's gun metal grey head as it bent over the table to inscribe my words onto the lined sheet that was to be my statement, 'for now,' as he put it. Abdul was bloody laughing at me.

How I had dreaded the arrival of the police as I stood in the street outside the telephone exchange. Two police cars had eventually arrived, quietly, with an ambulance and I had been escorted down the alley back to the bins. I had explained how I had clambered up the bin to look down and had seen Abdul's body lying there. I explained that the guy I had been with had done a runner.

'He was scared,' I said, but the young policeman just absorbed the information without comment before hoisting himself up the side of the bin and swinging his leg over.

Two paramedics and Duggan waited beside me. No chance of my doing a runner, not any more and I felt as guilty as hell standing there among the uniforms in the yellow light of the offices above. We could hear the young constable moving about and then the bin jerked as his head appeared with his elbows and the rest of his body launched out into the night. He came towards us brushing dust and debris from his hands.

'No pulse, Sarge.'

The paramedics moved away and Duggan turned away from me, but I hadn't been given permission to leave.

'Can we get the police surgeon in there?' he said.

'We'll need a ladder, or something,' replied the young policeman.

'OK, get her to verbally certify death and I'll get forensics out.'

The word made my skin prickle. Those guys could identify lipstick to the brand name. What would they find after all those boots had stomped around the body except that smear of lipstick on Abdul's shirt? And Chronic had done a bloody runner. It looked so bad, and how could I say I knew him, the Chronic? Tell them he was my dealer? I don't think so. Don't get me wrong, it's nothing fancy, no needles and tourniquets, no tinfoil and tumblers, no pipes and bowls. What I got from him for twenty-five quid a quarter was mostly bog-standard Moroccan with all the charm of a multiple blend of variable quality Japanese whisky. Chronic got his name because he dealt only in cannabis, which, despite Richard's remark, was showing something of a resurgence as a recreational drug of choice after its neglect by late Seventies youth in favour of glue and speed. For me, I just had to have something. My demand for alcohol had finally proved to be elastic. I had decided to mix and match and, like the true Thatcher's child that I was, my decision was based on sound economic principles of consumer choice. Alcohol was simply getting the better of me. physically and financially. I was finding I could drink gin all night, spend a small fortune and still have no fun, even though Aldous Huxley's great exciter of the *Yes* function was making me nod a good time at just about everyone in the bar. I couldn't even relax with it anymore. And sick? Oh man. But I had to stop the world somehow, had to have something to get me off limits and John 'Chronic' Delaney sold it to me in little cling film wraps so that at the very least I could dream at night.

I'd met him in a pub. I watched him play the machines for a while and having complimented him on his Terminator skills, we got talking. He wasn't a bad looker if you fancied the type who looked as if he changed his sheets once every six weeks. He was a slouching six foot two with stringy fair hair that parted in the middle and tended to fall across his face. He wore pale baggy jeans without a belt and an XL T-shirt that seemed to get sucked into his body by some internal vacuum. Chronic looked as if he needed to go to bed, or as if he'd just got up, and not a splash of water in between. He was an adolescent twenty-three, slightly spotty and he was jumpy, always, but I'd never seen him do a turn like the one he did when the sirens started. I was straight with him, most of the time. He introduced me to Abdul Malik because I'd said I'd wanted a cheap mobile phone like his, and Chronic, who knew I was a journalist, gave me the benefit of the doubt.

I'd walked down the alley to the front of the exchange looking for a phone. I should've taken poor Abdul up on his 99p deal and let him get that two hundred and fifty commission on something that had cost him thirty to fifty quid, stolen from some car or lifted straight from someone's ear. I'd have had something to ring 999 with and drop myself right in it.

It had got darker and the street lights were spreading pools of sodium yellow on the pavement. There was no-one around. I could've just gone, got the hell out of it. There was no helping him, was there? And how'd anyone know we had been there?

Our fingerprints were on the rim of the bin, but so what? Ours and others. I just couldn't believe he was wearing that shirt. He must have had it on for days and that wasn't his style. He was always immaculately turned out in his street gear, clean as a pair of heels. He'd smelt wonderful too, washed clean and spicy. Maybe, he wasn't dead and I should call an ambulance. My heart began to beat faster with the rush of life-preserving adrenalin. My God, what if he was alive? Bloody Delaney. What the hell had happened to him? I ran towards the river and crossed the fast road by the Embankment. I clutched the small gold tube in my sweaty hand while my heartbeat deafened me and the hairs on my clammy skin prickled up. Do it. Do it. Do it. Wait a minute. I reasoned with myself. If they ask, you've got to tell them. You've got to tell them because you can't lie. Knowing about the lipstick might save you. You can tell them how it was and how it got there. The lipstick could eliminate you, make them look for something else. The brown water below smelled of soil and metal. How far could I throw it? At low tide, would the shiny tube stick out of the mud? They'd know if someone wanted to hide something, they'd come running down here. They'd look, they'd find it and then they'd ask me why.

Such is paranoia when it grips the amateur, and I was an amateur. An indifferent killer could store a severed head in his freezer and live with it for six months before casually bagging it up for disposal on a beach bonfire of rubber tyres. A lipstick like mine in the hands of a professional would have surely ended up in the river and lain there forever next to the knives, revolvers and pistols that hordes of murderers had slung over the wall and gone home happy that they were disconnected from their crimes. An amateur panics. An amateur runs around like a headless chicken, around and around in helpless involuntary circles with nothing functioning but the memory of a thought process. I was hyper-ventilating. I needed a bloody drink, a bloody great double. I saw the telephone kiosk and ran for its stinking shelter. I dialled 999 asked for the police and ambulance and then I rang DI Robert Falk just to let him know what kind of trouble I was in.

'So,' he said, 'You were supposed to meet your friend but you found him at the bottom of the bin. Anyone with you?'

'Yes, a guy called Delaney.'

'What happened to him?'

'He ran for it.'

'Why'd he do that?'

'I don't know, he heard the sirens and panicked.'

'You were on a story though.'

'Yes.'

'A story about what?'

'I can trust you?'

'Come on, Mrs Powers.'

'A story about how easy it is to get access codes and key telephone numbers for national telephone exchanges.'

'This boy suggests that's what you'd find in the bin?'

'Yes.'

'Not as easy as he thought, was it?'

'Just remember I told you this, Robert. Just remember that I said we turned up and there he was.'

He started to laugh.

'You've told me everything of course.'

'Of course, I have.'

Yeah, everything. I might be an amateur but I wasn't about to start doing anyone's job for them. They had to ask me first.

'Don't forget, Mrs Powers, crime investigation is based on intuition and intuition leads to the asking of relevant questions.'

'Thanks for sharing that with me, you're a pal.'

I knew then that I'd done the right thing. If I'd thrown that lipstick in the Thames I would've been asked about it and I would've lied. Intuition would tell them that. Caught out in that lie, I would have had to tell them I'd junked it and wouldn't that have looked bad?

Poor Abdul, poor, poor, Abdul. The police surgeon donned her rubber gloves and pronounced him dead. She said his neck had been broken.

# Graeme Gordon

## Notes

I think I'm a humourist as much as a crime writer and a surrealist more than a realist. But life is far more like a collection of Bukowski short stories than a television soap opera. And there's nothing cosy or reassuring about life. It's a fucked-up assault course, not a logical, solvable puzzle.

I don't care about genre — if something's real to me, if it somehow touches my life, it gets my vote. Most of the time, I stare out of the window, wander the streets, read the papers or whatever — and see life as a sick joke on the human race. Which is why I write the way I do.

What influences me most are my surroundings. The setting for this story came to me before anything else — the kind of pub I might find myself drinking in, if the beer was cheap enough. Once I knew where I was, it was just a question of looking around, seeing who else was there and what they were up to. I normally feel very sympathetic towards my characters but the place was such a dump that I found myself focussing on someone equally unattractive.

I almost always write with music on — particularly if I have a deadline. This story's soundtrack was provided by Blur and Supergrass. My novel Bayswater Bodycount was mostly written to REM, so it probably has a slightly different vibe.

*My literary influences are pretty much all American — though films from both Europe and the States have probably made a greater impact on my creative consciousness. I'm far from thrilled by what little I've read of the traditional British mystery. But in the end, the only thing I really have to contribute to the crime fiction debate is my fiction.*

# *Friday Night*

## by Graeme Gordon

The beer was slops, the crisps were stale and the pool table was showing more slate than baize. A cosy pall of cigarette smoke hung in the air, lending a wholly bogus appearance of warmth to the place. The wallpaper was yellowed and peeling and the mirror behind the rack of watered spirits was brown and sticky with second-hand tar. As the door to the Gents banged open and shut, a sickly smell of alcoholic urine wafted out into the lounge.

John stood at the bar, swirling the dregs of a sixth pint of cut-price lager around the bottom of his glass. It was gone one in the morning, the doors were locked, most of the lights were out and there were only a few other regulars in the pub; very familiar faces — with a bit of effort he could have put first names to them — but not friends of his. Tom the landlord had gone to change a barrel more than an hour before, leaving his wife Pat to mind the bar. And she seemed more interested in breaking the sweet sherry speed drinking record than whatever might have happened to him.

'Is Tom coming back up?' John asked her.

'Same again?' she responded automatically .

He wondered whether a slap round the face would get her to pay attention any better. Or maybe a punch in the tits would be more effective.

'I wanted to have a word with him,' he said slowly and deliberately, straining to keep his voice under control. He was nearly thirty years old, but it still tended to break into a higher register the moment he started to lose his temper.

The vacant expression on Pat's face hardened into a disapproving grimace.

'If it's money you're after, you can think again because we ain't got none.'

John really wanted to be shrewd — just carry on asking for Tom until she went and fetched him, then touch the guy for twenty quid — but the urge to needle her straight back got the better of him.

'What's that in the fucking till, then — scrap paper and milk bottle tops?'

'Overheads,' Pat retorted.

As soon as it became clear that John was not going to be capable of coming up with another smart-arse remark, Pat smiled smugly to herself and turned away to top up her sherry glass. Which was fortunate, since it meant that she caught John's beer glass across the back of her head rather than fully in the face, as he had intended.

'Fucking bitch!' he shrieked in a grating falsetto, lunging viciously at her.

'Steady on,' muttered a crumpled old drunk in a sad brown suit, who was propping up the far end of the bar.

Nobody else made the slightest attempt to intervene as John wrestled the landlady to the floor, biting, punching and kicking her. In fact, two of the three potential interveners couldn't quite be bothered to watch.

Pat's soft, flabby body was robbing John of the pleasure he had hoped to get out of beating her up. His fists and boots were right on target but there was no feeling of any real contact. He had to imagine her vital organs rupturing under the force of his blows, visualise the internal bleeding, think about how the bruises were going to look the next day.

As his adrenalin rush played itself out, he began to lose interest in the battered pulp on the floor. Leaning back against the bar to steady himself for one last, big kick, he found his attention drawn irresistibly to the shiny new electronic cash register.

'Yes, thank you,' he said out loud, going up to it and examining the keyboard.

The range of options was utterly bewildering. There didn't appear to be any one button that simply opened the till drawer. John tried several different combinations in quick succession. The till bleeped and whined resentfully, then went dead. A message on its little display screen informed him that he had failed to enter a valid user identification code and so had been rejected by the system.

'Give me the fucking money!' he shouted, thumping the machine with both fists.

It didn't do any good; the cash register refused to cooperate. John swore at it some more, then stamped off through to the kitchen annex. He soon found what he was looking for — a long, broad stainless steel carving knife. When he came back out with it, the two younger men at the bar drained their glasses and left in a hurry. The old drunk stayed put, eyes closed, mumbling vaguely to himself.

John slid the carving knife into the narrow gap at the top of the till drawer and pushed up on the handle, trying to prise it open — but all he succeeded in doing was snapping off the tip of the blade.

'Fuck it!'

He grabbed Pat by the neck, pulled her head up and waved the knife in front of her puffy, mottled face.

'How do you open the fucking thing?' he demanded.

Being either unconscious or dead, the landlady failed to answer his question. A few deep cuts — along the line of one of her cheekbones, across the bridge of her nose, down the other side of her face — made her more interesting to look at but didn't make her any more talkative. John dropped her head. It hit the floor with a dull clunk, blood streaming from the freshly-opened wounds.

He was beginning to think that he was just going to have to leave the money, when he suddenly remembered that Tom was still in the cellar. The landlord was an intimidatingly large man, but he was really more of an overweight bloater than a heavyweight fighter. And John had both the element of surprise and the carving knife to his advantage.

Nevertheless, he felt distinctly apprehensive as he eased

open the door to the cellar and crept stealthily down the stairs. At the bottom, he found a small whitewashed room with a delivery chute to his left and a pair of aluminium swing doors in front of him. Trembling from a combination of the freezing cold and his failing nerve, he slipped the knife into the inside pocket of his denim jacket and shoved hard against one of the doors — hoping to catch Tom off guard.

At first, all he could make out in the shadows of the next room were a whole load of beer barrels. Most of them were stacked in a corner; a few in the middle of the room had clamps on top and plastic tubes running up through the ceiling to the bar. As John followed the path of these tubes with his eyes, he finally caught sight of the landlord.

Tom was hanging upside down from one end of a heavy chain at the far end of the cellar. The chain ran through a deadlocked pulley system bolted into the ceiling, which allowed him to raise and lower himself in maximum safety with minimum effort. Apart from a pair of his wife's none-too-sexy knickers, he was completely naked.

'What the hell are you doing in here?' he yelled angrily at John. 'I thought I locked that door.'

John continued to stare up at him, momentarily unsure of how to react. Tom yelled at him again.

'Get out!'

'Don't tell me what to do, you filthy fucking pervert!' John shouted back.

Tom grabbed the loose end of the chain and pulled up on it, swiftly lowering himself from the ceiling. John whipped out the knife and rushed over, sticking its broken tip a short way into the landlord's huge belly just as he got his shoulders to the floor. Tom came to an abrupt halt and watched as a trickle of blood ran down his chest to his chin, then dribbled off round his neck.

'Fuck!'

'Listen, you fat cunt,' John said threateningly, 'I'm taking you upstairs and you're going to open the till and give me all your fucking money.'

'Is that right?' Tom blustered.

John turned the handle of the knife, digging out a small chunk of flesh. The blood flowed more freely now, mingling with the tiny pools of sweat that had sprung up between Tom's goosebumps.

'Let's go,' said John.

Tom shivered, his eyes flicking back and forth from the knife in his stomach to the crazy leer on John's face.

'Right — yeah — okay,' he stuttered, 'I've just got to get down off the chain and put some clothes on — okay?'

John thought about it. He was quite sure that Tom wasn't above playing some spiteful trick on him. On the other hand, it was undoubtedly true that he would be unable to leave the cellar at the same time as staying chained to its ceiling. Perhaps the answer was to disable him in some way — but what would do the trick? Chopping off an arm? Both arms? An arm and a leg? The knife frankly didn't look heavy-duty enough to hack off a whole limb, even if he cut carefully at the joint.

As John reviewed the options, he developed a slight nervous twitch, which caused him to jiggle and twist the knife a little further into Tom's gut. The big man whimpered faintly, chewing on the inside of his cheeks to stop himself from crying out — scared of doing anything that might antagonise or, worse still, encourage his tormentor.

'All right,' said John, 'You can come down, but you don't need any more clothes than you've already got on.'

'But what about — what about...' The landlord's voice trailed off.

'What about what?'

'My wife,' he moaned pitifully.

'She might want her pants back,' John replied cheerfully. 'She might think you're a disgusting fat pervert — in which case she'd be right — or,' he grinned unpleasantly, 'She might just be way past giving a shit — in which case, everything'll be all right, won't it?'

He tugged hard on the chain, depositing Tom in a heap on the floor. Tom sat up quickly, gasping for breath. He made a clumsy attempt to untangle the chain from his ankles with just one hand, keeping the other clasped firmly over the hole in his stomach.

'Are you taking the piss?' asked John, stooping over him from behind and pricking his shoulders with the knife.

'No — no, I'm just...'

Tom didn't bother trying to finish the sentence. Using both hands now, he quickly freed himself.

'Get up!'

Tom did as he was told.

'Move!' John commanded, jabbing him hard in the buttocks to speed him on his way.

The landlord yelped and jumped forward a couple of feet, which made John really want to giggle. As Tom settled into his customarily slobbish stride, John could feel himself going red in the face from holding the laughter in. When they reached the double doors, he completely lost control, snorting and screeching hysterically.

Taking this as his cue, Tom swept open the doors, dived through and slammed them back in John's face. John fell heavily on his arse, bruising the base of his spine — blood streaming from his busted nose. But he managed to keep his grip on the knife and was soon on his feet again, seething with rage. Tom wasted vital seconds stripping off his feminine underwear, preferring to be seen as a naturist than a fetishist by any witnesses in the bar. By the time he was in a suitable state of undress and ready to tackle the stairs, John was already barging his way back into the room.

Tom saw him coming and threw a punch, but John ducked it and weaved on by, taking up a strategic position at the bottom of the staircase. The contest was more equal than before, but Tom still didn't fancy his chances against a knife-wielding psychopath. With the obvious escape route blocked, he could see only one way out — the delivery chute.

Not wanting to make the same mistake twice, he rushed over and started clambering up it without taking a moment to stop and think. It was only when he reached the very top that he both saw and remembered that the trapdoor to the pavement was padlocked shut, and remembered all too clearly that the key was in the pocket of his trousers.

He groaned helplessly and collapsed, sliding feet first back down the chute on his belly. He was prepared to admit defeat. His reputation would suffer for it, but the brewery would have to make good the loss — he was about to be the victim of an armed robbery, after all. He would even have the scars to prove it.

But John wasn't thinking about the money any more; when he licked his lips, he could taste his own blood. As Tom continued his descent, John paced purposefully across the room to the end of the chute. As Tom's toes touched the floor, he thrust with the knife.

The combination of Tom's downward momentum, the strength of John's assault and the sharpness of the blade drove the knife deep into its target. Before John knew what was happening, the knife, the hand he was holding it in and six inches of forearm had disappeared up Tom's backside.

Tom emitted a spluttering, gasping sound from both ends at once. His body quivered around John's arm, then went still. John tried pulling the knife back out, but it seemed to be caught in some internal crevice.

'Give me it back!' he shouted at the corpse.

After a brief and fruitless struggle, John decided that there wouldn't be any real harm in leaving the knife where it was — he had no further use for it. Once he let go of the handle, he found that his arm came slithering out as far as the wrist without him having to exert any pressure at all. And a gentle tug sufficed to extract his fist from the loosened grip of Tom's shredded anal sphincter.

As his hand plopped out, it released a stinking puddle of bloody diarrhoea. John recoiled in disgust, churning waves of nausea rising from the pit of his stomach. When he saw that his right arm was coated with the stuff to just bellow the elbow, his mouth watered incongruously. Coughing and spitting, he stumbled away from the body and leaned heavily against the nearest wall. After a few dry heaves, he choked up a large pat of vomit, followed almost immediately by a gush of watery slime.

'Fucking hell!'

Having discharged its contents, his stomach quickly settled down, leaving John with a numb, empty feeling inside. Breathing through his mouth in a vain attempt to block out the stench, he hurried off up the stairs. His first impulse was to go and get a drink, but what he really needed was a hot shower and a change of clothes.

Passing by the door that led back through to the bar, he went up another two flights to the pub's tied flat. It didn't take him long to find the bathroom and, a few minutes later, he was scrubbed clean and lightly perfumed with Pat's peppermint shower gel.

While he was drying his hair, he began to focus a little more clearly on the situation he had got himself into. He put on Tom's bathrobe and went and fetched a bin bag from the kitchen, packing it with his blood and shit stained clothes.

Just before he sealed the bag, he remembered to retrieve his wallet from his jacket pocket.

'Get it together, for fuck's sake,' he chided himself.

Although there was far too much mess downstairs for him to have any hope of clearing it up, he could at least avoid leaving actual personal identification lying around. Shaking his head at the thought of such idiot carelessness, he hustled on through to the bedroom and set about rifling the cupboards and drawers.

All Tom's clothes were way too big for him. Pat was nearer his size — but her silky blouses and flared trouser suits couldn't possibly pass for menswear. In the end, he settled on a pair of Tom's vast crimplene slacks — which he could only get to stay up by knotting a tie round the waist — and a baggy nylon darts shirt. A quick glance in the full-length mirror on the bedroom wall confirmed his worst fears: he looked completely ridiculous.

'Well, it can't be helped,' he snapped irritably at his reflection.

To make matters worse, his stomach had started to grumble insistently. He really was bastard hungry. It was too late for fish and chips or a kebab — and the local shop must have been closed for hours. He knew he had nothing to eat at home, but maybe Tom and Pat would have something.

As it turned out, their kitchen was very poorly stocked. John supposed that such a profoundly disagreeable couple were not often called upon to entertain an unexpected dinner guest. All the same, at the back of the top shelf of the food cupboard, he did find a large selection of slightly dusty Golden Wonder Pots.

Since the choice appeared to be between one of these and a joint of beef that would need at least two hours in the oven, John boiled the kettle and whisked up an instant chicken chow mein. As he ate, he immediately began to feel better. More strangely, he also began to get a hard-on.

Looking down at the sideboard he was standing in front of, he saw that while his right hand was digging a fork in to the pot meal, his left hand was caressing the raw joint of beef which he was sure he had put straight back in the fridge. As soon as he realised what he was doing, his penis stiffened that much more.

'Fuck it — what's wrong with you?' he hissed, snatching his hand away.

But he couldn't help wondering what it would feel like to hold the meat between his thighs — just for a bit, just to see. Glancing guiltily around the room, even though he knew there was nobody there, he unknotted the tie from his waist and let his trousers fall to his ankles. Then he picked up the joint of beef and rubbed it slowly up between his legs. As the cool, moist flesh pressed against his balls, he came — with sudden, startling ferocity.

'Christ almighty!'

He hurled the joint across the kitchen — smashing a mail order display plate — tore off a handful of kitchen roll, roughly wiped himself off with it, then pulled his trousers back up.

Feeling horribly panicked, he dashed back through to the bathroom, pocketed his wallet, grabbed the rubbish bag, and hurtled down the stairs to the bar. Disconcertingly enough, the old drunk was still there, raising his head and squinting curiously at John as he came bowling in through the door. John froze, heart pounding. After a long moment, the old man opened his mouth to speak.

'Evening, Tom,' he lisped, 'I think you've lost a little weight there, if you don't mind my saying so.' He paused to juggle his false teeth back into place with his tongue. 'I'm afraid I have to report that your dear lady wife's been neglecting me,' he complained. 'I'll have a pint of best, thank you kindly.'

John glanced down at Pat's body — which was obviously not about to leap up and start serving drinks — then opened the flap in the counter and let himself out from behind the bar. Now he felt oddly calm.

'It's self-service tonight, mate,' he said thoughtfully, 'But it's on the house.'

The old man's eyes lit up.

'What — even the spirits?'

'Everything,' John assured him.

On his way out of the pub, he looked back over his shoulder to see the old man happily helping himself to an extremely large measure of malt. He toyed with the idea of joining him for a swift one, but thought better of it; all he really wanted to do was sleep. Yawning widely, he wandered off down the street to the junction with Blackfriars Road, dumped the bag of soiled clothes in one of the big bins by the council block on the corner, then headed for home.

# Mike Ripley

## *Notes*

W hen asked — as crime writers usually are — 'Where do you
get your ideas?' my stock response is the truthful one: 'I
hang around in pubs.'

In the days when afternoon opening hours were a novelty and not a
chore, I was sitting in an empty pub off the south side of Oxford Street
and witnessed an Australian barman briefing a spotty youth on a
bicycle on his delivery run for that day. The delivery in question was a
couple of hundred 'Calling Cards' to all the phone booths and boxes in
the area.

Off went the youth and for the price of a pint, the barman told me
the ins and outs of the business, although he never said who was paying
him.

This was one of the stories written for the original Fresh Blood
anthology which never got off the ground, and was the second short
story to feature my series hero Angel. Maria Rejt of Macmillan's heard
about it and rescued it from oblivion by publishing it in Winter's
Crimes in 1991.

It is a period piece already, but at the time the cards on display in
London phone boxes were something of a novelty. Everyone noticed
them (and read them) but only after a year or so did the moral
crusaders attempt to clean up the streets of the West End. They

*failed. The cards are still around, better printed, delivered invisibly with the precision of a commando raid and, in content, more inventive than ever, colour printing and laser copying have made life easier and allowed the use of design and subtle imagery. It has been argued that they are a form of pop art and there was even an exhibition of them in a club off Duke Street in 1994. (It lasted for three days then closed.)*

*This story contains only minimal violence, no murders and no policemen. But there are lots of crimes here. And the placid acceptance of them is probably the biggest crime of all.*

# Calling Cards

## by Mike Ripley

There was fresh blood on the black guy's hand as he took it away from his nose. This was probably because I'd just hit him with a fire-extinguisher.

Well, it wasn't my fault. I'd meant to let it off and blind him with some disgusting ozone-hostile spray, but could I find the knob you were supposed to strike on a hard surface? Could I find a hard surface? Give me a break, I was on a tube train rattling into Baker Street and I was well past the pint of no return after an early evening lash-up in Swiss Cottage (what else is there to do there?). All I could see was this tall, thin black guy hassling this young schoolgirl. I ask him to desist — well, something like that — and he told me to mind my own fucking business, although he wasn't quite that polite.

So, believing that it's better to get your retaliation in first (*Rule of Life No. 59*), I wandered off to the end of the compartment and made like I was going to throw up in sheer fright. I thought I did a fair job of trying to pull the window down on the door you're supposed to open which links the carriages. (Think about it — if you're going to throw up, where else do you do it on a tube?) And, as usual, the window wouldn't open. So I staggered about a bit, not causing anyone else any grief as this was late evening and the train was almost empty. And while swaying about, which didn't take much acting the state I was in,

I loosened the little red fire-extinguisher they thoughtfully tie into a corner by the door.

You can tell someone's put some thought into this, because it always strikes you that it says 'water extinguisher' when you know that the tube runs on this great big electric line.

Whatever. I got the thing free from its little leather strap and staggered backwards, trying to read the instructions.

After two seconds I gave up and strode down the carriage to where the black guy was sitting and just, well, sort of rammed it in his face, end on.

He couldn't believe it for a minute or two, and neither could I, but I was ready to hit him again. Then he took his hand away from his nose and there was blood all over it. Then his eyes crossed — swear to God, they met in the middle — and then he fell sideways on to the floor of the carriage.

The train hissed into Baker Street station and suddenly there seemed to be lights everywhere. I had a full-time job trying to keep my balance and decide what to do with an unused fire-extinguisher.

The doors of the carriage sighed open and I felt the schoolgirl tugging at my sleeve.

'Come on! Let's blow!' she was yelling. 'He'll be coming at you hair on fire and fangs out once he comes round.'

It seemed a logical argument, the sort you couldn't afford to refuse. So I followed her, dropping the extinguisher on the back of the black guy's head, solving two problems in one.

It made an oddly satisfying noise.

Now to get this straight; she did look like a schoolgirl.

OK, so I'd had a few. More than a few. That's why I'd left my trusty wheels, Armstrong (a black London cab, an Austin FX4S, delicensed but still ready to roll at the drop of an unsuspecting punter), back in Hackney. I had been invited up to Swiss Cottage to a party to launch a rap single by a friend of a friend called Beeby. So you heard it here first; but then again, don't hold your breath.

It had been my idea of lunch — long and free, though I think there was food there too. And round about half-past eight someone had decided we should all go home and had pointed us towards the underground station.

Unfortunately, a rather large pub had somehow been dropped from a spacecraft right into our path and an hour later I found myself on autopilot thinking it was time I got myself home.

So I caught the tube and there I was, in a carriage on one of the side seats (not the bits in the middle where your knees independently cause offences under the Sex Discrimination Act with whoever is opposite) with no one else there except this tall, thin black guy and a schoolgirl, on the opposite row of seats.

At first the guy seemed a regular sort of dude: leather jacket a bit like mine, but probably Marks and Spencers', blue Levis and Reeboks and a T-shirt advertising a garage and spray-paint joint in North Carolina. Nothing out of the ordinary there.

But even in my state I had to do a double-take at the girl he was holding down in the next seat. Not, you note, holding on to or even touching up, but holding down. And when the train hit St John's Wood she waited for the doors to start to close just like she'd seen in the movies — and then made a break for it. And of course, she didn't make the first yard before he'd grabbed her and sat her down again next to him.

At this point, I lost what remained of my marbles. I interfered.

The thing was, she did look like a schoolgirl. Blue blazer, white shirt straining in all the right places, light blue skirt, knee-length white socks and sensible black shoes. She even had a leather school-satchel-type bag on a shoulder strap and — I kid you not — a pearl-grey hat hanging down her back from its chin-strap.

And this black guy was holding her down. So I asked him to let the young lady go. And he told me where to go. So I got a fire-extinguisher and hit him.

Did I hit him because he was black and somehow defiling a white schoolgirl? Bollocks. Did I step in to protect the fair name of young English maidenhood? Well, it would have been a first.

I did it because I was pissed, but it seemed the right thing to do at the time.

We live and learn.

'Move!' she yelled again as she pulled me down the station towards platform five.

Goodness knows what people thought, though I was in little state to care, as this schoolgirl dragged me down the steps to the Circle Line platform and bustled me into a crowded carriage, all the time looking behind her to see if the black guy was there and only relaxing when the doors closed and the tube shuttled off.

She breathed a deep sigh of relief. I could tell. We were close and the carriage was full. She noticed me noticing.

'I wasn't really in trouble back there,' she said, looking up from under at me in that up-from-under way they do.

'Nah, 'course not.'

I grabbed for the strap handle to keep my balance.

'It was just that Elmore wanted to deliver me — well, had to, really — to somewhere I didn't fancy.'

'That a fact?' I said, which doesn't sound like much but which I regarded as an achievement in my condition.

'You wouldn't understand,' she said quietly, biting her bottom lip.

'You could try explaining. I'm a good shoulder to cry on and I had nothing planned for the rest of the evening.'

Now in many circumstances, that line works a treat. On a crowded Circle Line tube when everybody else has gone quiet and is looking at this suave, if not necessarily upright, young chap chatting up what appears to be the flower of English public schoolgirlhood, it goes down like a lead balloon.

She saved my blushes. In a very loud voice above the rattle of the train she said: 'Then you can take me home.' And then, even louder: 'All the way.'

After that, what could I say?

All the way home turned out to be underground as far as Liverpool Street station, then a mad dash up the escalator and an ungainly climb over the ticket barrier to get to the mainline station just in time to grab two seats on a late commuter boneshaker heading east.

Trixie lived in one of those north-eastern suburbs which, if it had an underground station, would call itself London, but as it didn't, preferred to be known as Essex, but wasn't fooling anyone. There was nobody on duty at the station so we got out without a ticket again and she led me across the virtually deserted Pay-and-Display carpark to a gap in the surrounding fence. That led on to a sidestreet and just went to prove that for early morning commuters the shortest distance between two points is a straight line. I wondered when British Rail would catch on.

Her house was one of a row of two-down, three-ups which backed on to the railway line. The front door had been green once, but the paint had flaked badly and under the streetlights looked like mould. The frame of the bay-window on to the street was in a similar state but through a gap in the curtains I could see a TV flickering.

'Who's home?' I asked, not slurring as much as I had been.

'Josie, my sister. I told you,' she said.

She had too, on the train. Told me of fourteen-year-old Josie who was doing really well at school and had only Trixie to look out for her now that their mum had died. There had never actually been a dad, well not about the house and not for as long as Trixie could remember. And yes, Trixie was her real name, though God knows why, and she was thinking of changing it to something downmarket like Kylie.

She opened the front door and stepped into the hallway, calling out: 'It's me.'

I stepped around a girl's bicycle propped against the wall. It had a wicker carrying-basket on the front in which were a pile of books and one of those orange fluorescent cycling-poncho things which are supposed to tell motorists you are coming.

The door to the front room opened and Josie appeared. She was taller than her sister and she wore a white blouse with slight shoulder pads, a thin double bow tie, knee-length skirt, black stockings and sensible black patent shoes with half-inch heels. She had a mane of auburn hair held back from a clean, well-scrubbed face by a pair of huge round glasses balanced on her head. She held a pencil in one hand and a paperback in the other. I read the title: *The Vision of Elena Silves* by Nicholas Shakespeare. I was impressed.

'You're early,' she said to Trixie, ignoring me.

'This is Roy,' said Trixie.

Josie frowned. 'You know our deal. I'm the only one in this house who does homework.'

'It's not like that, honey. Roy's a friend, that's all. He helped me out tonight, saw me home.'

Josie gave me the once-over. It didn't take long.

'Well, at least you'll be able to press my uniform before school tomorrow,' she said to Trixie.

'Of course, honey, now you get back to your studying and I'll make Roy a cup of tea in the kitchen.'

In the kitchen, she said: 'Don't mind Josie, she doesn't really approve. Put the kettle on while I go and slip into something less comfortable.'

While she was gone, I plugged in the kettle and found teabags and sugar. Then I ran some water into the kitchen sink and doused my face, then ran the cold tap, found a mug and drank a couple of pints as a hedge against the dehydration I knew the morning's hangover would bring.

Trixie returned wearing jeans and a sweatshirt, no shoes. She busied herself taking an ironing-board out of a cupboard and setting it up, then plugging in an iron and turning the steam-control up. She began to iron the creases out of Josie's school skirt.

'It was good of you to see me home,' she said conversationally.

'Yeah, it was, wasn't it? Why did I do it?'

'And the way you sorted out Elmore... I hope he's all right, mind. I've known a lot worse than Elmore.'

Thinking of what I'd done to Elmore made my hands shake.

'You haven't got a cigarette on you?' I asked.

'Sure.' She picked up the school satchel she'd been carrying and slid it across the kitchen table.

I undid the buckles and tipped out the contents: two twelve-inch wooden rulers, five packets of condoms of assorted shapes, flavours and sizes, two packets of travel-size Kleenex, cigarettes, book matches and about a hundred rectangular cards.

I fumbled a cigarette and flipped them.

They were all roughly the same size, about four inches by two, but printed on different coloured card, pink, blue, red, white, yellow and red again. A lot of red in fact. The one thing they had in common was a very large telephone number. Each had a different message and some were accompanied by amateur but enthusiastic line drawings. The messages ranged from *Striking Blonde* to *Black Looks From a Strict Mistress*; from *Busy Day? Treat Yourself* to *Teenager Needs Firm Hand*. They all carried the legend: *Open 10am till late* and *We Deliver*.

I made a rough guess that we were not talking English lessons for foreign students or New Age religious retreats here.

All the cards had a woman's name on them: Charlotte, Carla, Cherry and so on. I split the pile and did a spray shuffle, then dealt them on to the table like Tarot cards.

'No Trixie,' I said.

'Are you kidding? Who'd believe Trixie? I'm Charlotte and Carla, among others.'

I ran my eye down the cards. Charlotte apparently demanded instant obedience and Carla was an unruly schoolgirl. So much for biographies.

'Working names?' She nodded. 'And tonight was Carla, the one who needs a firm hand?'

'Yeah, but not Mr Butler's.'

'Mr Butler?' I asked, pouring the tea.

'That's where Elmore was taking me. But he didn't tell me it was that fat old git Butler — if that's his name — until we were on the tube. I'd swore I wouldn't do him again, not after the last time. He is *molto disgusto*. Really into gross stuff. He waits till everyone's gone home, then he wants it in the boss's office. I know he's not Mr Butler, but that's what it says on the door.'

'Hold on a minute, what's all this about offices — and where does Elmore come in?'

'It's on the card,' she said taking a cigarette from the packet.

'I've seen hundreds of these things stuck in phone boxes. You ring the number and get told to come round to a block of council flats in Islington,' I said. Then hurriedly added: 'So I'm told.'

'Ah, well, read the difference, sunbeam. "We Deliver" it says.'

The penny dropped. Then the other ninety-nine to make the full pound.

'Elmore delivers you — to the door?'

Trixie blew out smoke.

'To the *doorway* sometimes, but mostly offices, storerooms, hotel rooms. Sometimes carparks, sometimes cinemas. Once even to a box at Covent Garden.'

'You mean one of the cardboard boxes round the back of the flea-market? Which mean sod was that?'

She caught my eye and laughed.

'No, chucklehead, a box at the opera. You wouldn't believe what was playing either. It was a Czech opera called King Roger, would you credit it? I thought that was a male stripper.'

'This wasn't one of Mr Butler's treats, was it?'

'Oh no, he's too mean for that. He likes humiliating women, that's his trouble. And I told Elmore never again, but he was just doing what Mrs Glass told him to do.'

'Mrs Glass?'

'Oh, never mind about that.' She turned off the iron and held up Josie's school skirt. 'That's better.'

She folded the board away and joined me at the table, indicating the cards I had laid out.

'Anything there you fancy?' she tried softly.

'Would you be offended if I said no?'

'Too right — I need the money. Josie's expecting to take thirty quid to school tomorrow to pay for music lessons, and I'm skint.'

'Elmore handles the money, right?'

She nodded and ground out her cigarette.

'Are you sure you wouldn't…'

I held up a hand, stood up and emptied the contents of my pockets on to the table. As I had been at a freebie all day, I hadn't thought to pack credit cards or anything more than a spot of drinking money. I had £2.49 left, which wouldn't even cover the train fare back to town.

'I was thinking of asking you if you could see your way…' I started.

She slapped a hand to her forehead.

'Just my luck,' she muttered under her breath. Then she quietly banged her forehead on the table twice.

'Hey, don't do that. I'll get us some dosh. What time does Josie go to school?'

She looked up. There was a red bruise on her forehead.

'Eight-thirty.'

'No problem. Do you have any black plastic dustbin liners?'

'Yes,' she answered, dead suspicious.

'And some string?' She nodded, biting her lower lip now. 'And an alarm clock?'

'Yeah.' Slow and even more suspicious.

'Then we should be all systems go.'

She gave me a long, hard look.

'I've heard some pretty weird things in my time… This had better be good.'

I slept on the couch in the front room and promptly fell off it when the alarm went at six. It took me a couple of minutes to remember where I was and what I was supposed to be doing, and another twenty or so to visit the bathroom as quietly as possible and get it together enough to make some instant coffee.

Then I pulled on my jacket and zipped it up, stuffing the pockets with the dustbin liners and string Trixie had supplied. Over my jacket I attached the fluorescent orange warning strip which I borrowed from Josie's bicycle, then I slung her empty school satchel around my neck to complete the ensemble.

I was ready to go to work.

In the station carpark, I pulled the dustbin liners over the four pay-and-display machines nearest the entrance and secured the open ends with string around the machine posts. It was still dark and I was pretty sure no one from the station saw me.

The first car arrived at quarter-to-seven and I was ready for it, leaping out of the shadows and holding the satchel out towards the driver's window as he slowed.

'Morning, sir. Sorry about this, the machines are out of action. That'll be two pounds, please.'

It was as easy as that.

After an hour, I got cocky and embellished it slightly. There had been an outbreak of vandalism and the machines had been superglued, or the mainframe was down (whatever that meant) but we were doing our best to repair things.

Then one smartarse in a company Nissan asked for a ticket and when I said I didn't have any, he said 'Tough titties then,' and almost drove over my foot.

He looked just the sort to complain once he got inside the station, though I bet he wouldn't say he parked for free. So I decided to quit while I was ahead. Josie's satchel had so many pound coins in it (no notes as everyone had come expecting a machine) that they didn't rattle any more. It was so heavy, I was leaning to port.

I waited for a gap in the commuter traffic and headed for the hole in the fence. When I got back to Trixie's we counted out £211 on to the kitchen table. I was furious.

At two quid a throw it should have been an even number. One of the early-shift commuters had slipped me an old 5p piece wrapped in two layers of tinfoil.

Somebody should complain to British Rail.

'So what are you going to do now?' I asked, distributing fifty of the coins between two pockets of my jacket and hoping I didn't distress the leather any more.

'Buy some groceries, pay a bill maybe.'

Trixie buttered herself more toast. Josie had taken her music-lesson money, satchel, bicycle and uniform, stuck a slice of toast in her mouth and left without a word to me.

'And then?'

'Oh come on, get real,' said Trixie impatiently. 'Then I ring Mrs Glass and go back to work.'

'When?'

'This afternoon probably.' She glanced at the piles of one pound coins on the table. 'How long do you think this will last? It'll take a damn sight more to buy me out. This is very useful but it don't make you my white knight or guardian angel.'

I bit my lower lip. I hadn't told her my full name.

She put down her toast but held on to the butter-knife, so I listened.

'I chose to go on the game, so there's no one else to blame. I don't like working for somebody else but I don't have any choice just at the moment, so that's that. OK?'

I picked my words carefully.

'This Mrs Glass, she has something on you?'

'Not her; she just runs the girls from her off-licence in Denmark Street. That's the number on the cards. It's her husband, Mr Glass, who recruits us. And we don't have a choice.'

'Is this Glass guy violent?'

'Not that I've ever seen.' She went back to buttering.

'Then why stick with him? Why not do a runner?'

'He'd find us. He's our Probation Officer.'

I got back to Hackney by noon, in order to collect Armstrong. The house on Stuart Street was deserted, most of the oddball bunch of civilians who share it with me not yet having given up the day job. Even Springsteen, the cat I share with, was missing, so I opened another can of cat food for him, showered, changed and left before he could reappear. I couldn't face one of his and-where-do-you-think-you-were-last-night? looks.

Before I'd left Trixie's, she'd leaked the basic details of the operation run by Mr and Mrs Glass. Talk about sleazeballs! But then, he who lives by sleaze can get turned over by sleaze and Trixie had given me plenty to go on.

I spent the afternoon sussing out the off-licence on Denmark Street. It wasn't difficult to find, there being only a dozen or so businesses left there now that the developers were moving in. There was just so much time even I could hang around a Turkish bookshop without raising suspicion, but there were still a handful of music shops left where the leather-jacket brigade could kill a couple of hours pretending to size up fretless guitars and six-string basses.

There was nothing obviously unusual about the off-licence's trade, except that on close inspection there did seem to be a high proportion of young females going in, some of them staying inside for a considerable time. And although they went in singly, they came out in pairs. Not surprisingly, Elmore hadn't turned up for work, so the girls were doubling up as their own minders and 'deliverers'. It was time to put in an appearance.

I retrieved Armstrong from around the corner outside St Giles-in-the-Field. As Armstrong is a genuine, albeit delicensed, taxi, there had been no fear of a ticket, even though I had parked illegally as usual. You had to be careful of the privatised wheel clampers, though, as those guys simply didn't care and slapped the old yellow iron boot on anything unattended with wheels.

There wasn't an excess of riches for the shop-lifter, that was for sure. Many of the shelves were almost bare or dotted with mass-market brands of wines — the ones with English names to make ordering easy. Only the large upright cold-cabinet seemed well stocked, mostly with cans of strong lager or nine per cent-alcohol cider which were probably sold singly to the browsers in the next-door music shops.

At the back of the shop was a counter piled with cellophane-wrapped sandwiches, cigarettes and sweets. Behind it, standing guard over a big NCR electronic till was a middle-aged woman who wouldn't have looked out of place serving from a Salvation Army tea-wagon or standing outside Selfridges on a Flag Day for the blind or similar.

'Need any help, love?' she asked. The accent was Geordie, but maybe not Newcastle. Hartlepool, perhaps, or Sunderland.

'Er… I'm not sure I'm in the right place,' I said, shuffling from one foot to the other, trying to look like a dork.

To be honest, I suddenly wasn't sure. She looked so – normal.

'Pardon?'

'Well… I was told you might have a spot of work going.'

Mrs Glass drew her head back and fiddled with the fake pearls around her neck.

'Work? What sort of work?'

'Err… delivering things.' I jerked my head towards the window and Armstrong parked outside. 'I get around quite a bit and a friend said you could always use someone to drop things off.'

'What sort of things?'

'Calling cards.'

She looked me up and down, and then at the till again, just to make sure it was safe.

'Who told you?'

She glanced over my shoulder at Armstrong's comforting black shape. And why not? Policemen, VAT-men, National Insurance inspectors and the Social Security never went anywhere by taxi. Or if they did, they didn't drive it themselves.

'A young lad called Elmore,' I risked.

'When did you see him?'

'Last week sometime.' When he could still speak; before he ate a fire-extinguisher.

She seemed to make a decision. She could have been judging jam at the Mothers' Union.

'It's twenty pounds a throw,' she said, businesslike.

'I thought thirty was the going rate,' I said, knowing that it was at the time.

'You'll be taking the taxi?' I could see her working out the possibilities. Who notices black cabs in London?

'Sure.'

'All right then, thirty. Wait here.'

She fumbled with a key to lock the till and I saw she wore a bunch of them on an expandable chain from the belt of her skirt. She opened a door behind the counter and stepped half in just as a phone began to ring. Holding the door open with one foot, she took the receiver off a wall mount and said 'Hello' quietly. Further in the back room I could see a pair of female feet half out of high heels begin flexing themselves.

Whoever it was must have arrived when I was fetching Armstrong; I hadn't seen anyone else come in. I hoped it wasn't Trixie.

'Why yes, of course Madame Zul is here,' Mrs Glass was saying softly. 'Yes, she is as cruel as she is beautiful. Yes, she is available this afternoon. When and where? Very good, sir. Madame Zul's services begin at one hundred pounds.'

I was straining my ears now and hoping no real customers came in. Not that Mrs Glass seemed in the least bit inhibited. Business was business. 'May I ask where you saw our number? Ah, thank you.'

She concluded her deal and replaced the phone, then, to the girl I couldn't see, she said: 'On yer bike, Ingrid my love. You're Madame Zul this afternoon.'

'Oh, bugger,' said the voice above the feet, the feet kicking the high heels out of my line of sight.

'Sorry, my dear, but Karen's tied up as the naughty schoolgirl.'

Somehow I kept a straight face.

Mrs Glass scribbled something on a sheet of paper and handed it over. A red-nailed hand took it.

'The costume's hanging up and the equipment bag's over there.' Mrs Glass was saying. 'You'd better get a move on.'

Then she turned back to me and she had a Harrods carrier-bag in her hand. She placed it on the counter and turned down the neck so I could see four white boxes, each about three inches by four.

'One of each of these four in every phone box, right?'

I nodded, knowing the score.

'British Telecom only, don't bother with the Mercury phones.'

'Wrong class of customer?' I said before I could stop myself.

She looked at me with a patient disdain normally reserved for slow shop assistants.

'The Mercury boxes are too exposed. They only have hoods, not sides and doors. The cards blow away.'

'Do you use the sticky labels? I've seen those around, you know, the adhesive ones.'

Mrs Glass sighed again, but kept her temper. She was good with idiots.

'If you're caught doing them, you get charged with vandalism 'cos you're sticking something to the box — defacing it. Right? With the cards, all you get done for is littering and they've never prosecuted anyone yet as far as we know.'

'But don't get caught.'

'Right. Now, the cleaners for the Telecom boxes are under contract to clean first thing in the morning every other day. Your patch is Gloucester Place from Marylebone Road down to Marble Arch and don't forget to hit the Cumberland Hotel. There's a bank of phone boxes in there and the place is always full of Greeks. Then work your way over the parallel streets in a square, OK?'

'Baker Street, Harley Street, Portland Place?'

'And don't forget the ones in between. There's a good mixture of foreign students, embassy staff and BBC in that area.'

Again, I thought she might be kidding, but she wasn't. She was obviously proud of her market research.

'We do a random check on you to see that the cards are up. If you're thinking of dumping them, then don't come back. If we don't get a call from one of these boxes within twelve hours, we assume you've dumped them.'

She pulled on her key chain again, flipped open the till to remove three ten-pound notes. She pushed them across the counter along with the boxes of calling cards. Then she added a five-pound note.

'Make sure Madame Zul gets to the Churchill Hotel by four o'clock, while you're at it, will you?' Then, over her shoulder, she yelled: 'Ingrid, this nice young man's going to give you a lift!'

Madame Zul, she who was As Cruel As She Was Beautiful, smoked three cigarettes on the way to her tea-time appointment, and as I drew up outside the hotel, she stuffed two pieces of breath-freshening chewing-gum into her mouth, picked up a sports bag which positively clanked, buttoned her trenchcoat around the black plastic outfit she was wearing and stomped off towards the lobby.

I watched her go through the sliding doors, then gunned

Armstrong and headed south-east, away from the West End and my card-drop zone.

She had not proved the greatest conversationalist. I had tried a few pleasantries and one obvious chat-up line. I even tried the heavy stuff and asked her whether, as a woman, she felt exploited.

'The punters need us more than we need them,' she answered curtly. 'And I could always work the check-out down the supermarket.'

I was thinking about that, wondering just why I was doing what I was doing, when I arrived at Peter's in Southwark.

Printer Pete's Place is tucked away in a smelly courtyard off Marshalsea Road not a spit away from the old Marshalsea Prison site. Somehow I always suspected Peter — he hated 'Pete' but there had been a typographical cock-up on his business stationery — took pride in that. He loved dealing in anything shady. Probably that's why he became a printer.

I showed him the boxes of calling cards. I had been prepared to scour the phone boxes of the West End collecting them, but now I had about a thousand in pristine condition, not one thumbed by a sweaty hand.

'Nice enough job,' said Peter, turning one over in his hand. '150gsm card, centred-up, neatly trimmed. Most of the girls working on their own do real hash jobs. It's like trying to see how many different typefaces you can get into six square inches.'

'Can you do what I want?'

'Sure. These babies'll go through the machine easy enough but I'll have to put one of my night-shift on it. This is what we in the trade call a hand job.' He roared at his own joke. 'Hand job, geddit?'

'Not often enough,' I countered.

'Got the numbers?'

I handed over a piece of paper with two 0181 London phone numbers and he laid out one of each of the four cards on top of a packing case of printer's ink. The four each had a different catch-line, but the same phone number and the words: *Open 10 till Late* and *We Deliver*. The messages were: *Carla, Teenager, Needs Firm Hand; Charlotte The Striking Blonde; Relax In Samantha's Firm Hands;* and, of course, *Madame Zul, As Cruel As...* and so on. You know the rest.

'So you want these 0181 numbers above the 0171 number?' Peter asked.

'If you can overprint easily.' He nodded. 'So how much?'

'A ton,' he said immediately.

'Get outa here,' I responded.

'Seventy-five, then. It's night work. Overtime.'

'Bollocks. Thirty.'

He squinted at me over his wire-frame glasses.

'Any chance of a freebie?' He waved vaguely at the spread of cards.

'Which one?'

He blushed and tapped the *Madame Zul* card with a shaking forefinger. Really, Pete, I had no idea.

'I had that Madame Zul in the back of the cab less than half an hour ago. I can certainly ask for you.'

'Ok then, thirty and you can pick 'em up tomorrow morning, first thing.'

'Thanks Peter, see yer then. But hey — let me tell you, this lady really can be cruel.'

So cruel, she could easily say no.

The best time to catch a Probation Officer is when the pubs and Courts are shut, so I was knocking time spots off a ten-pound phonecard from a booth in King's Cross station by nine the next morning.

He answered his direct line at the third ring.

'Islington Probation Service.'

'Mr Glass? Mr Colin Glass?'

'Yes. Whom am I speaking to?'

'Nobody if you've got this on tape, for your sake.'

There was a pause.

'There's no recording. State your business.'

The accent was northern, unexceptional and not as sing-song as Mrs Glass, your friendly off-licensee.

'I need to talk to you about some of your clients — and before you tell me you don't discuss clients, the ones I'm interested in are Carla, Charlotte, Samantha and Madame Zul, as cruel as…'

'Who *is* this?'

'Someone who is going to make you an offer you can't…'

'How did you get this number?'

I was getting annoyed with him. He was cutting off all my best lines.

'Get down to York Way in half an hour. Be on the flyover where it goes over the railway. Just walk up and down, I'll find you.'

I hung up and retrieved my phonecard, slotting it back into my wallet along with the white business card from Islington Probation Service which I had lifted from Trixie's handbag.

Very usefully it gave me Mr Glass's direct line at the office, as well as his home phone number.

I noticed an old, half-scraped off adhesive card on the side of the phone. In handwritten lettering it advertised *Black And Blue, The Strict Twins*. The number it gave seemed to follow the series of the phone box I was in and for curiosity's sake I checked. It turned out to be four booths away, a distance of maybe twelve feet.

Some people had no imagination.

I cruised up and down York Way, which is just around the corner from King's Cross, until I saw him hop off a bus and begin to look around. He was alone.

I parked Armstrong on the waste-ground which leads to the Waterside pub and Battle Bridge Basin where the longboats attract the groupies in summer (as most are owned by rock musicians) and locked him. I had two pockets-full of cards, which I had collected from Peter the printer at 8a.m.

Being out on the road at that time was almost a first for me. Wearing a suit was another one. I hoped the cards didn't spoil the cut of the double-breasted.

I put on a pair of Ray-bans (fakes, but good fakes) and marched up the road to meet him.

Colin Glass was a worried man. He was about fifty, short and thin and thinning on top. He wore a Man at C & A suit and as it flapped open I could see where a pen had leaked in his inside pocket. I pegged him as a civil servant who had changed to the Probation Service rather than be made redundant from some other department.

'Mr Glass, we need to…'

'Just what is going on?' he blustered. 'How dare you ring my office?'

'You'd prefer me to ring you at home?'

I reached into my jacket pocket and he flinched away from me. My hand came out holding a selection of calling cards. I fanned them like a magician.

'Go on, pick a card, any card.'

He picked a blue one: *Charlotte, The Striking Blonde*. One of Trixie's.

'So what the hell is this? What are you trying to say?'

'Ever seen one of those before?' I asked, dead polite.

'Of course not.

'Check out the phone numbers.'

'Jesus Christ!'

'I doubt it,' I said.

Below us an Inter-City train picked up speed and headed north. Colin Glass looked as if he wished he were on it. Or under it.

'Try another,' I offered, showing him the full wedge of cards from my pocket. Then I reached for my other pocket. 'Or how about teenagers in need of a firm hand, or Madame....'

'Who... did... this?' he spluttered.

'I have no idea, but unless certain things happen, about 1,000 of these things will hit the phone boxes this afternoon and there could be a specially targeted drop in certain areas of Islington. Not to mention a few through the post to various people.'

He was ashen now, but still holding the cards at arms length as if they would bite.

'There's... can we... ?'

'How many girls have you working for you, Colin? And do tell the truth. You know it makes sense.'

'Six in all.'

'All clients of yours?' He nodded. 'All on probation?'

'They are... or they were.'

'That's naughty, isn't it, Colin. Abusing your position and all that. What a story for the newspapers, eh?'

'Look, they were on the game anyway. If anything we made it safer for them, made them pool their efforts.' He was trying out arguments he'd rehearsed but hoped never to use. He wouldn't look me in the face.

'And I bet Mrs Glass made them cups of tea and saw to it that they had condoms on tap and probably did a bit of counselling on the side.'

He looked up and there was a faint spark of hope in his dead-fish eyes. I blew it out.

'Tell it to the judge. And the papers. And the Civil Service Commission.'

He bit his lower lip.

'What is it you want?'

'You out of business, that's what. This afternoon. Close up the Denmark Street shop — man, that's so obvious a front I'm surprised you haven't been raided by the drugs squad. Rip the phone out and pay off all the girls. Give them a grand each, cash. Call it their redundancy money.'

'Six thousand? I can't…'

'You will. Where's all the profit gone, eh?'

'You don't understand… the pension they give is pathetic.'

'Stay lucky and you might get one. If you don't come across by four o'clock this afternoon, these things go out.' I waved some more cards at him. 'By breakfast tomorrow you'll be giving press conferences — and so will your bosses. Mind you, look on the bright side. Your wife could pick up a bit of business overnight once this number here…'

'All right, all right, I'll do it.'

'Remember, a thousand to each girl. Got anyone else working for you?'

'No.'

I dropped a couple of the cards on the pavement and he scuttered after them before they blew into the gutter, moaning, 'No, please…'

'How about a dude called Elmore?'

'Only him. He sub-contracts jobs when he has to.'

'Then a grand for him too and tell him to retire. If any of them ask, just say it was a present from a Guardian Angel, got that?'

He stood up again, the knees of his trousers filthy from where he'd scrabbled on the pavement.

'Why are you doing this to me?' he asked nervously. 'What's in it for you?'

I looked up and down York Way. There was no one else in sight and traffic was light. I slipped my left hand into my jacket pocket.

'There's nothing in it for me,' I grinned. 'And I'm doing it because I don't like your attitude. You're supposed to be one of the good guys.'

It was the only answer I could think of and I didn't want to debate it, so I threw a fistful of his calling cards into the air and left him on his knees again, frantically trying to pick up every last one.

I told the story to my old and distinguished friend Bunny in a pub in Hackney about two months later.

Bunny is very interested in all matters female and feminist and for all the wrong reasons. He regards it the same way as opposing generals regard intelligence on troop movements.

'But what did you get out of it, Angel? A quick bonk?'

'Just a good feeling,' I said, not really knowing myself.

'So you did get to…'

'Please, curb that one-track mind of yours.'

'I can't help it if I'm over-healthy.'

I spluttered into my beer.

'What's wrong with that, then?'

'Nothing,' I choked.

We had got on to this subject because Bunny had found a red calling card stuck in the door frame by the pub's public phone. I hadn't read it properly until now.

'Well, I think it shows great initiative,' he was saying. 'A working girl's got to work, so why not employ the latest technology?'

He was referring to the card which listed an 0860 number — a mobile phone.

I read the legend: *Carla, Teenager, Needs A Firm Hand.*

I suddenly knew how Trixie had spent her redundancy money.

# Chaz Brenchley

## *Notes*

A story's genetics are seldom easy to unravel in retrospect, but it so happens that in this case I can track every step of its development. It began as a cheat, and got stuck; continued as an illusion, and got stuck; and finally found an ending when I realised that it wasn't in fact about anything that it had pretended thus far to be about...

Or more specifically, it began as an exercise at a day-school for wannabe crimewriters. I was supposed to be running this exercise, dammit, not participating; but the class ganged up on me and made me do what they were doing, viz write an impromptu opening to a crime story.

However, mine was not so much im— as totally, utterly promptu. I'd suspected at planning stage that some such outcome might be on the cards; so I'd been thinking about beginnings all week, and the first line of this story was already in my head. I liked the sound of it, it was punchy and a little unexpected, it would do very nicely to start an exercise.

I wrote the opening couple of pages at the day-school, cheerfully conning the class into believing that I'd thought it all up there and then; and then I put it aside, having no idea where the story might be going, and really no intention of ever finding out.

But it so happened I was doing the world's strangest job at that time, being crimewriter-in-residence on a sculpture project in Sunderland; and I was using the opportunity to write a book's-worth of short stories. I'd more or less run out of ideas, so I picked this up again largely to look busy on the job, to have people think I was working. Next thing I knew, I'd written ten thousand words or so, which was simply too much to waste; besides which, I'd got interested in Joe. But I still couldn't see what he was doing there, where the story was.

Until, in the pub one afternoon, I remembered — à propos of nothing at all — something a friend had said to me once about my first book: that the characters were all too honest with each other, that they only ever said what was true. Which gave me suddenly a whole new angle to work from: how if that were not at all true of Joe, what would it do to the material I'd already written, what new direction would it give the story? I walked home and spun the whole thing on its axis in the space of a paragraph or two, and the second half was a romp.

Received wisdom has it that the best short stories spring from a single clear thought, one idea examined in isolation. I think this is nonsense; in my experience the stories that work best grow from a synthesis, two or more separate ingredients that react dangerously together.

I also think that fiction rooted in reality makes for a better read. I'd never have made it to the pivotal point of this story if I hadn't been in Sunderland, with those streets and that river to write about. Joe's character grew from there, from the place and the people I saw and talked to every day; and plot, of course, grows from character, though ideas can come from anywhere.

# My Cousin's Gratitude

## by Chaz Brenchley

My cousin left me his cat, and it almost killed me. Honest, it did.

I was fourteen, for God's sake, I didn't know what I was doing. I'd lived half my life in Cousin Albie's pocket, trying to please him any way I could. That was instinct, or training, or maybe just fair exchange: he'd taught me to read and write, back when I was seven or eight and having mega problems at school. Even after I'd caught up with my classmates, he wouldn't let me go. 'Education's crucial, Joe,' he used to say. 'You learn everything you can now, it'll all come in useful later.' So two or three days a week I'd be round at my cousin's, taking lessons; and he always sent me home with a book or two from his shelves. He had more books than I'd ever seen in a private house before, did Albie. His books and his cat, that's all he lived for, I used to think, unless it was his books and his cat and me.

But Cousin Albie was old, in his fifties somewhere, and his cat was older, or seemed so to me: a decrepit beast, white-muzzled and slow, so slow. Albie was suddenly slower, though. The cancer had shrunk his speed more than his body, even, and it had shrunk that badly. He asked me, he said, 'Will you look after Tommy, Joe? If I go first?'

'Course I will,' I said, not thinking about it. Not thinking at all what it might mean. You don't look to the future, do you? Not when you're fourteen, and you're confronting death for the first time. You promise anything, or I did, just because it was easier. I couldn't get round it in my head: this man was dying, and he was asking a favour of me, and saying no would probably have been the worst thing in the world just then, for both of us. Besides, I always did say yes to Cousin Albie.

My parents weren't thrilled, they'd never been big on pets. Best I'd ever done before was a goldfish brought home from the fair, that I'd won for myself with an air-rifle and three quid's-worth of trying; and that should've had a love-by date stamped on its tail, it should've come with its own matchbox for burying. Didn't last a week, before I found it belly-up in its lemonade bottle.

Come to think of it, maybe my parents' guaranteed antipathy was another reason why I said yes so quickly. Fourteen again: a bit of rebelling never hurt anyone, at fourteen. I was sniffing at every fence they'd built for me just then, testing my own strength and theirs. They'd never been wildly keen at the way Albie had adopted me, I guess they felt criticised and grateful both, and those are both difficult to live with; but this was different, this was special, this was sanctioned by death and they couldn't even give me a hard time over it.

'It's for Albie,' I said, 'he was really worked up, what's going to happen to Tommy when he, when he dies; so of course I said yes, what else was I going to do?' And they grunted, they sighed, and they nodded reluctant agreement in the end, as they had to.

So Albie died, and they let me see him dead before the undertakers took him. That was mega, and maybe some recognition from them at last that I was growing up a bit. Unless it was meant to be punishment in advance for the cat, sort of 'You let us in for this, so here's a nightmare or two, here's a little reminder that we're adults and you're not.'

Whatever the reason, they let me go upstairs and look at him, pale and cold on his bed, dressed in his best suit and his glasses off his nose so that I almost didn't know him, he looked so different. It wasn't right, to dress his body up and strip his face naked that way.

I'd have put his glasses on for him, only I couldn't see them. Instead I just touched his cheek, half apology and half curiosity and ever so wary, worried about leaving a mark so that everyone would know I'd done it; and he wasn't stiff like I'd been expecting, he was only cold and a bit damp-feeling, like chicken waiting for the oven.

I was up there a long time, too long for my mother, who came to fetch me down. Then I carried sandwiches all afternoon from my aunts in the kitchen to my uncles in the lounge. They called it a wake, but it was a half-hearted and sorry thing. Didn't go on late enough to keep any of us awake, didn't make near enough noise to wake Albie.

We were last to leave, taking all the crockery with us because we'd brought our own round for the tea. 'No one wants to eat off a dead man's plate,' my mother said to excuse it, though I thought it was more that she wouldn't eat off Albie's plates, cracked and stained as they were. And when we left, when we carried the boxes of china down to the car, we carried the cat also, in his basket.

My cat now, my basket.

It was the next week that I got the letter. Long white envelope, neatly typed and addressed to me, *Joseph McLeod, Esq*; oh, my parents were curious. I'd left for school already when it came, I didn't know a thing until I got home after football practice and found it waiting, with my parents waiting too. They hadn't opened it, but I reckon that was a close-run thing. You could see where they'd been looking, trying to read bits of it through the envelope, there were smudgy fingerprints all over; but it was dead good paper, good and thick, they couldn't have made out a word of what was inside.

So I ripped it open, with them behind me and peering over my shoulder; and it was from Albie's solicitor, about his will.

I don't remember the words, what it actually said, though I must've worked my way through it twenty times, that day and the next; but what it meant was dead straightforward, amazingly easy to understand given that it came from a lawyer.

Albie wanted his cat to have the best of everything, that was the gist, and he knew how much it cost to keep a cat in luxury. So he'd left this money in a building society, and the interest on it would be enough to cover everything that Tommy needed, for as long as he lived.

And then when the cat finally died, the letter said, all that money would be mine. As much as there was left in the account, free and clear, no strings attached.

Ten thousand bloody quid, there was in that account when Albie left it to me. Ten thousand quid's-worth of my cousin's gratitude; and all right, fair-do's, that's what nearly killed me in the end. It was the money, not the cat. But I wouldn't have got the money without the cat. And I've never had a cat since, and I wouldn't take one even if you paid me twice or ten times what Albie did. The money's just not worth the grief.

Back then, though, I was desperate for it, I wanted that money with a passion; and I couldn't believe how long the bloody cat hung on. Tougher than Albie, it was, or just more determined. I never got fond of it, no one could; it was a foul, stinking creature with a lousy temper and worse habits. It used to shit in the bath, or else in corners of the lounge. My cat, my job to clean up after it: always me who got down on hands and knees to scrub the carpet with disinfectant, and always me who got yelled at before and afterwards. Half a dozen times, when we were expecting visitors and the lounge was reeking still, I swear my mother was going to kill the cat bare-handed, except that then I wouldn't have got the money. The letter had been dead clear about that. I wasn't even allowed to have it put down if it was suffering. A natural death in its own time it had to have, or all the money went to charity.

So I kept it alive, I got bruises off my mother just holding her back from hurting it; and at last it did die. I came down one morning to find it stiff and stinking in a pool of its own piss, and suddenly I was rich.

Sixteen I was by then, and more than ten grand in the bank; and my parents couldn't touch it, it was mine.

First thing that happened, suddenly everyone who hated me wanted to be mates. All my friends really *really* loved me now.

And my girlfriend, she loved me too. She said so as often as I wanted her to, as often as I made her.

Her name was Carol, and we'd had this awkward thing going for a few months, that had probably only lasted that long because to keep seeing each other was actually easier than breaking it off. It had given us both someone to go with, someone to be seen with; and that was points in our world, that put you on the successful side of average.

Now, though, now she was keen; now she was hot for me, coming round and asking for me, something she'd never done before.

'She's only after one thing,' my mother said, with a sniff of deep contempt; but I knew that, and that was fine. I was only after one thing also, and I didn't mind paying for it.

Didn't even cost me that much, really. We were just kids; neither one of us had had time or opportunity to acquire expensive tastes. I bought her a few tapes and a few bits to wear, some pizzas and some concert tickets. That was enough, that was plenty. Every present brought greater rewards, from lessons in French kissing on her doorstep to the keys to her big brother's bedsit, times he was away. By then we were both learning, both making mistakes; and if I hadn't had the money, I reckon I wouldn't have got further than the first mistake, when I managed to hurt her and get stains on her new black skirt, all in under five minutes.

But I bought her another skirt, and with it bought myself another session on the bed, another chance to get it right. I guess she was as aware as I was that there was a queue of other girls behind her, only waiting their chance to spend some of my money for me; so she was more patient than I deserved, maybe. Anyway, I was happy and so far as I could tell so was she. We had good times together and we were both getting what we wanted, and the way I saw it then you couldn't ask much more than that.

So money can buy you happiness, never mind what they say. At least a bit, for a while. And something else it can do, money can buy you more of itself. Just give it the chance, and money *breeds*.

If you're careful, if you get it right.

Like this, like me and Ronnie. Ronnie had been almost a good friend of mine for a term and a half, a couple of years before; and now he came to me in the street, first time he'd spoken to me in six months, and he said:

'Joe, mate, can we talk?'

'Sure.'

'Down here,' he said, with a sideways jerk of his head; and I followed him slipping and skidding down a steep bank of new shrubs ankle-scratching high, to where the tide had sucked the river halfway dry and there was kind of a rock beach to jump about on, with stinking mud waiting for when our feet slipped between the rocks. We used to come here all the time, and not worry what we took home for our mothers to wash; but now I was wearing new Filas and Calvin Klein jeans, and I wasn't any too comfortable down there.

So I found a solid perch where I could just stand until the rock dried, maybe sit on it then if this took that long; and I said, 'What, then? What's up?'

Actually, I already knew what was up. I'd known him well two years ago. Better than he'd meant me to, perhaps; certainly well enough to be wise, to let the friendship slide as soon as I found a safer companion. I'd shared bottles with him, but not as often as he'd asked me to. I'd shared joints in his back yard and sniffed his poppers at discos and parties, but that had been enough for me. I didn't want to get any deeper into him or the things that he did, the things that he did to himself.

'I'm skint,' he said, not the first time that I'd heard that. Of course he was skint, he was always skint.

'Yeah?'

'I'm hungry.' Not the first time I'd heard that, either. It wasn't true, though, not literally. He didn't mean hungry for food. His blood was jumpy; all his skin twitched and shivered in sympathy, no matter how he rubbed it.

'So?' I wasn't going to help him out, not yet. He wanted a favour, no need for me to make it easier to ask.

'Lend us,' he said. 'Just for a bit. A couple of weeks, till I get some cash together...'

'How are you going to do that, then?'

'Oh, you know. The usual.'

Again, I did know; but I knew something else too, that the pickings weren't good for him at the moment. If they had been, he wouldn't need to ask for money. And I had no reason to suppose they might get better, in the next couple of weeks or couple of months or ever. If I asked about it he'd only lie, though, he'd have some story of a bonanza coming up; so I didn't ask, I didn't challenge him. I just said no.

'No,' I said. 'I'm not lending you money for skag.'

'For God's sake Joe! I *need* it, man! When did you get so fucking righteous, anyway?'

'I'm not,' I said. 'I don't care what shit you shoot up. It's your body, you screw it any way you like. Doesn't hurt me. All I'm saying, I'm not lending you the money to do it. I'm not soft, man. I'd never see it back, would I?'

'Sure you would,' he said, meeting me eye to eye, oh so earnest. 'Straight up, Joe. Soon as I got it, I'd pay you...'

'No, you wouldn't. You'd be hungry again by then, and you wouldn't bother.' Too easy, borrowing off a pal; he was more likely to do the other thing instead, come and ask for more.

He argued a bit, but I wouldn't shift, so then he tried a different angle. 'I thought you were my friend,' he said, accusing.

'Did you?' was all I said, but my eyes reminded him: six months without a word, with no contact at all though he lived only two or three streets from me. A friend in need, that's all he was, all he'd ever been. When he needed something, he was such a friend...

And oh, he needed now. I could see it in him, that hunger, doing more than fret his fingers against his twitchy skin. He looked too cold in the sunlight, in the heat of the day; he was sweating, sure, but he still looked cold. I didn't think that sweat had much to do with the sun, either. Sour and cold, not a good sweat at all: just another expression of his body's hunger.

'Tell you what I will do, though,' I said.

'What?' He was instantly hopeful, thinking me soft as shite after all.

'I'll buy your bass off you. That'll give you money.'

I think he was genuinely shaken, at least for a second or two. His mouth went all slack as he shook his head, as he said, 'Joe, mate, I can't sell my bass.'

'Not to anyone else, you can't,' I said, thinking, *not so soft after all, am I, Ronnie mate?* 'You can sell it to me, though. I'll buy it. And I don't give a fuck what you do with the money.'

He was suddenly desperate, putting his hands up to deny me as he saw how serious I was, how very much I meant it. 'Joe, no. It's all I've got...'

It wasn't, though. He had two things, he had his bass and he had his habit; and this was crunch time. He'd have to trade one of them in, and I knew which my money was going on, however much he whimpered.

The bass was a Fender fretless, and it was worth a lot of dosh. Sold straight, it was worth a small fortune; only Ronnie couldn't sell it straight, could he? Matter of fact, he couldn't sell it at all. No one local was going to touch it. A thing that valuable from a known addict with a dozen convictions for theft and no proof of ownership, just when the police were giving second-hand traders a really hard time, checking everything against the register of stolen goods? No chance. He might as well turn himself in at the station, that's where he'd end up anyway if he tried touting a Fender around.

Me, though, I could sell it. I didn't have Ronnie's disadvantages: I didn't have a record, and I wasn't broke. I could travel down to London or Birmingham or Manchester, and off-load a Fender bass with no trouble at all; but not Ronnie. If he'd had enough for a bus-fare, then he wouldn't have been so hungry. He'd have spent it already on skag or Temazepam or whatever he was on these days, and he wouldn't have been hungry till tomorrow.

He said no again, he loved that bass, he said; and he did, I knew that. He really didn't want to sell it, though that was what he'd pinched it for in the first place. So I shrugged and said okay, no skin off my nose, I said, and see you around; and I turned to go, and he said wait.

'Wait,' he said, 'listen,' he said, 'how's about this, how's about if I sort of pawn it to you? You lend us the money and take the bass, and if I don't pay you back, then it's yours? How's about that?'

I didn't even stop to think about it, I just shook my head, straight off. That would be just the same as a loan; he'd always be asking for extra time to pay, 'just a couple weeks more, and you could just give us another fifty in the meantime, couldn't you, Joe, you've not lent us half what it's worth...' I wasn't getting into that sort of shit. All or nothing, I said, and meant it.

And after another five minutes of fretting and fidgeting and rubbing at his clammy, sticky skin, he said yes.

Didn't even ask what I was offering. I could have screwed him hard on the deal, but I didn't; he knew a lot of my friends, and that wasn't the reputation I was after. I offered him a quarter of what it was worth, figuring I could sell it on for half. He knew that was fair, he'd done enough dealing with fences in his time. So he nodded, and I sent him home for the guitar while I went off to the building society.

So I bought Ronnie's guitar and sold it again, all in three days; and I made myself a nice piece of money on the deal, and the start of a reputation too.

Not as a fence, that wasn't what I wanted. I wasn't fussy, I'd take pinched stuff if it came my way, so long as I thought it was safe and worth the extra care it demanded; but mostly I dealt straight. That's what I liked, the dealing. I'd always got a buzz out of trading this for that, one favour for another, even before I found myself in cousin Albie's debt. Albie always drove a hard bargain, I had nothing for nothing from him and didn't expect it; under his tutelage, I'd learned to do the same. And that morning on the beach with Ronnie had shown me a way to use that skill to my advantage. A lot of my friends had gear they'd grown out of or didn't use any more, that was going to be worth money to someone else, only they didn't know where to look for a buyer or couldn't be bothered to find out. Or if they had nothing to sell then their cousins did, or their parents or their aunts; or else they knew this funny old gadgie, just down the road from them, had a house full of junk and lived off sardines, Joe, you should go see him, might be something there worth a bit and he'd be dead glad of the money...

Before I knew it, almost, I had a business on my hands. I left school and didn't need a job or a training place, didn't need anything from anyone else. Or thought I didn't, cocky little bugger that I was. Anything I did need, I could pay for.

Like I needed transport, so I bought an old pick-up and paid a mate with a licence to drive for me — on the quiet, of course, he still kept signing on — until I'd had another birthday and learned to drive myself.

And soon I needed storage space, Dad's garage wasn't big enough any more; and I needed space for myself also. Living at home was starting to cramp the style I was striving to achieve.

I looked at shops and warehouses, any place I could trade from; and I looked at flats and houses, any place I could live. I asked about rents and heard what they were thinking, clear as day: how easy it was going to be, they were thinking, like taking candy off a baby, cheating a kid like me. Trouble was, they were very likely right. I had no experience; all I knew was that it can be dead hard to know when you're being cheated. And it was only the potential cheats who would even listen to me; the straight landlords didn't want to know. You're too young, they told me, come back in a few years' time. We don't rent to children.

So I asked about mortgages, and got the same again. Legally I was a child, and no one would even consider it. Never mind how healthy the accounts looked, I was still only a kid playing Trader Jack...

Mooching along the river, my constant magnet, the path took me past smart estates and offices, past the church and the new university campus; and then suddenly I was out of the development area and back to the river as I'd always known it, dark and dirty but no darker, no dirtier than the buildings on its banks.

Houses or factories, they were old and dodgy and half of them were derelict, freshly burnt out or else fallen long since into decay. The footpath was heading the same way, sometimes narrow and dangerously crumbly where half of it had slipped away into the water, sometimes stained black where a hopeful fisherman had lit himself a little bonfire to keep warm. I didn't think of turning back, though. I liked it like this, on the seedy side; felt like a different river. Felt like my river, the one I'd grown up with, only that there wasn't any noise now. I couldn't fool myself I still had the shipyards at my back and the colliery ahead, just around the bend. I'd come a couple of bends too far for that, grown a couple of years too old.

Right here the bank was cut away into an old company dock; and never mind that the company was long gone and its factory gone after it, nothing but a broken road and a mound of rubble now. The dock survived, and so did the big old barge that had been there for as long as I could remember, moored and abandoned in the dock's deep water, out of exploring reach for any kid who didn't have access to a boat.

I don't know how long I stood there looking at her. All I know is that when I'd stopped, I hadn't had an idea in my head except to stand and look because I was bored of walking; but when I left, when I turned and started jogging back downstream, my mind was buzzing and I knew just exactly what I wanted.

First thing, I wanted access to a boat…

I had friends at the new marina, the last few blokes who fished out of there in their old cobles, resisting the rising charges and the subtle and not-so-subtle pressure to move, to follow the rest of the fleet to its new home on the opposite bank. These were north-bank men and this was their dock. Call it a marina, call it any fancy name you liked, it was still their dock and they'd always fished from here and they weren't going to move just because some posh gits had brought their prissy little yachts in and were making a fuss about dirt and smells and such…

I had no patience then, except in deals. I wanted everything to happen right now, I wouldn't willingly have waited a minute, a second extra for anything; if none of my friends had been available I'd have screamed and cursed, I'd have behaved just like the immature kid that everyone kept telling me I still was.

Luckily Tad was there, hosing down his foredeck. I yelled from the dockside as soon as I'd got my breath, though I think he'd seen me already and was deliberately making me wait. He waved an arm in acknowledgement, and started to coil up his hosepipe. I danced a jig on the concrete, reckless with frustration; at last he jumped down into his dinghy, and rowed himself over.

'Something you'll be wanting, then, Joe lad?'

'Please, yes. That old hulk in the Culverton dock, you know the one?'

'Aye.'

'I want to get aboard. Will you take me?'

In the end, I took him. He made me row the dinghy all the way, against current and tide both. But that's just life, deals all down the line; and that particular deal was doubly worth it to me. I was into hard exercise, making my body work, polishing up my image. Money was good, but muscles and money together would be irresistible.

And then came the true reward when we reached the barge, when I hauled myself aboard aching and trembling and gasping for breath, sweated dry but still grinning, feeling my head spin as the endorphins fizzed in my rampant blood. When I stamped warily on the deck, and my foot didn't go through the boards; when I tried to kick open the door that would let me below and the screws that held the padlock didn't loosen their grip by a fraction, so that I had to work them out with my penknife and break a blade doing it; when I explored the depths of the hold and smelt nothing but bilge-water down there in the dark, no rotting wood, no soft destructive fungus.

Hard work brings its own rewards, my mam used to say to me, time and again she said it; and that day, sure enough, she was dead right.

Hard work brought me a home and an office and a warehouse, all in one. And a cage and a killing-chamber too, but that was later.

Took an age, mind, to establish title to the hulk. What with my being the age that I was, took an age and a couple of quiet back-handers even to have the authorities take me seriously. And no one was planning to spend any money that far upriver, so one abandoned boat came nowhere on anyone's priority list.

Finally, though, the council took possession of it after a bit of an argument with the NRA, and then I was free to buy it from the bailiffs. Got a good price, too: an excellent price on paper, if you don't factor in another wee chat in a pub and another wad of cash in an unmarked envelope.

Good people to have on your side, the bailiffs. 'Specially in my sort of business.

Then I bought a couple of days of Tad's time. We went over that hulk from stem to stern, from top deck down to bilges; I was counting on his seaman's eye to spot problems that I wouldn't even recognise as problems, but even he found nothing to worry me. What he did find for me, he found a friend with a dinghy for sale, and argued him a long way down from his asking price. Proud as I was, I wasn't too proud to have someone else do my bargaining for me every now and then; I listened and learned, I paid Tad a commission and still came away with the best of the deal.

And, of course, with the dinghy. Another long haul upriver, only this time it was my choice and I timed it right. I could have stuck the boat in the back of the pick-up and driven it all the way, but that would've felt like cheating; so young man waited for time and tide and hitched a lift on the rising river's back. I still had to work, of course, and in places I had to work hard against chaotic eddies set up by contrary currents in the dark water, but it was easy in comparison. I'd made and earned my luck the first time, and now I was floating on it as the hulk — *my* hulk, my barge, my beauty — floated in the dock.

I left the dinghy chained to a rusting ring in the dock's wall, with the oars chained together and the rowlocks in my pocket against a chance boat-thief passing by. I trotted up to the nearest bus stop and went home for just long enough to collect my sleeping bag, my radio, my torch and my teddy bear and whatever I could raid from the fridge for supper; then I drove back to the river, back to the dock and the dinghy, where a few more easy strokes were enough to carry me across the water, just enough to bring me home.

I got pissed that night in solitary splendour, sipping my way through a slowly warming six-pack while the radio sang soft on the deck beside me, and I watched the river flow and the city light itself up against the encroaching dark.

When I couldn't trust my balance any longer, when I got star-spin every time I lifted my head to look up, I pushed away from the rail I'd been leaning on and staggered over to the hatch. Thinking that maybe this wasn't the smartest state to be in on a boat I didn't know well yet in the dark, I fumbled down the companionway to the cabin where I'd left my things, kicked my boots off and slithered into the sleeping bag. Mister Bear was there to make a pillow for my head, of course, nothing more than that.

My mind twisted at right angles to the world, and I toppled into sleep like a man might topple from a bridge, falling and flailing and afraid. But I dreamed of nothing and woke to the sounds and the smells and the gentle movements of a different world, first day of a different life.

And woke also to a hell of a hangover, and no paracetamol; to a bladder ready to split, and no toilet; to a parched and sour mouth and only river water available and even I wouldn't risk drinking that.

Pulled my jeans on, groped my way up into savage sunlight, pissed over the side and no, I really didn't want to drink the river, thanks — and found the radio with its batteries flat, after I'd left it on all night.

Leaned against the side of the wheelhouse and started to giggle, despite my tender throat. Slid slowly down till I was sitting on the deck, hugging myself against the surges of laughter that shook my bones; and then croaked, 'Stuff it,' and hauled myself to my feet again. Dropped my jeans on the deck, vaulted over the side and plunged feet-first into deep and murky waters, and never mind what poisons ran under the surface.

When I pulled myself out into the dinghy, a dog-walker was watching from the footpath with her mouth hanging open. I just waved at her, scrambled butt-naked onto the barge, picked my jeans up and went below.

No surprise, when the police drove down and hailed me from the dockside. By then I was dry and decent; I rowed myself over and was very polite to the constabulary. Yes, I'd been skinny-dipping but no, I hadn't waggled my willie at her, officer; I'd been taking a bath on my own doorstep, hadn't realised there was anyone in ogling-range and would be more careful in future, sir, certainly I would. And yes, indeed this was my own boat, and I intended to live on it; and yes, that was also my pick-up. Sadly the paperwork was still at my parents' house, if their officerships wanted to peruse any or all of it to assure themselves of my *bona fides*…

Which they did, shock horror; they trailed me back into town and went through everything, including the contents of my dad's garage. I didn't care. It was all clean just then, so let them dig as deep as they cared to. They'd bother me less later, if they were sure of me now. They could even be useful. So I smiled and smiled, made them coffee with my own bare hands, learned their names and called them 'sir' and gave them quietly to understand that deals could be done, should they ever find themselves wanting anything I could provide.

Bargain basements and auction houses, those were my magnets now. Furniture I needed, carpets and rugs and oil lamps; light and comfort and warmth, they were the priorities. And a calor-gas cooker and a chemical toilet, that's the only thing I bought new. A proper bathroom could come later, when I had the cash for home improvements; for now I could boil water to wash in, swim while the weather stayed warm and visit parents or friends for hot showers and baths.

I found an old cast-iron stove in a junk shop, and spent a morning with a wire brush, cleaning off the rust. The afternoon I spent driving round scrap-yards, looking for some pipe of the right gauge to make a chimney. Came home triumphant and worked into the dark, along with a couple of mates I bribed with dope and beer; and before we crashed out on bare mattresses, our mouths still working though our brains had long since packed it in for the night, the barge had central heating.

Had a name, too. We'd argued it all around the houses, all evening while we worked. Being lads, we'd gone through every girl I'd had and every girl I'd wanted, in fantasy or fact. None of them suited, though; so we'd moved on to joke names, and — being lads — they were most of them dirty. It was fun, but I didn't want that either.

'Name it after your cousin, then,' Nick said in desperation, 'show your gratitude. You're always saying how he gave you the start, none of this would've happened without him, so…'

'Or his cat,' Ali spluttered, choking on a throatful of smoke. 'Call it after his bloody cat.'

'Can't,' I said, twitching the joint from Ali's fingers and drawing smoke deep, grinning at the idea none the less, hissing a white cloud out through my teeth. 'They're both blokes. Boats can't be. Mike.'

'Unh?'

'Mike. We'll call it Mike.'

'But you just said…'

'Not that Mike,' I said, giggling. 'Not Mike short for Michael. Different kind of Mike altogether, this Mike.'

'What, then?'

'Not telling.'

And I didn't tell, even under torture. They were good mates of mine, Nick and Ali both — hell, I was letting them sleep aboard, wasn't I? My first guests, they'd have to be good mates to be so honoured — but some things need to be kept publicly private even from your best mates. They need to know you've got secrets, that they're not let in all the way. Keeps them one pace back, which is where a mate should be.

So they never knew it, then or later, but they slept that night aboard the good ship *My Cousin's Gratitude*, Mike for short. The way I saw it, the way I'd always known it, gratitude had to be female at heart, whichever sex it came from.

They were the first visitors to stay the night, but only the first of many. In fact they stayed the whole weekend; we declared war on draughts the next morning, and spent all day nursing our stiff necks and plugging every last crack in the cabin walls, with the stove burning to make it good and stuffy in there. By the time sunset came round again there were a dozen of us, and it was an official boat-warming party. Which ran on all the next day, like good parties do; but I made them work for their fun. Before the last of them left, I'd picked up a job-lot of industrial silver foil from a scrapyard and we'd wallpapered both the main cabins with the stuff. Looked strange until I got it covered over with woodchip, but it was brilliant insulation. Killed one hundred per cent of all known draughts, dead.

*My Clubhouse*, Mike could've been short for, those first months aboard. A lot of my friends were still living with one parent or both, had nowhere to go to be private; so they came to me, singly or in couples or in gangs. Girls and boys, turning up by invitation or just on spec; wanting to mooch or to party, to watch the silent river or to talk all night or maybe to take each other to bed somewhere they didn't have to scramble into their clothes again when the front door banged.

Sometimes they wanted to take me to bed. Carol was still around and still willing, sometimes, though she wasn't the only one now. We'd learned a lot from each other, but variety made for more fun than loyalty. It was free market economics, winning out every time over a state monopoly; though all I said, all I thought was that I fancied playing the field a bit, not being tied down. And Carol felt the same, or said she did. She always seemed to be available for me, mind, when I called to ask. And I never saw or heard of her going around with anyone else. If I thought about it at all, I figured that was just the money thing again, her not wanting to upset the honey-pot; but I didn't think about it much. Her life, she could run it her way. I got my share, or better than, and that was all I cared about back then.

Sometimes I had other visitors, wanting other things. I did a lot of deals, on that barge. Other people asked if they could do the same thing, use Mike as a trading-post, and they were offering generous commissions; but I always refused. No way would I risk getting busted for drugs or other things that weren't even my own trade goods. Not worth it. Closest I came, I let Ronnie come out a few times to shoot up and drift the night on one of my mattresses. Only Ronnie, and only a few times. Mike wasn't a shooting gallery; but Ronnie was useful to me, so I offered him that much hospitality.

I had so many unexpected visitors early on I had to hang up a length of rusting iron pipework on the dockside, with a shorter piece to clatter against it like a gong, like a doorbell, let me know that someone had turned up. Not everyone saw it, or understood it, or chose to use it; I still kept half an ear open for someone shouting, whenever I was aboard.

And when I wasn't, when I was away I always left the dinghy chained up and took the oars and rowlocks with me in the back of the pick-up, against unexpected uninvited guests.

Once, just once, that system let me down; but once is enough. Once can change everything, once can change the world.

Once I came back late to the boat, after a night's hard clubbing. I'd left the pick-up parked way up on the road, a long way from the dock, with the oars hidden under a tarp in the back. With the dinghy on its chain and that distance for insurance, I figured my home should be safe enough.

Wrong.

I knew something was wrong, a long time before I reached the water. I'd taken a taxi from town, and paid it off by the pick-up; I'd retrieved my oars, no worries there, and come down swaying under the burden of them and maybe singing a little, as I was alone tonight and private, drunk and happy, all sweated out; and halfway down the track I saw the warm lights glowing through Mike's ports, where no light should be. I didn't leave her lit, that would be sheer folly. Oil and naked flames, and me not home to watch them? No way.

But the lights were burning, so someone was home, if not me. When I got closer I could see the dinghy tugging at her painter, trailing the barge like a Lap-dog on a leash, though I had the oars under my arm, rowlocks in my pockets and the key to the padlock on my belt-clip.

Okay, you could paddle a boat with your hands, that short way over still water; but no one else had a key, and the chain was locked.

Had been locked. The chain was there, dangling from the ring in the dockside wall. And the padlock was there also, tucked through a link in the chain but the staple left cockily open, like a message, *I don't need a key to undo your locks, son.*

I could have shouted, I suppose; or I could have rung the bell, clattered my iron bar till he came out looking to see what all the noise was about.

But Mike was mine, and the dinghy was mine, and I wouldn't wait for a thief to let me aboard. Nor phone the police on the mobile in my pocket, the other obvious option. *Look officer, I'm just a kid, and some man with clever fingers has stolen my home away* — no. I had too much pride for that. I needed to sort this by myself, just to prove that I was old enough to handle my life without help. Even if I was the only witness, the only one there to prove it to.

I was drunk, sure, but sobering up fast now; and chill brought me down the rest of the way, as I stripped off to my jeans and nothing on the dockside and slid quietly into black water.

Stupid, this was, and I knew it was stupid even as I did it. Alcohol ain't ice, it doesn't melt into harmlessness so fast, however it might be feeling; and it ain't oil either, it doesn't float on water. It certainly doesn't help the human body float.

And the night was dark, with only the barge to light it; and I was swimming into those lights, going half naked and quite unarmed, brutally cold and unprepared into confrontation certainly, maybe into real danger...

I knew all of that, I measured those risks against good sense, made allowance for the alcohol in my brain wanting to override good sense — and still I did it, stupid or not. Christ, I was young, wasn't I? Stupid's allowed, I reckoned, when you're young. Young and angry, as I was that night.

Young and angry, proud and pissed: turned out to be a fatal combination.

I swam a tight, steady breast-stroke, though my muscles wanted to churn and kick against the bone-cold shiver of the water. Slow and quiet I came out across the dock with never a splash, only my dark head bobbing against dark water to betray me. I avoided the shimmering paths where light fell from the barge's ports and came round sneaky to the stern, to where the dinghy bobbed on its painter.

I'd long since given up worrying about the water. The river was my regular morning bath now, and a common pool for skinny-dipping parties by moonlight. There were knotted ropes hanging into the water like ladders at strategic points port and starboard. Hauling myself up one of those would make Mike rock unexpectedly, though, enough to warn anyone that she was being boarded. More discreet to slither first into the dinghy as I did, and use that as a platform: to stretch up from there and get my hands flat on the deck, and then to kick and heave, shoulders and elbows and roll aboard under the stern-rail as smooth and secret as I could manage.

Got to my feet and felt how the deck was barely pitching beneath me, just a hint of movement stem to stem, my heavy old lady whispering a greeting that with luck wouldn't be noticed; took time to squeeze the water out of my hair so that it wouldn't be dribbling down my face, at least, however much it might pool around my feet; and then I stepped softly forward to the companionway that led below.

Sweetly silent in wet bare feet, I came down to the door into the main cabin, thought about kicking it open like a film hero, and didn't. Might damage something, part of the door or part of me; and why bother anyway? Even my anger was cold now, after that swim.

I turned the handle, opened the door, walked through into light and warmth and change.

Again, I didn't know what I was doing. Given the choice, given a second chance I'd be smarter: I'd turn round and swim back to the dockside, get dressed and walk or maybe run away, wet and wise and grateful.

But I was young and stupid, young and angry, proud and pissed; so I walked unthinking into the muggy comfort of my own cabin on my own boat, and found myself utterly usurped.

Not relaxed, you couldn't ever say that he relaxed: but he sat at his ease on the old heavy leather sofa-bed I'd rescued from a skip up the posh end of town. His thin, clever fingers went on calmly building a joint — and using one of my sacred *Viz* annuals to roll it on, I noticed, which felt just as much a trespass, if not more — and he didn't even glance up until he'd struck a match to heat the wee gobbet of resin that he held between finger and thumb.

Then he lifted his head to look at me, while the flame rose broad and yellow and steady as his pale gaze.

He didn't say a word, and nor did I. All the words were there in my mouth, ready to spew out like a sewer discharging; and my body was up for it also, my muscles shivering with need as much as cold, wanting to grab and haul, to drag this thief out of my home and toss him into the dock; and all I could do was stand there stupid, stare and stare.

Heavy yellow-white hair swept back and hanging to his collar; skin that lay loose and a little baggy on him, throwing shadows on his face, showing me all the bones of his skull; a wide straight mouth, full lips a little parted; and all of that only a frame for his eyes, his bleached-blue eyes with stained whites cracked scarlet...

But maybe it wasn't the face, the way he looked or the way he looked at me. There's nothing in the words even to describe how he seemed, let alone to explain it. But oh, he was hypnotic, filling my sight and my mind, draining me of anger and intent.

And then a thread of white smoke thickening to a string, drawing itself like a line in the air between us, snaring my eye like a wire; and I looked down to see how the dark little lump of dope was smoking in the flame, and how the flame had spread all the short length of the match now, and still he held his fingers in it, entirely still while he looked only at me.

He didn't move until the match burned out, a thin twist of charcoal from end to end, all the way to where his fingers held it in a pinch. And when he did move it was no more than his head, just an inch or two forward. The dope was alight now, a little flicker of flame curling around his unflinching fingers; but his breath killed that, unless it was the glance of his eyes. And then the rising twine of smoke shuddered and bent, it leant towards him as he was leaning towards it; and then it was caught, or else it saw its way at last, and it climbed into one broad nostril like a seeking worm.

The thought, the image of that was right there in my head: this blind, probing, living thing questing in through his nose and down his gullet, coiling in his belly or his gut. I nearly puked, I could see it so clearly; but that's what I wanted to see, that's what I was focusing on fiercely, not to see anything else.

Not to see his face on my boat, with all that that implied.

But I never was too hot at lying to myself; and he was there, and my eyes were trapped by his face, whatever pictures my mind was painting behind them. So I did see him, and I did see him smile; and I did see how the smoke leaked out through his stained teeth, and I did hear him say my name.

'Joseph. Little Joe. *Nice* this...'

His voice was soft, sibilant, slightly slurred, just as it always had been; and he might have meant the dope, the boat, our reunion or all three; and he probably did mean them all, but mostly I thought he meant how nice it was for him to sit there and look at me standing half-naked and running wet, three years more grown than the last time.

'Yeah,' I said, 'nice,' I said; and felt my face start to smile, wanting to please him, wanting to make it true. I never could say no to Root.

Nor could my cousin Albie...

Okay, so I lied to you before, maybe, just a little. Back at the start there. Or I just didn't tell all of the truth, that's a better way to say it.

Not just the cat, my cousin had to be grateful to me for. The cat was only cover. There was plenty else, and the ten grand wasn't simply to say thanks, it was to buy my silence for the future. I'd always understood that. Albie needed to be certain, he couldn't have gone peaceful else; he needed to know that even after he was dead, I'd keep his secrets.

Root's secrets.

Others too, there were always others; but it all came back to Root.

Well, it would, wouldn't it? If ever a bloke was well named, that bloke was Root. And I don't mean because he carried his name marked out on his back, though he did that. I'd known him half my life, and he was always the man who made things happen. It wasn't only me and Cousin Albie; everyone listened, did what he said, wanted to keep him smiling. We were scared, I guess, kids and grown-ups both. I'd seen big men go pale, when Root wasn't happy. But it wasn't just fear that worked for him. Root had the magic in him somewhere.

It worked that night on the boat, just like it always had. I stood there shivering from more than the cold and the water, and I smiled because that's what you did for Root, he liked to see you smile; and if he'd said what he always used to say, if he'd just said, 'Let's lose the jeans, then, little Joe,' I guess I'd have done that too, just like I used to, every time.

But he didn't, he only said, 'You want to get dry, kid? You're dripping.'

'Yeah, right…'

That wasn't a dismissal, that was go get a towel and come back; but as soon I was out of the cabin — out from under his compelling, hypnotic eye — I remembered that this was my own boat, bought and paid for and very much earned before ever I got the money. Root said jump, I wasn't going to argue, I wasn't that stupid; but Christ, I wasn't a kid any more, and he was on my territory. I could surely find space to assert just a little independence…

So I didn't go running back with a towel in my hands and nothing else changed, no different. I took time to have a piss in the head and find some other clothes, get myself dried off in private.

But even so I hurried, and I didn't pretend to anyone that I was in control here, or anywhere near it. I went back into the cabin in baggy T-shirt and cut-offs, not to give Root any signals he didn't want to see; he was a leg man, always had been. And I dropped down cross-legged onto the floor at his feet and rubbed the damp towel slowly through my hair, well within touching if he should choose to touch.

I glanced up at him a little sideways, a little tentative, just the way he used to like it; and his long arm swung leisurely over and his tar-stained fingers touched my lips, but only to hold the roach there for me, offering a toke like a peace-pipe, *suck on this*.

All my skin felt clammy still, nothing was dry but my lips were. The cardboard was wet, where he'd held it in his mouth; and as I closed those dry lips on it, as I obediently sucked, a bubble of memory closed my throat, hard as glass and hurting. And shattered like glass, and hurt more. Just for that moment between drawing and tasting smoke, all I tasted was Root: strong and rancid, bad meat on the turn, he tasted like the buzzing of flies or the slow drip-drip of sewage seeping through a crack in the plaster. All threat and certainty, *something worse is coming your way...*

And oh, that was so familiar to my tongue and my throat, to my mind and all my body at once, every muscle jerking acknowledgement as though he'd twitched a leash. His smoke filled me and reclaimed me, took possession of his wandering lad; and his soft chuckle said it all, *I'm back now* and no words needed.

Nor later, when that joint and the next were stubs squeezed dead between his calloused fingers and dropped heedless onto my carpet; when my head was dizzy with smoke and memory, fear and sickness and coming home to rest against his leg, too heavy for my neck to hold up any longer.

When the long-promised touch came at last, his fingers beating a light tattoo across my skull, tugging and twisting at my hair to hear me yelp again for old time's sake, sliding down inside my T-shirt to pinch and tweak my nipple, to tease disapprovingly at the new-found hair on my chest.

When touch turned to grip, when he hauled me up and over to the tangled bedding on the mattress where I slept, when his strong and knowing hands had me stripped to nothing before we got there...

Call it sleep, call it unconsciousness from too much dope on top of too much beer; call it hiding if you like, doesn't matter what you call it.

Whatever it was, I woke or came round or came out in the end, at the last, when I had to. My head pounded and all my body ached, except for those sharp little places that hurt too much to be aching; and my heart stuttered in rhythm with my memory of the night before, and if I had a soul it was trembling and cowering in corners, and feeling deep shit sorry for itself.

Root was back, he'd found me; the bedding smelt of him already, edged and sour, so that I tasted stale smoke and sweat and other reminders with every small breath I drew. Small because he was somewhere there in the cabin, I knew that, my skin was twitching; and I wasn't consciously trying to fool him — you didn't do that, you didn't lie to Root even about the little things, or never more than once — but instinct and long training both held me in their familiar grip. Breathing soft and keeping still were more than habit, they were basics, lessons in survival.

Breathing soft and keeping still, I could hear a faint rasping, repetitive without being regular and no part of the sounds and rhythms of my boat.

Slowly, reluctantly I opened my eyes, because I had to do it sometime and curiosity has its spurs. Root was standing at a porthole with his back to me, wearing my jeans still damp from the swim last night and scraping a razor down his jaw, dry-shaving while he watched the river.

The skin of his face might be loose and hanging, but on his back it was taut still, stretching easily over lean muscles and bones you could count; but no one ever counted Root's bones, first time they looked at his back. Couldn't ever see his bones, first time, for looking at his name-tag.

He had a thick, seamed ridge of scar tissue that curled like a living whip from his back ribs to his belly, but you couldn't see that either, until your fingers found it.

What you saw, all you were ever going to see that first time was the tattoo that grew from under his ivory hair, that reached down his spine and spread out in fingers and fronds and sinister little hairs to grip all his body from shoulders to arse in a tangled mass of roots that writhed as his muscles worked beneath them, that seemed to creep and stretch further through his skin every time you looked.

Not true, or it must have reached face and toes and everywhere by now, I'd been watching that root so long, so many years; but that was how it seemed even to me, even still. I thought I could watch it growing as he shaved.

'Good morning, little Joe.'

He hadn't turned to see, and still didn't; and I'd made no more noise or movement than my eyelids fanning the air as I blinked, but still he knew I was watching.

I grunted, all the sound my tight throat could make. He chuckled.

'Not so little any more, though. Are you? Little boys get bigger every day. Alas. Your best days are gone, Joe lad. Like your voice is gone, and your looks are going. That's the bugger of it, that the day a man gets into a kid's jeans,' and he patted his butt through my denim but that was only for the pun's sake, it wasn't what he meant, 'he can already hear the clock ticking, and he knows fine well it's running down.'

*A man like you.* I thought, *maybe*; but it didn't matter anyway, even to Root. He didn't care. There would always be other kids, that's how the world runs for men like him. Like clockwork.

And right on the heels of my thought came his words, 'You'll have friends, though, Joe boy? Little friends? It's nice here, and I'd like to meet your friends.'

Yeah, I had friends, little friends by the dozen. I still did some deals with schoolkids; and my mates had younger brothers or cousins. Or sisters and girl-cousins also, Root wasn't fussy. He'd take anything, so long as it wasn't too well-grown.

Except that I wasn't handing any of my little friends over to Root's untender training. I'd sell almost anything to anyone, but not this. Myself, sure: I'd spent half my life selling myself to Root and his kind, my sweet cousin Albie and all his circle of friends. And yes, I'd survived; I thought I'd come out pretty well except for being deep shit scared of men with tattoos in general and one painted man in particular; but I guess I'd been tough or lucky, or both. Others I'd known or known about hadn't made it look so easy.

Not by a very long way.

So no, Root wasn't getting his hard hands on any of my kids. No matter what it cost me; and it would. With Root there was always a price to be paid, even when you did what he wanted.

'Sorry,' I said, 'I don't mix with little kids. Not now. I'm grown up, right?'

You didn't lie to Root; but that was only half a lie at most, because in fact I didn't mix with the little kids I knew. I did business with them if it was worth my while, or I tolerated them for the sake of the company they came with, but we didn't *mix*. Not really.

And besides, Root knew I didn't lie to him, he was safe to remember what had happened the only time I'd dared; so he was going to believe me this time, straight off, no worries. Wasn't he?

Well, maybe he was. He didn't shift, his feet didn't stir; his hand never twitched as he went on dragging the blade of the razor over his stubble. All I heard was a sigh, a little sigh of regret; and maybe that meant *ah well, too bad. Never mind*. Maybe I'd got away with it, maybe I'd fooled Root. One and only time, if I had; but there could always be a first time, right? And I was grown up now, not a kid any longer; and a businessman to boot, bound to be a better liar, yeah…

Anyway, that's how it went. Two things I never did, telling lies to Root and saying no to something he wanted; and I did them both that morning, more or less. Both in one sentence, thirteen lucky words. And the sky didn't fall on my head, nor Root's chill anger; and he didn't bring it up again, any suggestion that I might pimp for him. Didn't show any signs of doing it for himself, either, finding kids at the age he liked and tempting them back to the boat for fun or profit, 'Hey, kid, wanna see my tattoo?'

Actually, though, he never had. That was Cousin Albie's role, gentling the innocent. Root liked his playmates sussed. Not willing, necessarily; reluctance turned him on, I guess, and resistance even more — he'd smiled when I was obstinate, and given me bruises I could still remember, long years on — but he didn't have the patience to teach even a young dog new tricks.

What surprised me was that he had the patience to do without, seemingly; what appalled me was that this wasn't just a flying visit, seemingly. Not just *hi, Joe boy, remember me?* and a cruise that failed. At first I had this dream that Root would shake his white head in sorrow and depart when I let him down so badly, when I didn't drop sweeties into his lap. Held onto it as long as I could, I did, till it was fraying to nothing between my fingers; and still he showed no signs of moving on.

This was the payback, then, I supposed. I'd not given him what he wanted, so he was giving me in return what I emphatically didn't want, himself with no sign of relief.

I couldn't ask him outright, *how long you staying, then, Root?* Say it any which way, it was still going to come out like a hint, *when are you moving on?* Once bolshie it seemed I could get away with, now I was grown; twice bolshie I wasn't even going to try. The first time had been stupid enough.

So I did the other thing, kept quiet and watched him settle, watched him come and go; hoped every time he went that he wouldn't come back, and was every time disappointed.

He let me sleep alone, after that first night. That had been only repossession rather than desire, reclaiming a territory long left abandoned; he'd meant exactly what he'd said the next morning, that I'd grown too big to please him. Bed was a haven for me, with him dossing in the smaller cabin; but it was a tainted haven at best. Not my bedding, because I'd had that up to the launderette first chance I got, but the whole boat now smelled of Root and I couldn't escape it. His constant joints, his oily sour skin, his clothes claggy with dirt, that he wore and wore and never washed: poor Mike was rank with him, I thought I'd never get her clear again. Certainly I'd never get her clean while Root remained.

I lived in Root's dirt and stink and hated it, wanted no one else to see me do it; but that was only one and the least of my reasons for trying every trick I knew to keep my friends away. Growing soft, I was, reluctant to let people look after themselves the way I'd always had to, the way I'd never given a second thought to till now. I'd taken a crazy chance to save a few kids some grief, and now suddenly I was trying to do the same for everybody, I wanted to keep the world away from Root. Even though that meant keeping him to myself, or letting him keep me…

Try hard, you can work miracles; but not on everyone, and not all the time. I spread the word as far and as wide as I could, as fast as I could manage. I told different people different things, whatever was most likely to stop them dropping by. A few, like Carol, I even told the truth; or a part of it, at least. 'There's this bloke,' I said, 'he's moved in on the boat, and he's trouble. I can handle it,' I said, 'don't worry, I've known him forever; but he won't shift, and I don't want him messing with you, so just don't come, okay? I'll phone you when I can get away, and we'll meet in town, or your place...' *Though there won't be much of that*, I remember thinking, stroking her arm in a silent promise I knew I wouldn't keep. Mike was my first true home, though Root had poisoned her; she was sickened with his infection, and I wasn't happy to leave her alone and him rampant within her.

Others I lied to, or left messages for; but there was always going to be someone I didn't reach, like there were always going to be times when I wasn't aboard. Just my luck — or his, or maybe Root's — that it was Ronnie didn't get the message, or ignored it; and something more than luck, maybe, some evil sod in the Fate department brought him down to the boat when I wasn't there to shelter him.

Coming back at sunset, pick-up loaded with the clear-out from some rich bastard's redundant garden shed — tools still sharp and rust-free, *two* lawnmowers, a barbecue hardly used and all its bits: you wouldn't believe what people want rid of sometimes, just because they've played that game now and they're tired of it — I found the dinghy missing from the dock, and had to ring my own front door bell, banging away furiously at the dangling, jangling pipe till a shadow stumbled up onto Mike's deck, slithered over the side and rowed awkwardly across to fetch me.

And that was Ronnie and he was well gone already, his eyes were huge in the half-light and he stank of Root's sweet smoke; and of all the people I knew, I think maybe Ronnie would've been the very last I wanted to see like this. I'd have risked Carol against Root, sooner than this. At least Carol could say no. Ronnie was an addict; he couldn't even say no to himself.

I didn't say anything, though, just dropped down into the dinghy and took the oars myself to save getting soaked by Ronnie's splashback, the way he was already. Pulled over and tied up, gave Ronnie a boost onto Mike's deck because it looked like he'd never manage alone, and then followed him down to the cabin.

Nothing worse than dope on display, no needles: something to be grateful for, I supposed. And something else, Root was well pleased with this new company. Smiled and nodded at me, and passed a new joint for Ronnie to light it without in any way inviting me to share. Coward that I was, I seized on that to go topsides and spend an hour hauling to and fro across the water, unloading the pick-up and stowing all the gear in Mike's hold.

I was hungry then and too tired to cook even for me, let alone for all of us; Root never ate much, but Ronnie must have the munchies bad by now, so high he'd been getting. Those two could look out for themselves, I decided; there was plenty of bread, and stuff in tins. Me, I walked up to the road and got myself fish and chips and a can of Coke, and had supper in the pick-up's cab with the radio on but the lights not, in case Root or Ronnie looked out .

Back to the boat one last time tonight, and I tethered the dinghy firmly, already guessing that Ronnie wouldn't be going home till morning. That was no major grief; I'd shared a bed with him before when there was need, and he slept like a rock when he was stoned. Most people did.

Went inside, and learned that I wasn't as sharp as I thought I was. Sure, Ronnie was out for the count already, though it wasn't late; but I would never have thought to find Root so solicitous for his comfort, settling him down for the night in the little cabin where Root himself slept.

Which of course left Root and me to share the big cabin and my big bed, not big enough but nothing ever could be. He didn't want to play that night, or not with me, but that was small relief. One final joint and he was as gone as Ronnie, too heavy asleep even to be snoring; but I didn't sleep, not for hours. I had too much nightmare in my head to find any space for sleep.

Ronnie would sell the moon, I thought, to someone who could get him well fixed in return. He'd sold me his bass, after all; and he'd loved that more than anything else in his sad life. For him, Root would be better than Jesus: a man who could spread his fingers wide through the city and claw in any drug Ronnie fancied, any time.

And Ronnie had a couple of little sisters he didn't love much at all, and any number of schoolkids in his ken. Often they were the same kids I dealt with: they'd sell to me, then take the money to Ron to buy little silver packets of hash or ecstasy. Offer them a free smoke and some pocket-money on top — a private little party on a boat, maybe? — and they'd follow him like he was the Pied Piper.

All the way to Root…

By first light I was no closer to making any kind of decisions what to do about it, only that I had to do something. That alone was still a source of wonder to me. I didn't understand it; but wherever the hell this sense of responsibility had come from, it was very real.

Fortunately, it hadn't made me stupid. I wasn't about to go busting in on Ronnie sleeping, hustle him off the boat and tell him never to darken my bow-wave again. Root would ask, *where's Ronnie?* — and because I had no hope of lying to him directly, I would say *I shooed him away, to save some kids your delicate attentions* or words to that effect. And then there would be pain and darkness, for as long as Root chose to administer them; and all of it for nothing, because after he was done he would send me to bring Ronnie back to him, and I would go. I knew that, no question.

I could go now, of course. Chase Ronnie off and run myself, just abandon boat and business, find somewhere to hide. Down the other end of the country would be best…

My boat, my business. And — fuck it! — my responsibility, all the kids in town now, if I left Root unregarded in such a welcome bolt-hole. Christ, he could do anything he liked on Mike, so far from being overlooked or listened to. I knew some little of what Root liked; but if once he felt free and uninhibited they'd maybe start finding little bodies floating down the river, he could go that far…

So no, I wasn't running either. Something else I needed, some master plan; and needed something more before I could construct one. Information was the secret of all success in trade, and all life was a trade-off, this against that. Only know what you were dealing with, and you could be honest or not, as you chose; but I'd never buy a pig in a poke, nor would I try to sell one.

I slipped out of bed and dressed as the sun came up, moving quiet and slow, though there was little chance of disturbing Root this early. Left Ronnie sleeping also, marooned them both aboard as I paddled the dinghy over to the dockside. They'd keep, for a little; and please God they could do no damage there, except to themselves or each other.

Well, Root could damage Ronnie. No one, I thought, could damage Root. Old and hard and wickedly twisted, sunk beyond reach of man, that was what I thought of Root.

Some things are hard to do, and rightly so; some things that should be hard are easy. But the opposite is also true, that what looks easy is sometimes harder than anything.

It shouldn't, it never should be hard to go back, to walk those streets you walked or ran or cycled as a kid: to follow familiar routes past park and post-box, to turn a corner without thinking and find that one door among dozens, where many memories are hid...

Shouldn't be hard; but Christ, it was wicked hard for me that day. Even in the truck, perched on high wide wheels now to remind me how far I'd gone from here, I could feel a tremble all under my skin as those streets filled the windscreen like a private showing of my secrets, just for me. Maybe this was another reason why I'd loved Mike so much when I found her: that she gave me a home by the town but not in it, separated from the network of streets that all seemed suddenly to lead here, to this little patch where I'd grown up, where every eye-blink hurt like shards of glass.

I wanted vengeance all of a sudden, all in a rush. For the first time that I could remember, I wanted someone to pay for the fuck-up that had been my childhood. Family or friends, I didn't care: just then I'd have punished any of them, all of them for blindness or ignorance. Wilful or not, they'd let it happen; and that seemed as much a crime as what cousin Albie had done to me, or Root, or half a dozen others.

Albie was gone, Root was back and it was the others I was looking for this day, though not to punish. Usually it had been Albie's house they met at, but not always; I knew where each of them lived, even those I'd never been to visit. Call it a child's curiosity or else some deeper wisdom, an early understanding of the power and uses of knowledge — and I'd always under-stood things early, I'd had to — but I could remember the trouble I'd taken sometimes to find out who these big men were, how big their cars and houses.

Nor was that all I'd learned about them. Position was good, but personality counted for a lot also; I'd measured them all against a future need so that now, when that need was on me, I knew who were the weaker links in this tight-forged and secretive chain, who could be leaned on safely and who might be dangerous to go to, who should be avoided.

Harry was the man for me. Harry the Head we used to call him, though he'd never been head teacher and I doubted if he was yet. He taught in a different school from where I'd gone, in another part of town — they none of them shat in their own back yards, these clever men; well, none except Root, who didn't care — and the last time I'd seen his face had been on telly, trying to talk up his chances as a candidate for the local council.

Time before that had been in big messy close-up, doing something that would've got him barred from any political club in the land, never mind putting him behind bars also; but even without that being known, I hadn't rated his chances in the election. He was never going to be better than a placer, wasn't Harry, bridesmaid to the core: good enough to get selected sometimes, no way good enough to win.

Unless he'd moved or married since — and he wasn't the type to do either one, he didn't have that much ambition — he lived alone in a small, drab-looking bungalow squeezed between semis on a fifties estate, and he parked his tired Volvo in the road outside. 'Nuff said, really. Even the running-for-councillor bit, I reckoned, was more disguise than anything else. These guys, they needed to look respectable.

Except for Root, of course; but Root had never really been one of them. Which was what I was counting on. Harry would remember that, whether their little ring was still active or not; and he'd remember other stuff too. He might not feel so loyal to a man who didn't only frighten the kids.

Might not. We'd see.

It was a weekday, a schoolday, but I was well early; and yes, there was a Volvo parked in the street just where I was looking for one. Not the same car he'd been driving when I knew him, it couldn't be; but it looked like it. Same sort of colour, same sort of age, same sense of a man who drove a car only because he'd missed the bus.

I left the pick-up with its nearside wheels on the kerb, not to block the road altogether, and strolled up the path to his faded front door. Hands in pockets and very casual, in case he was watching from behind his dirty nets: cool and just a little threatening, just a hint of danger. Root wasn't the only one who could frighten grown men, it was a talent I meant to develop myself; and nothing's more frightening than knowing your secrets known.

Watching or not, Harry came pretty quick to his door when I thumped it. He was Cardigan Man now as he always had been, M & S Man and utterly unchanged; but not so I, and it took him a while, took him a second or two of blankly staring before he twigged. Then he pulled the back of his hand across his mouth where toast-flecks were clinging to his lips, and he said, 'Joe...'

'Yeah,' I agreed, smiling slightly and hoping it didn't look too friendly. Friendly was not what I was here for. 'Nice of you to remember. Come in, can I? Just for a bit?'

He nodded slowly, and stood back from the door. He didn't say anything, but his hands did, jumping and fluttering, making a messy fumble of it when they tried to close the door. I turned away, to hide a genuine grin. Gotcha, I was thinking; I'd have no trouble here.

I walked straight through into the kitchen, old habit not dead yet; and was glad to be ahead of him, where he couldn't see my face, because all my skin twitched at once when I saw that he hadn't changed a thing in here. Brown embossed lino on the floor and the walls just painted plaster patched with Polyfilla blotches; and I a kid again, sitting how many times at that same table, looking at the floor or looking at the walls or watching my fingers curl around a cup of cooling coffee, waiting only for him to say...

'Well,' he said, as he always used to; and I could have screamed, maybe, I could have given myself away totally if the tone of his voice had been different. But I wasn't a kid any more and it wasn't me scared and sullen this time, wanting this not to be true. I heard it in him, how far I'd turned the tables; and then I could get a grip, I could look at him and cock a silent eyebrow, wait him out.

'Well,' again, 'what can I do for you, Joe? You're looking, looking well...'

'Yeah,' I said. 'Root,' I said.

'I beg your pardon?'

'What's Root been up to recently, what's he about? See much of him these days, do you?'

'No. No, not at all. We were never, Root and I, not exactly friends, you know…'

'No.' Only business partners, if you could call it that; and I was sure that Harry would. There was always give and take in business, it was an exchange, benefits to both parties; and he'd like, no, he'd need to see it that way, what he'd done to me and others. What he still did, chances were, with the same or other partners and a new crop of kids. Clever men, cautious men, not likely to be caught or blabbed about; and I couldn't see any of them stopping, not of their own choice.

Root was the exception, not cautious at all. Just as safe, though. People talked about Root, of course they did; but only softly, and only to each other. Nothing was ever going to leak out to where it might be noticed.

As witness Harry not talking now, but only stammering and denying, lying in his teeth.

'Come on, Harry,' I said. 'Get real. So maybe you don't see him any more, I can believe that; but you'll know where he is and what he's doing. What's the gossip?'

'None, Joe. Truly, none. He's gone, I think.'

'Yeah? Why would he do that, then?'

'Well, it's not surprising. I mean, really. After…'

'After what?'

'After what happened with that lad.' He looked at me and frowned with surprise, reading my next question on my face. 'You must have heard about that, surely?'

I shook my head. 'I've got other things on my mind now, Harry. I don't keep in touch.'

'Well, but it was in all the papers…'

'What was?'

'A boy hanged himself, in his dad's garage. He didn't leave a note, apparently, and the inquest's been adjourned. It was suicide, no question; but — well, you know how the papers get hold of things, cases like this. Signs of abuse, is what they're saying. And we knew, you see? We knew the lad…'

'One of Root's, was he?'

'Yes. Yes, he was. And Root's left town since, I think, unless he's lying very low indeed. Why do you want to know, anyway, what are all these questions for?'

I shook my head, and got out of there.

Walking in the air, we'd called it at school, looking to find a laugh in it somewhere. There'd been two of them while I was there, a girl who'd screwed her exams and this weird boy, skinny as shit, who always had bruises on him somewhere even before he gave himself the big one, all around his neck. Some lads I knew had found him, swinging from a tree in the park; and we were talking about it later, lying in the grass with a four-pack of lager and our eyes very much on that tree, and someone said that's what he must have looked like as he kicked, like he was walking in the air. And someone else started singing that bloody song off *The Snowman*, and that was it...

So Root's loving interest had sent some poor kid for a stroll on the wind, and now — yes, Harry — he was lying very low indeed, down on my old boat. Not trusting the newspapers or the coroner, perhaps, not certain that there actually was no note. If anyone ever was going to blow Root open, I thought perhaps that was how it would be: a final desperate message to a world that failed, *Ask Root* and goodbye. And maybe that's what the police wanted to do, maybe they had lots of questions they wanted to ask Root; so maybe they'd hushed the coroner and the papers both, maybe they were out there now, looking and looking...

Or maybe not, but Root had thought the chances good enough to look for a bolt-hole, and some bastard contact had given him Mike and me.

It was a curious idea, Root being careful, Root laying low; but all care is relative. He obviously didn't feel threatened enough to stop doing what he did. The spider was spinning a new web, that was all. Laying low wouldn't stop Root digging in. Filaments were stretching already, slithering into fresh ground, groping for food.

And would find it, and would bring it back to Mike to feast in comfort, feeling safe as houses, safer, safe as boats...

No. There are things that happen because they have to, and there are things that happen because no one can be bothered to stop them happening; and this wasn't either one of those. I could stop it, if I was ready to pay the price. And one thing for sure, this deal would cost me.

Might cost me everything, which was no kind of fair trade.

Time and again that morning I found myself shadowing policemen down the street, or else driving oh so slowly past the station and pretending to myself that I was looking for a place to park, that I was only minutes from walking in there and talking cold, cold turkey.

Didn't do it, of course. Never had any intention of actually *doing* it. This was dreamland, *let's pretend it's easy* when easy was the last thing, *let's pretend we'll do it tomorrow* when tomorrow was already backing off, shading into next week or the week after that.

Done with games and done with dreaming, I headed back to the dock about midday. Root and Ronnie had only moved from dream to dream, though they seemed quite comfortable with it, sprawled on the rugs and poking lengths of wood into the roaring stove, passing joints and laughing. Well, one of them smiling and the other giggling; and I thought only one of them stood any chance of seeing their dreams come true.

I nudged Ronnie with my foot, nice and gentle although what I really wanted to do was kick him into kingdom come. *Sold one of your sisters yet?* I wanted to ask him, and didn't. *Are you taking bids on little boys?*

Actually, I only said, 'I want you, Ron. I need a hand shifting some stuff.'

'Ah, shit, Joe, not today...'

'Yeah, now.' And now I could work the toe of my boot a little harder into his ribs, I could lean on him a fraction in a way Root would doubtless be approving, even though I took his smoking-partner from him. 'Come on, you owe me a favour. Several favours. And I'll pay you, so you win both ways...'

At last I got him on his feet and out of there, though he was little enough use to me. I did all the heavy work myself, moving things around in the hold and loading some into the dinghy while he watched dizzily and got in my way. And then he was scared of the jump down from the deck and sure enough nearly missed it, except that I'd gone first and was there to grab him, to save him going head first into the water.

'Maybe I'd better just take you home, eh, Ronnie?'

'Nah. Nah, I'm fine, Joe, I'll be fine...'

*I don't want to miss out on the cash*, is what he meant; but for once in my life I didn't mind being ripped off, I was just glad to have ripped him off the boat.

So I let him sit in the cab while I drove around town making deals, making money; and I didn't even wake him when he fell asleep. When he woke himself, coming up dusk, and asked blurrily where we were, I said, 'Nearly home, mate. Five more minutes.'

He only grunted, and closed his eyes again. Maybe he thought I meant, *nearly back at the boat*, because he looked confused and pretty pissed off when I did the other thing, when I delivered him to his own home rather than mine.

'Go on,' I said softly when I saw him hesitate, despite the twenty quid I'd tucked into his shirt pocket. 'Get some food inside you, Ronnie, get some proper sleep. Spend a night in for once, why don't you? See if your mum remembers what you look like...'

Probably he wouldn't do that, not with cash in hand; not unless he'd already got a promise from Root, *come back tomorrow and I'll see you fixed*. If he could count on a good deal in the morning, maybe he wouldn't risk street skag tonight.

Maybe.

Whatever, I was rid of him, and on my own in town; which of course meant Root on his own aboard Mike, and he'd have a job getting off with the dinghy dockside. Couldn't see Root swimming it...

He was used to this, though, with me coming and going every day and only the one dinghy between us. He really was lying low, it seemed, or else this was how he always preferred to live, passing time in a chemical haze and rarely stirring out of doors except to replenish his stocks.

So. No worries — *yeah, sure, no worries at all, Joe mate* — and nothing but time to kill; I drove down to the coast and sat in the cab eating a carry-out with my fingers and watching the trawlers go out, shrinking to pinpoints of glimmer against the rising dark. Then I went to the movies in a big complex out of town, just one more vehicle in a crowded carpark and one more face in the crowd, even to myself I could feel anonymous and private.

Coming back after midnight I parked up on the road, not to disturb Root with the engine's roaring if he was asleep already. Walked down to the dock and rowed myself quietly over, climbed aboard and found him in the main cabin still, sprawled on my mattress and well out of it. No need to tiptoe, though I did, just to be sure. The stove had died down to a dull glow; I fetched in the bag of briquettes I'd hauled up from the hold that afternoon, and banked it up enough to last all night.

Then I got out of there, shut the door nice and quiet, went back on deck. Fiddled about up there for a minute or two, tossed a mental coin and did what it told me to, jumped down into the dinghy and pulled over to the dockside.

And went up to the road and repossessed the pick-up, drove round to Carol's and parked down the road a little way, not to wake her parents.

Doing things properly, standing under her window throwing stones, I had to swallow hard against the giggles rising like pebbles in my throat, threatening to choke me.

At last, the *chink, chink!* was getting through; I saw a shape move behind glass, saw her open the window and peer down.

And tossed one last little bit of gravel lightly, gigglingly up to tangle in her tangled hair.

'Oy!' she hissed. 'Stop it! Wharra fuck do you want, anyway? I was in bed...'

'Good.'

'Eh?'

'I was lonely,' I said.

Nothing more than that; but she was still for a second, as I'd known she would be, and then she nodded, just as I'd known that she would. 'Wait, I'll come down...'

'Nah, just drop the key and I'll come up. It'll be quieter...' And I knew the way, even in the dark; I wasn't going to trip over the cat or get my foot stuck in a saucepan.

The key dropped glinting into my hand, and a minute later I was slipping softly into Carol's bedroom to find her on her feet by the dressing-table — a big art deco affair I'd picked up at an auction for her Christmas present — and fumbling to knot the cord of a dressing gown.

'Don't do that,' I murmured, closing my hands over hers to hold them still. 'Get back into bed, if you're cold.'

'Uh-huh. You're coming too, I suppose?'

'Yeah. Please,' added a breath later, on a quiet grin.

'You're a pig, Joe McLeod. Never even phoning for weeks, then coming round any time you fancy just expecting to hop into bed with me... What if I'd had someone else here, eh? What then?'

'I'd have slept lonely tonight,' I said. 'Unless you threw him out, of course...'

'What, for you? Dream on, boy...' But her eyes were big and happy in the dark, and her fingers were busy with my jacket already, unzipping it and slipping it back off my shoulders; and I thought she would have done, maybe, would have put any other boy out of her life to make room for me.

Whatever, she made room enough in her single bed. Next morning too was familiar to me, as known as her body: being shaken awake too early, dressing in whispers, sidling barefoot down the stairs for a last kiss at the back door before the postman or the milkman or the paper-boy were anywhere in sight. Walking on the grass borders not to crunch the gravel and then whistling cheerfully back to the truck, ready to wink back at any part of the world that chose to wink at me...

Oh, I was a carefree lad to any eyes that were watching; and for the first time, though I took all those precautions, I was secretly hoping that Carol's parents' would be. There's trouble and trouble, and *You had a boy in your room last night* would be nothing, absolutely nothing to the trouble waiting for me back on the boat.

But I drove down to the dock like a young man quite untroubled, keeping up appearances to the end; and splashed my merry way across the water, hauled myself lithely aboard and went below to find Root.

And found him, right enough; and came up coughing and spluttering, and had to bend over the stem rail to retch cruelly on an empty stomach before I could fumble with clumsy fingers for my mobile phone and punch three nines, *hurry hurry!*

'Hallo? Ambulance, ambulance please... Yeah, could you send an ambulance to the old Culverton dock, please? It's the north bank of the river, couple of miles upstream, behind Corporation Road… Yeah, right, that's it… I don't know, there's this guy been sleeping on my boat and he's, he's so cold and he won't wake up, I think he's dead… I don't, I don't know what the hell happened but the air's dreadful, I couldn't breathe down there…'

Five minutes, they said, and don't try to do anything, don't go back down. Wait for the professionals, they said.

Very far from going down, I went up instead, as high as I could: clambered onto the cabin roof and squinted into the low sun and the long shadows, and couldn't see even a dog-walker on the towpath, not a body moving.

Almost immediately I was jumping down again, couldn't keep still; and I dropped into the dinghy and pulled awkwardly for the dockside, to be there ready for them when they came.

When they did come, they came with the fire brigade also, big men made bigger by their alien masks and air-tanks. They let me ferry them across, but not board Mike myself; nothing I was allowed to do but watch from the dockside while they went below with a stretcher, came up with that stretcher so much heavier, a shrouded figure strapped to it.

By then the police had arrived, and I was telling them everything I could. This bloke I used to know when I was a kid, I said, he'd been staying with me on the boat; and I hadn't come back last night, I'd wanted some space so I'd gone down to the coast, had a pizza in the cab, seen a movie; and I still didn't want to come home so I'd slept the night with a girlfriend, that was all. And then I came back this morning, and the air in the cabin didn't smell right, and I couldn't wake Root up…

Yeah, Root, that was his name. All the name I knew. He had this tattoo, see…

That was where they really got interested, the police. They took me down to the station, before they'd even got the body off the boat. Not to worry, they said, I wasn't in trouble, they only wanted to talk to me; but I was that young, I could have my mother there if I liked, they'd fetch her down for me…

No, thanks, I didn't like. I wasn't that young, I said, and this was, you know, private… They nodded quietly, and glanced at each other with eyes that sang victory.

I made them happy people, those police. Something you learn fast, when you're a kid trying to please grown-ups: you learn to give them what they want. It was a knack I still had, you don't lose it, and I handed them everything they could have dreamed of except for living men.

So much for my cousin's gratitude, the bonds of trust and money he'd meant should buy my silence. I'd taken his money gladly, but he was dead, and so I broke his trust.

Root and my cousin, I said, those two. No one else, I said. They didn't believe me, of course, they kept coming back to it, asking again; but no, I said, just the two of them, I didn't know of any others. Could be others, I said, could be dozens, hundreds, what did I know? But they didn't touch me, I said. Just those two.

That was years ago, I said, I'd not seen Root for years; but then he turned up at the boat, and what could I do? He scared me, I said, no lie that; and he still had this magic, I said, so that I only wanted to please him like I used to. He needed a bed for a while, what was I going to do, say no? Tell him to go?

But he made me uncomfortable, I said, hanging around so long; so I kept away as much as I could. Like last night, finding more and more reasons to stay out, and then finally spending favours with a girlfriend, I said when I still didn't want to go home even to sleep. And yes, of course, here was her address; but send someone discreet, eh? She wasn't under age or anything, but she lived with her parents and they were funny about boys sleeping over...

And then this morning, I said, I slipped away early not to bump into those funny parents, kissed Carol goodbye and went back to Mike and found Root cold and stiff as a root, sprawled on my own bed there, and what the hell *happened* to him?

They weren't certain, they said, not till the autopsy results came through; but what it looked like, he'd heaped the stove high with charcoal and left the door of it wide open, and then he'd smoked himself stupid and passed out, unless he just fell asleep.

And God knows what went wrong, they said, we're looking at that chimney you cobbled together, they said; but whatever, either it got itself blocked or the wind just blew all the fumes straight back down into the cabin. No smoke, they said, to wake him, charcoal doesn't; but plenty of carbon monoxide coming off and other stuff too that they put in the briquettes to keep them regular, and none of it good breathing. And all the doors and the portholes closed and not a draught left in the cabin, we'd done our work too well there, seemingly. Root just ran out of air, they said. Slipped from sleep into coma, and then all the way down into death.

Wouldn't have known a thing about it, they said, as if that was any kind of comfort.

As if I needed any kind of comfort.

I wouldn't be allowed back on board Mike, I knew that; not today, at least, maybe not for several days. But I went down to the dock again anyway, just to watch the work, watch the water.

There was a constable waiting with a car there, doing nothing; not much older than me, he would have been, and we got talking, the way you do. I told him what I'd told his bosses, and what they'd said about the charcoal and the fumes; and he nodded and said, 'Nasty stuff, that. I remember when I was a kid, we had a barbi in my dad's garage because it was raining. It was cold too, so we'd pulled the door down, even. And we were all choking and our eyes were stinging, someone had an asthma attack; if we hadn't got that door up in a hurry, I reckon they'd have found ten dead teenagers in there in the morning.'

I nodded, grinning faintly. 'Yeah. Us too, we did the same thing. He never should've put charcoal on the stove anyway, if I'd known he was going to do that I'd have stowed it away in the hold...'

'Mustn't blame yourself,' the constable said. I just grunted and watched the water, wondering where it was now, the old shirt I'd plugged the chimney with last night. Wondering how far it had got after I pulled it out this morning and tossed it in the river, for the current and the tidal suck to take it away to sea...

'How come you're living on a barge, anyway?' he asked: making conversation, I guessed, trying to take my mind off any guilt I was feeling.

That was nice, so I told him some of it at least: my cousin's gratitude, the cat, the money. He sucked air through his teeth and shook his head, and said, 'It's unlucky, you know. Taking on someone else's cat, it always brings bad luck.'

'Is it? Seemed like the other way round, to me. All that money...'

'Yeah, but now you've got this, haven't you? And you could've been on board last night. It could've been you in that cabin, not your friend,' politely, making no assumptions. 'Could've been your body we lifted off this morning, yeah?'

'I suppose, yeah...'

'Well, then. Nearly got you killed, didn't it? That cat? It nearly killed you.'

'That's right,' I said; and that's the way I tell it now, to strangers. My cousin left me his cat, and it almost killed me. Honest, it did...

# About the Authors

**Nicholas Blincoe** was born and grew up in North Manchester. He has worked in radio and newspapers and was once signed to Factory Records. His first novel about a transsexual's bloody return to the Manchester drug scene, *Acid Casuals* was published to major acclaim in 1995.

**John Harvey** is the creator of the popular series featuring Nottingham police sleuth Charlie Resnick, who has also appeared in television adaptations. His latest outing was in *Living Proof*. Also a poet and scriptwriter, Harvey now lives in London, where he often performs readings with jazz bands.

**Stella Duffy** was born in the UK but grew up in New Zealand. She now lives in London where she works as an actress and comedian. She has written two novels featuring lesbian detective Saz Martin, *Calendar Girl* and *Wavewalker*.

**Russell James** is a marketing consultant who lives in Cheltenham. He has written four darkly realistic crime novels, *Underground*, *Daylight*, *Payback* and *Slaughter Music*.

**Maxim Jakubowski** followed a career in publishing by opening the Murder One bookshop in 1988. He writes, edits and publishes in many areas of genre fiction, including mystery and erotica. He reviews crime in a monthly column in *Time Out*, is a contributing editor to *Mystery Scene* and a winner of the Anthony Award.

**Mark Timlin** is best-known for novels featuring hardboiled ex-cop and south London private eye Nick Sharman (currently filming for television), a man known for his quick line in repartee and a penchant for casual violence. A former roadie for The

Who and T Rex, Mark seldom leaves his shady South London pastures.

**Ian Rankin** is a Scottish writer currently living in France. A winner of the Raymond Chandler Fulbright award and the short story Gold Dagger, he is the creator of the popular Edinburgh sleuth Inspector Rebus, as well as a series of fast-paced thrillers written as Jack Harvey.

**Derek Raymond** was the pen name used by **Robin Cook** who died in 1995. His 'Factory' novels have become cult classics and the first, *He Died With His Eyes Open* was filmed in France, with two others currently in development for the screen. His last published novel was *Not Till The Red Fog Rises*.

**Joe Canzius** is a pseudonym for a well-known British crime writer. His first novel under this name *Fast Road To Nowhere* will be published in 1996, and represents a departure from his usual series sleuth.

**John B Spencer** is a respected songwriter and musician who published his first two Charley Case offbeat mystery adventures in the '80s. Charley makes a welcome reappearance in 1996 with *Quake City*, a companion title in the *Bloodlines* series.

**Denise Danks** is a past winner of the Raymond Chandler Fulbright award and the creator of computer journalist/sleuth Georgina Powers, who has so far appeared in four novels. Denise lives in east London with her husband and two daughters, and has recently completed *Torso*, her first film script.

**Graeme Gordon** was born in Epsom and lives in London. He has been a struggling actor, a struggling playwright and a struggling filmmaker. His first novel *Bayswater Bodycount* was published in 1995, and as the title indicates, includes much mayhem and many corpses.

**Mike Ripley** (when not writing) is Director of Public Relations for the Brewers' Society, and says he has to drink a lot of beer for a living. He is the creator of Angel, a popular and award-winning crime bon-vivant who has appeared in seven novels so far, the latest being *Family of Angels*. He is also crime reviewer for *The Daily Telegraph*.

**Chaz Brenchley** is the author of six dark suspense and horror novels, the most recent being *Dead Of Light*. Born in Oxford, he now lives in Newcastle and has been writer in residence in Sunderland, where he has worked with local artists in multi-disciplinary collaborations.